YC3
signed

FIRE IN THE HOLE

Fire in the Hole launches the University Press of Colorado's *Women's West* series. Fiction and nonfiction, the series recognizes the exciting contributions of women in the American West.

The American West is an integral part of the nation's psyche. Yet the role that women of all cultures played is largely unknown, or captured only in a few stereotypes. Women did more than stand by their men. Recent scholarship reveals that women in the West were individuals of pluck, stamina, and amazing accomplishment. They came west for the same reason men did—to look for freedom and opportunity.

The University Press of Colorado's series is a tribute to these strong women.

FIRE IN THE HOLE

SYBIL DOWNING

To Paula,
with best wishes for good
reading —

Sybil Downing

UNIVERSITY PRESS OF COLORADO

Published by the University Press of Colorado
P.O. Box 849
Niwot, Colorado 80544
(303) 530-5337

The University Press of Colorado is a cooperative publishing enterprise supported, in part, by Adams State College, Colorado State University, Fort Lewis College, Mesa State College, Metropolitan State College of Denver, University of Colorado, University of Northern Colorado, University of Southern Colorado, and Western State College of Colorado.

The paper used in this publication meets the minimum requirements of the National Standard for Information Sciences—Permanence of Paper for Printed Library Materials. ANSI Z39.48—1984

Library of Congress Cataloging-in-Publication Data
Downing, Sybil.
    Fire in the hole / Sybil S. Downing.
      p.   cm. -- (Women's West series)
    ISBN 0-870871-380-3 (alk. paper)
    1. Coal Strike, Colo., 1913-1914--Fiction. 2. Women lawyers-
-Colorado--Fiction. I. Title. II. Series.
PS3554.09348F57 1996
813'.54--dc20   96-11175
                                                CIP

10 9 8 7 6 5 4 3 2

This book is dedicated to my husband.

Acknowledgments

The list of people who offered their encouragement and support for this project is long. Particular thanks must go to Elaine Long, Jane Valentine Barker, Kathleen O'Neal Gear, Jeff Long, Jerrie Hurd, and Glenda Riley, who read the manuscript, believed in it, and suggested improvements. I also wish to acknowledge with gratitude the following individuals and institutions for their assistance in providing technical advice and historical background: Judge Martin I. Steinberg; Dr. Sherburne Macfarlan; Peter Crouse; Elizabeth Downing; Dominic Ferrera; Roger Martinez; Joe Belotti; Gerald Stokes of the Trinidad Historical Society, Trinidad, Colorado; Paula Manini of The Bloom House, Trinidad, Colorado; the Denison Library, University of Colorado School of Medicine; Norlin Library and Western History Department, University of Colorado at Boulder; Western History Department, Denver Public Library; The Carnegie Library of Trinidad, Colorado. Finally, I owe my thanks to my agent, Susan Gleason, and to Luther Wilson, former director, University Press of Colorado.

Author's Note

Although this novel is based on historical events, it is a work of imagination.

The violent strike in the southern Colorado coalfields that occupied the nation's headlines in 1913–14 first came to my attention when I was doing research connected with the biography of my great-grandfather, Thomas M. Patterson. During the early stages of the strike, Patterson, a former U.S. senator and political reformer, was asked to mediate a settlement. Later, two of Patterson's law partners served as the defense attorneys for the union leader, John Lawson, accused of murder.

I knew nothing more about the strike. Was it a tragic incident of only regional interest or did it have national implications? Stirred by these questions, I began my search for answers. I walked land once occupied by union camps and talked to descendants of miners and residents of Trinidad who had lived during that period. I read hearings records, newspaper accounts of the day, and scholarly work focused on the strike.

Predictably, what emerged was an account of a violent and ruthless power struggle between classes, between capital and labor. Yet the story was of the men and women whose actions and attitudes forced the nation to truly look at itself, however briefly, and examine what it had become.

Most of the characters are fictional. Others were suggested by individuals, such as State Senator Helen Ring Robinson, who toured the union camps during the strike. A few of the characters were actual players in the events: John Lawson, the union leader; Louis Tikas, miner and union activist; John Osgood, a mine owner; Jesse Welborn of the Colorado Fuel and Iron Company; A. C. Felts, supervisor for the Baldwin-Felts Detective Agency; Frederick Gates, Rockefeller executive; Horace Hawkins, attorney; Edward M. Keating, congressman; and John D. Rockefeller Jr. Careful research was done to present them accurately. Only those who knew them at the time, however, can be certain whether the characterization is as precise as it might have been.

FIRE IN THE HOLE

The miner lit the fuses and ran down the drift, shouting, "Fire in the hole!"

Chapter One

Denver, Colorado; December 1913

Through the half-open door of her law office, Alex MacFarlane became aware of a voice rising above the day's orderly hum. It was a woman's voice, firm, insistent, with a thick eastern European accent. Alex looked up from the brief she was reviewing, listened as the voice continued until, thoroughly curious, she rose and stepped out of her office into the reception room.

One of the secretaries was arguing with a handsome, fashionably dressed woman with great dark eyes. As Alex approached, the stranger caught sight of her.

"Mrs. MacFarlane. Please, I must speak with you. It is a matter of greatest urgency."

Alex had no memory of ever having seen this woman who seemed to know her. "I'm sorry, have we met?"

"My name is Irene Vaska."

Alex nodded, though the name meant nothing to her. Ignoring the secretary's look of disapproval, she asked the woman to come into her office.

The exotic scent of Miss Vaska's expensive perfume filled the room as she took the chair next to the desk. "I must apologize for my rudeness, but I did not have time to make an appointment."

"That's quite all right." Alex was grateful for the unexpected interruption in an otherwise routine day. She went around the desk and sat down. "Miss Vaska, I have a confession to make."

The woman gave the barest of smiles. "You do not remember the name, do you?"

"No. I'm sorry."

"I have come about my brother Stefan—Stefan Vaska—who is in the Trinidad jail."

Alex started at the mention of the southern Colorado town, now gripped in a violent strike. Ten years earlier, at the outset of another strike, her husband had died in a mine explosion near there. She reached back into her memory, struggling to recall the name Vaska. It came to her, and her heart skipped a beat. So much had happened since then, so much deliberately put aside. "Good Lord. He's the boy who tried to rescue my husband."

The woman's smile broadened. "I knew you would remember."

"You say he's in jail. But on what charge?"

"A man telephoned yesterday. He told me Stefan was arrested for starting a riot in a place called Sandoval, somewhere near Trinidad."

"Miss Vaska, before you go on, you need to understand our firm does not handle criminal cases."

"Yes, I know, but my attorney tells me he does not have the proper influence."

"And we do?"

The woman leaned forward. "Mrs. MacFarlane, you and your father know General Chase. My lawyer does not."

"General Chase?"

"The military is the law there now. My attorney tells me Stefan cannot even be released on bond."

Alex frowned. A strike in Colorado had been the last thing on her mind. She had just returned from a month in London, visiting an old college friend, where the conversation at dinner parties centered around whether Germany would go to war with Britain and France. She was out of touch with domestic matters, only vaguely recalling the newspaper stories that told of the National Guard being called in and, when the violence had escalated, of military law being invoked.

"Who exactly is this General Chase?"

"He was a dentist here in Denver."

"You don't mean Elmer Chase?"

Miss Vaska nodded.

Alex instantly pictured the rotund social climber her father detested. Yet when it came to the use of military law as a means to maintain order, she knew her father and the general would agree. She almost smiled at the irony.

"We do know him, but only as an acquaintance."

"Mrs. MacFarlane, I see your name in the society columns. And your father is often mentioned in the company of senators and other important men. Your firm represents the owners of the coal mines. I am willing to pay for that influence."

Somehow Alex wasn't surprised by the bluntness of the offer.

Stefan is innocent. He should not be in jail, the woman's dark eyes pleaded with her.

Alex swung around to gaze out the window at the building across the way. Miss Vaska was probably correct. Influence would force her brother's release prior to a court hearing. Alex's father could bargain with Chase: Vaska's release for an introduction at the Denver Club. Stefan Vaska had risked his life for her husband. Surely, what his sister asked in return was not unreasonable.

She turned back. "As I have said before, we don't handle this kind of case, but given the circumstances, Miss Vaska, we'll do what we can."

"Thank you. From the bottom of my heart, thank you."

Alex shook her hand, admiring the quality of this woman, her level gaze, and determined smile that said, *to be fully lived, life has to be shaped from whatever hope is at hand.*

Alex walked down the oak-paneled hall to her father's door, identified by a discreetly lettered gold plate engraved JONATHAN RUSSELL, ATTORNEY AT LAW. She knocked and entered.

Her father was standing by his desk, telephone receiver in hand, barking into the mouthpiece. He signaled her to sit down, said something more to the person on the other end of the line, and hung up.

Though a slight man and shorter than Alex, what Jonathan Russell lacked in height and weight was made up for by his ramrod posture and meticulous grooming. Even at seventy, he was a handsome man.

"Why the frown, my dear?"

Alex studied her father, assessing the best way to state the situation, and decided to plunge ahead. "I just talked to a woman by the name of Irene Vaska."

His eyes widened. "The madam of a house of ill repute? In this office?"

"I don't know anything about her being a madam. I do know she wants us to represent her brother, Stefan. Remember? The man who tried to save Robb?"

Her father seemed not to have heard. "I'm told it's the finest one in town. A French chef, silk sheets. That sort of thing."

Alex ignored the gossip and went on. "He's being held in the Trinidad jail on charges of inciting a riot. At the moment, General Chase controls the legal system."

"Of course he does. The area is under military law."

"That's just the point."

"Which is?"

"The general in command is none other than Elmer Chase. He's been wanting you to sponsor him for membership in the Denver Club for years. We could easily use all that social ambition to our client's advantage."

Her father reddened. "I wouldn't ask that idiot for the time of day, much less for a favor such as you're proposing."

"Surely, you agree we owe Stefan Vaska—"

"We owe him nothing, Alexandra. After the accident, we paid his medical bills and then some."

"You paid his bills, not I."

His mouth went tight.

"Father, I accepted the case."

His dark eyes blazed. "Then you will have to telephone the woman and tell her we can't help her."

"Father—"

"Can you imagine this firm representing a miner, a striker? Our clients are the men who own the mines, not the ones who work in them."

"I thought justice was blind."

"Oh, come now."

"Stefan Vaska is a man, a human being. He deserves a fair hearing, and we have the influence to see he gets it."

Her father's expression hardened. "If you insist on becoming involved, you will do nothing but place yourself in an awkward position."

"How so?"

"To date, your entire experience in the practice of law has been in the shelter of my firm."

"Somehow I'd been under the impression we were partners."

He ignored her, continued. "A woman attorney is still considered a curiosity, not to be taken seriously. If you insist on representing this man, you will do nothing but prejudice his case."

Alex felt a rush of resentment. Her father apparently was blind to what she dealt with every day. She might not try cases in court, but she handled most of the firm's real estate transactions, meeting regularly with men on a professional level. In spite of their suggestive smirks and comments, she'd never been bested once when it came to knowledge of property law.

"In short, Alexandra, I will have no part of this scheme of yours."

"You're not willing to help Stefan Vaska?"

"I am not willing to sacrifice my reputation for a striker, nor will I ask Elmer Chase to circumvent military procedure."

Alex reached up to massage the back of her neck, which had started to ache.

"Furthermore, you know how I feel about violence and mobs."

She glanced away for an instant, feeling her anger mount. "You have no idea what the situation is down there."

"Nor do you." His tone was hard, unbending.

The secretary tapped on the door and reminded her father of his next appointment.

Alex strode back to her office. She was furious. She was thirty-three years old, a partner in the firm. Yet her father treated her as if she were still a child who needed his protection. Enough. She was perfectly capable of making her own decisions. Stefan Vaska deserved first-rate legal representation. She intended to see he had it.

Chapter Two

Plumes of steam whooshed out from under the railroad car and hung suspended in the cold air as Alex MacFarlane descended the steep steps. She wasn't sure what she'd expected Trinidad to look like. Its Spanish-sounding name conjured pictures of dark-skinned men and women with shiny black hair, of perfumed nights filled with guitar music. What confronted her on this December evening seemed quite commonplace: the usual depot with the dimly lit waiting room; beyond it more tracks lined with freight cars; farther on, a variety of buildings with the look of warehouses strung along a dirt road.

The other passengers had left her standing alone in the shadow of the train. She glanced about for a porter to take her two valises and guide her to a taxicab, but didn't see one. A flick of uneasiness rose within her.

Out of the corner of her eye, she caught sight of two figures—men, climbing down from the engineer's cab. As they came closer, she saw they carried rifles. They were dressed in long, khaki coats and stiff-brimmed hats. Soldiers attached to the Colorado National Guard, she realized. She was relieved to see them.

As they neared, walking abreast with an arrogant swagger, her momentary sense of security vanished. There was something about their manner that frightened her. She caught in her breath. When they reached her, the taller of the two grinned at her in an insolent way. She forced herself to meet his gaze, to disguise her anxiety. They asked her business in Trinidad.

"Legal," she said, evenly, though her voice sounded thin and unfamiliar to her own ear.

Still grinning, the taller soldier licked his lips, and they waved her on. She picked up her valises and strode purposefully down the platform, feeling the soldiers' gazes as they watched her, fighting the temptation to run toward the few passengers she saw clustered around some parked automobiles and rigs.

When Alex reached the end of the platform, she put down the valises and caught her breath. An older man, gray-haired, in a velvet-collared overcoat and wearing a bowler hat, came forward and offered her his cab, the only one in sight. She smiled, flooded with relief. Her heart slowed. She was back in control. After a moment of polite discussion, they agreed to share the ride into town.

The Ford touring car rumbled over the bridge onto a brick-covered street choked with wagons and automobiles, past brightly lighted saloons and commercial hotels and shops. The sidewalks were filled with men, many working men, judging from their plain dress. Alex wondered if they were miners. There were more soldiers. Roving about in packs, they were given wide berth as they passed. The town was larger than she'd expected, and it had a menacing feel that made her shiver. Denver was only two hundred miles to the north, yet it was as if she had entered another world.

"May I take the liberty of introducing myself?" her companion finally asked in an affable way. "Leslie Baxter, at your service. Counsel to the Colorado Fuel and Iron Company. Or CF&I, as it is often called."

Alex glanced at him, surveying him carefully. The mention of Colorado Fuel and Iron reminded her of the front-page stories about John Rockefeller's purchase of controlling interest in the company and most of the mines that supplied its coal. The mines in Sandoval, where Stefan Vaska had worked before his arrest, might be part of its holdings.

"I'm Mrs. MacFarlane."

"My pleasure." Above the smile, his eyes were sharp. "Might I inquire, madam, what brings you to Trinidad in these troubled times?"

Somehow his question struck a wrong chord. Was he implying she shouldn't be there? Or was he merely being nosy? She smiled as her mind raced to decide how best to respond. The cab stopped in front of the Columbian Hotel, where her secretary had telegraphed ahead for a reservation. A uniformed bellboy hurried out through the large etched-glass doors to take the bags.

Mr. Baxter got out and offered his hand. The need to give him an answer had passed.

"Thank you again for the cab, Mr. Baxter."

He gave a small bow. "Trinidad is a small town, Mrs. MacFarlane. I have every hope we shall meet again."

After a debate with the desk clerk about whether she had a reservation, Alex was shown to a suite on the third floor. Stepping inside, she looked around the small sitting room, noted the gunmetal gray striped wallpaper, a small desk with a telephone, a divan and two chairs upholstered in dark brown, patterned velour. The bedroom was tiny, barely large enough for the narrow bed, a chiffonier, a nightstand. For the price, the accommodations should have equaled the elegance of Denver's Brown Palace. Still, it was adequate; the windows had a view of the main street, and she had a private bath. She tipped the bellboy and closed the door behind him.

Alex opened her bags and hung her clothes in the wardrobe. After some tugging to open the drawers of the chiffonier, she arranged her underthings and nightgown. She placed her silver-backed brush and comb on the top, put a novel she'd brought with her on the nightstand. That finished, she telephoned the front desk and dictated a telegram to be sent to her father, telling him of her arrival. She was still irritated at his stubborn refusal to understand her point. But there was no reason to worry him unnecessarily.

She debated whether to go downstairs for dinner, then decided instead to call down for a sandwich and coffee. Until now, she hadn't realized how tired she was. As she waited for her supper to arrive, she slipped out of her traveling dress, corset and stockings, into the comfort of her nightgown and robe.

Alex began to brush her hair. Normally, the feel of the bristles against her scalp revived her at the end of a long day. Tonight she felt strangely distracted. She put down the brush, went into the bathroom, and filled the sink with warm water. She picked up the bar of soap, glanced about for a washcloth but didn't see one. Using her hands, she washed her face, the back of her neck. Eyes closed, she groped for the hand towel that hung on the nearby rack.

As she rubbed the towel across her face, she was strangely conscious of her cheekbones, the shape of her chin, her nose. She had inherited her mother's good bones. Her father, other men—and at one time her husband—had always told her she was beautiful. She wasn't sure she'd disagree. She dried herself, hung up the towel. Some day she might turn into a withered old crone. At the moment, the prospect seemed unimportant.

She went to the window of the sitting room, stared down at the street, her mind turning to the problems she was about to tackle. She thought again of the soldiers she'd seen, grim reminders of the fact she'd have to deal with military law. Irene Vaska undoubtedly was right. Influence, the prestige of the firm would be the key, the determining factor. She guessed she'd also have to deal with local politics. Though undoubtedly different than those of Denver, politics were something she understood.

Even if the situation proved more formidable than she imagined, she didn't care. She looked forward to the challenge. Hadn't she been the only woman in her law school class? In the brief period before her marriage, when she'd worked as a reporter for the *Rocky Mountain News*, she'd persuaded the city editor that a woman could cover the juvenile court. Her father's opinion to the contrary, she was not like some delicate hothouse flower.

Yet her life had become so humdrum, so consumed with details that there were days when she was certain nothing would ever happen again. She wasn't disintegrating. She simply wasn't living. She had allowed her father to control her life, until she couldn't claim a single accomplishment as her own. Stefan Vaska's case would help her change that, and it would give her the chance to repay an obligation that had haunted her for years.

Tomorrow her first order of business, before she called on General Chase, should be to contact the district attorney. He might know the particulars of Vaska's arrest, and he'd know the town, which was bound to be helpful.

She sat down at the desk and opened the slender telephone directory to find the listing and the address for county offices. The address was there, but the name of the district attorney wasn't given. She'd have to wait until morning to learn whom she would be dealing with.

Chapter Three

Bill Henderson stood in front of his office door and fumbled to insert the key in the lock. Ever since the military had taken over, he'd felt the need to lock up, a fact that annoyed him.

The key finally found its notch. He turned it, twisted the knob, and opened the door. The office was small, furnished with the customary oak filing cabinets, a glass-fronted bookcase, and two wooden chairs. Several framed diplomas hung above the desk, which was covered with a stack of papers he'd left there the night before. The ochre-colored walls still held the smell of fresh paint.

He hung his hat on the rack by the door, unbuttoned his coat, and glanced out the window. The morning beyond the limestone courthouse was overcast, heavy with the promise of snow. He thought of the poor devils huddled in union tents clustered near the mining camps across Las Animas County and its neighbor to the north. He wondered how long they could hold out in this cold.

His coat still on, he picked up the stack of papers from his desk, stared at it, then put it down. Morosely, he dropped into the ancient swivel chair he'd brought from his old office and swung toward the window. The grounds around the courthouse, barren of any vegetation, were riddled with hummocks of frozen earth left from the recent construction. The building was the pride of Trinidad, a monument to justice. Bill snorted at the thought, turned back toward the desk.

Such justice as there was now was dispensed by General of the National Guard Elmer Chase, formerly of Denver, where he'd been a dentist of no note. When Bill had called on him last night at his headquarters to object to the practice of holding men in jail without charge, the general had made it eminently clear who made the decisions now.

Bill heard a knock on the door, glanced around. Deputy Sheriff Buster Kinkus, a great bear of a man with brown eyes somehow set too close, filled the doorway.

"Mornin'."

Bill nodded.

"Thought you'd like to know they brought more of them strikers in last night."

"What're the charges?"

The big man grinned, his eyes nearly disappearing in folds of fat. "You're kiddin'."

"Sorry. I nearly forgot."

The deputy sheriff frowned. "It's the way it is."

Bill almost launched into a tirade over "the way it is" but caught himself in time. Losing control was stupid. "Where'd they come from this time?"

"Up by the Forbes camp. Claimed they was walkin' to town, mindin' their business."

"They probably were. That's the hell of it."

The deputy sheriff stared at him for a moment. "Yeah. Well. You said you wanted to know."

"Thanks." Bill tried for a smile.

"Any time." The big man stepped backward into the hall. "See ya."

"Yeah." Bill closed the door, sat down again. He thought about the men downstairs in the jail being held without charge because habeas corpus and due process were now things of the past. They probably weren't even aware those fundamental rights ever existed. Somebody told him once that twenty-three different languages were spoken in the mining camps. Though few of the miners understood English, most had come to this country with the hope of finding something better than the misery they'd left behind. If that was so, they'd have had to come straight from hell.

His door opened again, and Eloise Peyton, Judge Southard's secretary and second cousin, a gaunt woman in her forties, came in. He liked Eloise, felt sorry for her. She deserved better than the shabby life she had.

"Mr. Henderson, the judge wishes to see you." Miss Peyton's lips always seemed glued to her teeth, resulting in a kind of sucking sound when she spoke.

"Any time in particular?"

"Right now."

Bill didn't move. He wouldn't argue with her about whether he intended to comply. Eloise Peyton was only a hapless messenger, dependent on Limon Southard for her existence. As was her habit when she was upset, her eyes began to mist. "The judge is awful mad, Mr. Henderson."

Bill eyed her. "About what?"

"About your calling on General Chase last night."

"Well, at least the rumor mill is still in good working order."

Her eyes took on a confused look. "He said he was going to fire you."

Bill straightened the chair and stood up. That the judge believed he could fire him caught his fancy. It was absolute proof of the insanity that gripped the entire county. "Fire an elected official? Well, now."

Eloise Peyton frowned with such apparent distress that Bill wished he'd kept his sarcasm to himself.

"But you've roused my interest, Miss Peyton." Bill took off his coat, hung it up, smoothed his hair, and went to the door. "Come on, let's see what the judge really has on his mind."

Judge Limon E. Southard's bland, pleasant face framed by a mane of snow-white hair made him look more like a kindly grandfather than a county judge, especially one who sold his soul and his services to any and all who met his price. As usual, he was immaculately dressed. Today he wore a well-cut suit of dark gray tweed, with a huge diamond stickpin planted in the center of his black tie. Seated behind a massive desk in a high-backed leather chair, he beckoned for Bill to come into the office.

"Pull up a chair." He smiled, blue eyes crinkling in feigned good will.

"I'll stand."

The judge's smile held as he moved his hands slowly back and forth over the sleek wooden surface of the chair's arms, looking for all the world like a cat sizing up its prey. Bill leaned against the long table intended for use in conferences between attorneys and their clients, and folded his arms.

"Bill, you're a fine attorney. If I didn't think so, I'd have never offered your name in nomination as district attorney."

Bill studied the judge's seamless face. It occurred to him the man had no conscience. Why else would someone of his years show not a single sign of worry or regret over the chaos around him? "Miss Peyton indicated you want to fire me."

Southard laughed. "Which, of course, is absurd."

"I know."

"The truth is you worry me, Bill."

"How's that, your honor?"

"It was bad enough for you to try to interfere with Governor Ammons. Now this business with General Chase. Good Lord, man! What possessed you?"

Bill took in a deep breath. "I was elected to protect the people of this county, your honor. There are men in our jail being held without charge."

"For Christ's sake. We're under martial law down here. Due process is not our business. If there is any prosecuting to do, the general will do it."

Bill caught a hint of desperation in the judge's tone. "And what am I supposed to do?"

"Draw your pay. Keep your office open. Until martial law's lifted, General Chase is in charge. No questions asked."

Bill regarded him coldly.

"You're to keep your nose clean and your mouth shut."

Bill stepped away from the edge of the table. The judge's words constituted an order, as direct as any General Chase might give the rabble that he called his troops. Standing closer now to the judge, Bill thought he smelled whiskey. It was said the judge kept a silver flask in the bottom drawer of his desk. "And if I don't?"

Bill studied the blue eyes, hard as steel. Judge Limon Southard had read the law but never bothered to pass the bar exam, though that, in itself, was not unusual among Colorado's county judges. What was unusual was to have as his district attorney a man who had graduated top in his law school class, clerked for a U.S. district court judge, and worked in one of the state's most distinguished law offices. Bill Henderson was an object of pride for the judge. But when all was said and done, Bill was dispensable, and he knew it.

"Don't push me, Bill. I mean it."

"I'm sure you do, your honor."

The judge would never allow anyone to jeopardize his cherished lifestyle—tailor-made suits, good whiskey, expensive whores up in Denver. Whatever it took. He wouldn't blink an eye about hiring a couple of the Pinkerton toughs roaming around town to beat Bill up, to make sure he toed the line.

Bill had lived by his wits all his life. He could take care of himself, but the Pinkertons were experts.

Chapter Four

The morning after her arrival, Alex rose, washed, and put on a suit of deep green gabardine, the hem of its narrow skirt just above her ankles. Though the cut was severe enough to convey the seriousness of her purpose, the color was becoming. She adjusted a matching hat over her thick auburn hair, pinned a delicate pendant watch to her suit jacket. She glanced in the mirror to give herself a final inspection.

Her gray eyes appeared darker than normal and she looked pale. Whatever the reason—the shock of the town, the soldiers, the unfamiliar mattress, speculations about what was ahead—she hadn't slept well. She rubbed a little rouge across her lips and on her cheeks.

She wondered whether to telephone the district attorney for an appointment, then decided it probably wasn't necessary. Downstairs, she moved through the lobby, past men's curious stares to the dining room, where a waiter guided her to a small table by the window. She ordered tea and toast. At the last moment, she added a three-minute boiled egg to her order. Afterwards she was still hungry. She vowed to have a more substantial lunch, but she was anxious to get on with the day.

Once outside, she stood on the sidewalk for a moment to get her bearings. The air was dry, cold. The sunshine was so bright she almost had to squint. According to the street sign, she was standing at the intersection of North Commercial and West Main. The desk clerk had told her the new courthouse was one block south and east, up the hill.

Most of the buildings were several stories high, constructed of massive blocks of sandstone, the emphasis on utility rather than pleasing design. Stolid, uncompromising, like the mountain that rose directly behind them.

As they had been last night, the streets were filled with rigs, wagons, and automobiles. She dodged the red streetcar rumbling down Main Street and hurried across, down the block, past a modern department store. The large windows were gaily decorated for Christmas and, to her surprise, held attractive displays of stylish clothing. All the amenities of a modern town seemed to be in place. On the surface, Trinidad was a normal, thriving center of commerce.

Yet soldiers were everywhere. As she walked, she realized she had seen few women. Knots of rough-looking men, smoking cigarettes, lounged in doorways and on street corners. She wondered who they were. The feeling of danger was everywhere. She glanced about for a policeman, but didn't see one.

Her mood was somber as she entered the imposing limestone courthouse and checked the directory for the district attorney's office. She climbed the stairs, noting the gleaming brass balustrade. The hum of voices and the sound of heels clicking along the halls held an air of purpose. Her spirits brightened. From all appearances, Las Animas County still was carrying on its regular business.

Halfway down the hall, she found the door marked DISTRICT ATTORNEY. She knocked and stepped in. Standing at the window, an unlit pipe in the corner of his mouth, was a tall man—over six feet—with broad shoulders and a solid look about him. His brown hair needed trimming. At the sound of her footsteps, he turned, and instantly she was certain she knew him.

"Can I help you?" he asked, absently.

"I'm looking for the district attorney."

"That's me."

She looked at him more carefully. "By any chance . . ." Yes, she was sure of it. "You're Bill Henderson, aren't you? We went to law school together."

He stared at her.

"I'm Alex Russell MacFarlane. We were in the same class."

His pale blue eyes turned hard. "I remember."

His reaction took her aback. She forced a smile, uneasy in spite of herself under his gaze. The eyes were as cold as they had been that first day of law school when, sitting in the front row, she had felt them. Finally, she'd turned and seen him, staring at her, his eyes aglitter with such loathing she almost gasped. Over the next three years, his eyes never warmed. Occasionally, she had been tempted to confront him, to ask him what she had done to deserve his contempt. But she never did.

It was plain neither his eyes nor his contempt had changed.

Chapter Five

"What can I do for you, Mrs. MacFarlane?" Bill drew up a chair for her.

"Alex. Please." She smiled.

"Alex it is."

He stepped around his desk and sat down. The first time he'd seen Alex, she'd been what? Twenty-three? Slim with full breasts, burnished copper-colored hair, alabaster skin, chiseled features. The most beautiful girl he'd ever laid eyes on. She'd turned into a stunning woman.

Watching her as she sat erect, so sure of herself in her fashionable clothes—like a duchess—he felt the return of all his old resentments. Law school had been like a game for her. All the bills paid by daddy. A way to pass the time. Whatever she would claim as her reason for coming to Trinidad, he knew it served the same purpose.

She took off her gloves and arranged them on her lap. "I'm here to inquire about a man named Stefan Vaska. I understand he was a miner somewhere nearby. I've been told he's in custody in the county jail. The charge, I believe, is inciting a riot."

What in hell was she doing representing a striker? "Actually, no formal charge was entered."

"I'm afraid I don't understand."

"It's simple. General Elmer Chase, and only General Elmer Chase, calls the tune down here," he said. "He and his particular brand of martial law run this county and everything in it."

"I've been out of the country recently, but it seems to me I remember reading the general is operating the two counties as a military district."

"More precisely, a military district under martial law. Never formally proclaimed, of course, but that's what we've got."

"Yet, surely as district attorney, you—"

"You may recall from *Black's Law Dictionary*, Mrs. MacFarlane—"

"Alex."

"Alex." He shifted in his chair. "Black said when martial law is in place, civil authority—including the district attorney—is nonexistent." He said the words slowly, so she'd be sure to understand, like when he talked to the Spanish or the Greeks or Italians who had come to him with injury claims and spoke little English.

"I understand. But you must have access to information about my client. At this point, I'm completely in the dark."

"Strictly speaking, you don't have a client. Not now. Anyway, I don't know any more than you do," he said, bitterly. "When Chase took over, he made certain I didn't get so much as the time of day."

Alex gave him a dubious look. "Surely, the governor doesn't intend that—"

"Apparently, the governor has been convinced Las Animas and Huerfano Counties are in a state of war. I telegraphed him, asked him point blank if he had declared martial law. He hedged. I shot back another telegram. Same story. He said he had given General Chase orders to restore the peace according to his best judgment. Those were his words."

He smiled grimly. "The result is obvious. Habeas corpus, free speech, all civil and judicial administration—the whole shebang is out the window." The extent of the situation still overwhelmed him.

"The local newspaper? The city fathers? They've agreed to this?" she asked, wide-eyed.

"Hell, they were part of the bunch that pressured the governor into calling for this military district the general's set up."

"Have you asked for a judicial ruling?"

"You must be joking," he said, straining for patience, remembering his morning conversation with the judge. Alex MacFarlane either had her head in the sand or was one of the world's most naive souls. "Even the Colorado Supreme Court is controlled—bought and paid for—by the same men."

"Who are?"

"The bankers, the coal company owners, investors."

"I presume you talked to Ed Keating," she persisted.

"The congressman?"

She nodded. "He's a Democrat."

"So?"

"The governor is a Democrat. The president is a Democrat. In short, the Democrats are in power."

"Maybe so. But it's Republicans who run this county, Alex. Run the state, in spite of a Democratic governor."

Her cool gray eyes irritated him.

"Sure, the congressman came down on a whirlwind tour right after the strike began. Even the state commissioner of labor appeared for a few days."

"And?"

He was tired of her questions. "And nothing."

"What do you mean?"

"Just what I said. Nothing happened."

"But Ed Keating came before martial law—or whatever the governor wants to call it—was enacted, didn't he?"

"So?"

"Well, if he understood the situation now, I know he'd press for a full investigation."

Bill leaned across the desk. "First, you need to understand this isn't the first time martial law's been declared in Colorado. Besides, a federal grand jury was impaneled not more than three weeks ago. Though the U.S. attorney didn't allow any warrants to be issued, it still was an investigation."

"Maybe."

"Next, you apparently aren't aware of how difficult it is to get a resolution for a congressional investigation of a strike through the Rules Committee."

"It wouldn't be easy, I know."

"Face facts. Las Animas and Huerfano Counties are under martial law. Regardless of the reason for it, that's what you have to deal with."

"Are you saying there's another reason for martial law—beyond the strikers' rioting?"

He snorted in disgust. Did she really believe just what she read in the newspapers?

"All right then, what is it? Politics? What?"

It was politics all right. The kind he hated most. The kind driven by money. Impossible to fight.

"I'd appreciate knowing," she persisted, quietly.

He gave her a level look. Even with every dirty detail, she wouldn't understand. The life she led with its gentility and patina of manners was her armor plate against reality. Yet, at the very least, she needed to know how it started. "The real trouble began when the state ran out of money to pay the militia and a group of Denver bankers offered to loan the state the money. Back when the governor first sent in the National Guard, order was restored. The militia had money in their pockets. The shootings stopped. Thinking back, I'd say the union seemed to welcome the troops. I suppose they thought of them as protection against the company guards, who were nothing but a gang of vigilantes."

Bill gazed past Alex, remembering the day he'd gone out to the Ludlow camp with a group of soldiers and they'd played baseball with some strikers. The union pitcher was a wild Greek by the name of Tikas.

"But after awhile, regular members of the militia began to complain about being away from their homes and jobs." He picked up a pencil, rolled it between his hands.

"Gradually, new faces began to turn up—all of them company guards or strikebreakers from back East. As far as the strikers were concerned, the company had changed the rules. If they wanted to play rough, they would, too. All hell broke loose again."

He snapped the pencil in half. "Strikers beat up any militia they could find. Militia dragged men—and women—in without charge and beat the hell out of them while they were in jail. Shootings on both sides became the norm again."

Alex shook her head, her unlined, beautiful face set in an appropriately grim expression, like an actress playing a dramatic scene.

"Look. We've got a governor who's for sale, a general who is drunk on power, a town full of citizens—a state full of citizens for that matter—who don't give a damn, and so-called leaders blind with greed. As long as General Chase's martial law exists, there's nothing you can do for your client, or anybody else, in that jail."

"You may be right," she said, though the snap in her eyes told him she wasn't convinced. "Still, I want to speak with the general. Can you tell me where the military headquarters are located?"

"In the Columbian. Second floor. But if you think you'll get in to see him, forget it. You won't get past the sergeant."

"Actually, the Columbian is where I'm staying." She rose. "As to whether I'll get in to see General Chase—well, since I have no other alternative, I'll have to try. In any case, I'll also be seeing my client. If nothing else, I want to get his side of the story."

"Look," he began as he got to his feet.

"I know. I may not get in to see him either." She went to the door and opened it.

"It's too bad you had to come all this way for nothing."

She glanced over her shoulder at him and, as if she hadn't heard him, said in a brisk tone, "Well, good to see you again, Bill. If you like, I'll let you know if I have any success." Without waiting for his reply, she strode down the hall.

The sound of her heels striking the floor made his head throb. She had referred to the congressman by his first name. He wouldn't be surprised if she knew the governor, the president of every coal company. She was part of that world. Hell, she might get her client special privileges—in spite of martial law.

Alex MacFarlane defending a hapless miner was about the same as her tossing a coin in a beggar's cap. She and her father represented the very bankers who were financing the militia. What she was doing was an impulse, nothing more. He had no idea why she had taken on the poor sonofabitch. Frankly, he didn't care.

Bill glared at the bookcase across the room. Her perfume lingered in the air. The timing of her unexpected appearance couldn't have been worse. If she succeeded in persuading the general to release Vaska, it would be one more piece of evidence that there wasn't a shred of justice left in the world.

Chapter Six

Alex strode along the sidewalk. By now, the courthouse was out of sight. She probably shouldn't walk in unfamiliar territory, but she wanted to be alone to make sense of what she had gotten herself into. She'd never anticipated Bill Henderson's open antagonism or his determination to discourage her. If she took his word, there was no way around martial law.

She crossed one street, then another, lost in thought. The sidewalks stopped, forcing her to walk down the road. She could feel the pebbles through the thin soles of the boots she'd bought in London and sought out the smoother patches. She walked on, ignoring the cold, past small houses—hardly more than shacks—until she found herself on a hilltop covered with a mixture of winter-brown grass and sage.

Shading her eyes with one hand, she watched a hawk circle lazily, air currents carrying it higher and higher into the cloudless sky. From here, the prairie seemed to stretch endlessly toward the east. Turning, she could see, off in the distance, the snowy tips of mountain peaks etching the blue sky. A rough-hewn line of hills, running north and south, lay in the foreground. Here and there were clusters of rooftops, perhaps those of coal towns. In one of them, Vaska allegedly had incited a riot. Now he was in a jail cell.

Bill Henderson had told her wealth and political pressure were at the root of martial law. Miss Vaska must have been right. She'd also been right to assume Alex knew most of the players involved. So once she explained the situation—a lone man, a miner, undoubtedly caught in the midst of an unfortunate incident—she was confident General Chase would understand the merits of extending a favor and release him. She was impatient to get to work.

The moment she returned to the hotel, Alex went up to General Chase's headquarters on the second floor. An enlisted man sat at a table placed midway down the hall. When she asked to see the general, he eyed her, demanded her name and her business.

Telling her to wait, he went down the hall, knocked at the far door, and entered. A moment later he returned. "Sorry. The general's in a meeting."

Alex looked around and saw a chair placed near the head of the stairway. "If you'd be good enough to bring that chair over, I'll wait."

For two hours, fingers drumming on the pocketbook in her lap, Alex sat a few feet away from the sergeant seated behind the small desk. Slouched in his chair, his attention fixed on a pulp magazine, he seemed to have forgotten she was there. Her anger at the indignity of being put off mounted. Twice soldiers marched past her, forcing groups of hapless prisoners at bayonet point through the door at the far end of the hall. She almost asked the sergeant what was happening. But it occurred to her he might use the question as an excuse to send her away.

Finally, the door where the prisoners had disappeared opened. The man who walked toward her was not Elmer Chase, she realized, but Phil Van Howe, an attorney whose office was down the hall from her father's in Denver's Equitable Building. Approaching with a brisk step and shoulders squared, he was dressed in a smartly tailored uniform with shiny captain's bars on his shoulders.

"Phil. Good heavens. What on earth are you doing here?"

"Alex." He smiled stiffly. "When the sergeant said Mrs. MacFarlane was here, I thought it must be you. But I couldn't imagine what you'd be doing here. How are you?"

"Fine. Though a bit tired of waiting."

"I'm sorry about that. General Chase asked me to see you. He's tied up."

She regarded Phil with some amusement. He seemed quite taken with himself. Gone was the apologetic manner she recalled. Perhaps it was the uniform.

"A client of mine, a miner by the name of Stefan Vaska, is being held in county jail without charge." She tried to keep an even, business-like tone. His supercilious air made her suspect he would like her to plead for his help. "I understand he's a military prisoner subject to the disposition of the commanding general. That's why I need to see General Chase."

"The name of the man you mention doesn't sound familiar."

Alex decided to test whether civil law really was as absent as Bill Henderson claimed it was. "I want to arrange for bail."

"I'm afraid that's impossible."

"I see." She decided to try another tack. "When does General Chase plan to appoint an officer for my client's defense?"

"That usually isn't considered necessary."

She took a deep breath, trying for patience. "Phil, I really must see General Chase. I'm quite prepared to wait."

He gave her a quizzical look. "Why are you doing this, Alex? The man you say you're representing is a striker."

She raised an eyebrow. "I thought you'd never heard of him."

"Alex, they're all strikers." The tone had a hard, cruel edge to it.

She decided she should let the matter go. "The general does know I wish to see him, doesn't he?"

Phil gave a curt nod. "As I said, he sends his regrets."

She stared at him, tried to digest the fact that Chase had deliberately refused to see her. Apparently, the uniform and the power had replaced Elmer Chase's social aspirations. She would have to change her approach. "In any case, I'd like to see my client. I trust you can arrange it."

"Alex, within a military district, civilian representation is not appropriate."

"Ah, yes. I quite forgot." She fought the urge to slap his smug face. "But surely you won't deny a man visitors."

"Circumstances here are difficult. We have to move with utmost care."

She gave him her most understanding smile. "The man's sister has no idea how he is, Phil. A few moments with him. That's all I ask."

Van Howe pulled out his pocket watch. Snapping open the lid, he stared at it intently before he looked at her again. Finally, he said, "If you can wait a moment, I'll go with you."

Alex was stunned as the guard led Stefan Vaska into the small room. She realized she had expected to see a young man of seventeen, which was absurd. Ten years had passed, and the man who stood before her was nearly thirty.

He was of average height and slender build with dark brown hair. The muscles in his shoulders and arms showed through his rough shirt. His skin was dusky, his face pockmarked, with a half-healed gash about an inch long on one cheek. His heavy eyelids gave him a sleepy appearance, but the dark eyes themselves were bright, wary.

"Mr. Vaska, I'm Mrs. MacFarlane. You may remember my late husband." She waited for his response, but he continued simply to stare at her. "I've been retained by your sister, Irene, to represent you."

He said nothing.

The one-way conversation was unsettling. "Do you know why you're being held, Mr. Vaska?"

He shrugged.

Alex looked around at the guard. "Would you excuse us, please?"

"Long as he's here, I'm here," the guard said.

She was tempted to say something about attorney-client privilege, but guessed he would ignore her.

She turned her attention back to Vaska. "Was there an incident that occurred at the time of your arrest?"

"I asked for my mail."

"Do you belong to the United Mine Workers' union?"

He didn't reply.

Gaining any information from Vaska was going to be difficult. All she could do now was to acquaint him with his situation.

"Mr. Vaska, it's important for you to understand you and the others in the jail are being held as military prisoners. The legal system of the county is in the hands of the National Guard. This means the usual procedures— like posting bail so you can be free until your trial or hearing—well, those procedures have been suspended. As a consequence, until circumstances change, you must remain in custody."

He folded his arms, his penetrating eyes regarding her with suspicion.

"I can't tell you how long that may be."

He shifted his stance, as if impatient for her to leave. "You tell Irene I'm okay."

"I will. She's been very worried." Alex moved toward the door, though hesitant to leave when so little had been resolved. "If I can, I'll be back in a day or two. In the meantime, if there's something you need, I'll let the guard know where I can be reached."

Walking back to the hotel, she burned with fury at a system that allowed her client to be held without bail, on what for all she knew were trumped-up charges against him. He had made it plain he didn't want to talk to her. Like most men, he probably was reluctant to be represented by a woman. The guard's presence undoubtedly had made him uneasy. Still, something about his manner made her suspect he understood far more about the situation than she did.

The streetlights along Main Street came on. The day was nearly gone. In the bright sunshine of the morning—in spite of the ominous military presence—she had been full of hope she could negotiate a reasonable resolution of the charge against her client. All that had changed.

The district attorney, who might have been a source of help, had turned out to be a man who for some reason disliked her so much he probably wouldn't help her even if he could. General Chase had refused to see her. Then there was the matter of her client. If he didn't care what happened to him, why should she? Yet she did.

Her pride, her sense of honor, would not let her quit. Clearly, she would have to approach the problem with different strategies. She had to find a way around the present roadblocks. Right now she had not the slightest idea how to proceed.

Chapter Seven

Alex pushed through the crowded lobby and trudged up the stairs to her room. She wanted to let Irene Vaska know the situation. Then she'd grapple with the problem of what to do next. Going to the telephone, she gave the operator Miss Vaska's number.

Finally, a distant voice asked, "Hello? Mrs. MacFarlane? Is that you?"

Alex's heart ached for her. "Miss Vaska, I'm afraid I have bad news."

The line crackled.

"Is Stefan all right?"

"I talked with him this afternoon. He's in good health." There was no point in telling Irene about the gash across his cheek. "But he seemed reluctant to have me represent him."

"It is just his way," Miss Vaska said. "You must pay no attention. He's a good boy. When he gets to know you, you will be friends."

Alex was not so sure. "I've also been unable to see General Chase, though I did talk with his aide, Captain Van Howe."

"He will release Stefan?" Miss Vaska asked.

"He tells me your brother's case will be handled strictly according to General Chase's wishes."

"What does that mean?" Irene Vaska asked, the poor connection failing to mask her anxiety.

"It means that until martial law is lifted, there is nothing I or any other civilian attorney can do for him. It's possible a board of officers might be appointed by the general to review his case. They would make their recommendation to the general, who would then decide Stefan's guilt or innocence."

"No, no. You must see the general. This captain you talk of is a nobody."

Alex smiled ruefully at Miss Vaska's description of Phil Van Howe. "I will continue to try, but I can't offer much hope. I'm sorry."

She paused. When there was no response, she added, "Miss Vaska, you must understand—"

"Please. You are Stefan's only hope. You will find a way."

"The situation is difficult."

"But—"

"It's possible there may be another way to get him out, but it will take time."

"You will not give up then?"

Alex hesitated for only an instant. "No, I will not give up."

Alex sat in the hotel dining room, glared at the unappetizing pork chop and fried potatoes on her dinner plate. She wished she had someone to talk to, someone to examine the motives of the various personalities with her. But she was on her own. So be it. The arrogance of Phil Van Howe and Elmer Chase was intolerable. Both of them were nothing but power-hungry egomaniacs.

She gazed across the room full of uniformed men, hating the sight of them, and thought about the strike that had brought them. She didn't know much about the coal companies, but she suspected socialists were behind the union. Though she didn't approve of strikes or the violence, martial law was hardly the solution.

She bit into the slice of bread left on the butter plate and thought about the politics of the situation. The men who owned the coal companies were Republicans. Yet they had been able to pressure the governor, a Democrat, into calling up the militia, into allowing martial law. Odd. Particularly since it was common knowledge the union had put its weight and money behind the governor's election campaign. But how much weight? And how much money? Obviously, the coal companies' contributions were larger.

The union might not have known it had been outbid by the companies. Why else would they have gone ahead with their plans to strike? Was this strike some sort of a watershed, for both sides? She sipped at her coffee, which had grown cold, and let the questions simmer.

Her idea of Ed Keating calling for an investigation surfaced again. The mere idea, of course, was insane. An individual, an ordinary citizen, simply didn't sit down and decide a congressional investigation must be called.

And yet why not? Ed Keating was the area's congressman. He was also a friend since their days of working on the *Rocky Mountain News*. In spite of his being a freshman, she believed he had the political savvy to somehow get the votes. Her contribution would be her presence in Trinidad, with the advantage of day-to-date observations and insights that Ed, in Washington, could never get but had to have. Once she'd been a good reporter. It was time to get to work again.

She signaled the waiter to take away her dinner plate. She felt a surge of excitement at the possibilities. Stefan Vaska's case was taking on larger dimensions. No longer was she just her father's associate, sitting on the sidelines as she had for so many years. She and Ed Keating would be full partners. But for him to get the votes, there would have to be a public outcry—a great deal of outcry—loud enough to force his fellow congressmen to heed.

As she watched the waiter put a piece of apple pie before her, she pondered what the focus should be. A strike in itself wasn't news. Even the presence of the National Guard wasn't unusual. Martial law, then, must be the centerpiece.

Twenty years ago, the general population had tolerated martial law, but times were changing. The Progressives had forced the Pure Food and Drug Act through Congress seven years ago. There were regulations of interstate commerce. Yet with all that, there was still strong national sentiment against strikes.

Alex pushed her dessert plate away. It was a long shot—a very long shot—but it was worth a try. Her heart began to race over the possibilities. Testimony at the hearings could set the stage for corrective, even-handed legislation that would completely eliminate the need for strikes. In the process, martial law would be lifted. Stefan Vaska would have his day in court.

She'd write Ed Keating tonight. Come to think of it, Congress was on the verge of its Christmas recess. She'd send the letter to his home and suggest she visit him so they could work out the details.

Bill Henderson had pooh-poohed her suggestion about trying for an investigation. Surely, once he understood the focus she intended to use, he'd want to be involved.

Chapter Eight

Bill eyed her, trying to figure out Alex's cockeyed scheme.

"So who should I interview first?" she finally asked.

They sat across from each other at a small table in the Newhart Cafe, a block west of the Columbian Hotel. Because the place was a favorite breakfast spot, it was crowded. The noise level was so high he had trouble hearing her.

"Let it go," he said.

He'd been surprised when she'd telephoned the night before to set up a meeting and almost put her off with the excuse of too much work, but he decided she wouldn't believe that. Then it occurred to him it might be a good idea to know what the hell she was up to.

The waitress placed their plates of eggs, fried potatoes, and slices of bacon before them.

"It'll be Christmas in a couple of days. Go home."

"I have a job to do."

"Maybe I didn't make it clear yesterday," Bill said, picking up his fork. "Questioning the motives of either side is straight-out dangerous. Small towns don't appreciate out-of-towners nosing around in their business even under normal circumstances."

"I have no intention of investigating motives. I just want to get the facts. Is that so threatening?"

"What do you think?" he asked, loading his fork with potatoes, wishing he hadn't come, stalling in the hope he could figure out a way to discourage her enough so she'd go home. "Listen, even without martial law, these counties aren't exactly centers of free speech."

"You say that and you're the district attorney?"

He chewed the potatoes, swallowed, recalling his conversation with Judge Southard again.

"So you won't give me any names, is that it?"

"It's not a matter of names," he said. "It's a matter of being realistic."

"I'm perfectly realistic."

"You think I'm exaggerating? Take a look at the two men sitting behind me over by the door."

Alex glanced past his shoulder.

"They're Pinkerton detectives. Brought in by the Victor American mine owners from Kansas City last week to take care of anyone—and I mean anyone—who causes trouble."

"But—"

"Those birds are not gentlemen. They're here to do a dirty job. I'm telling you, this strike isn't child's play. The stakes are as high as they get."

"I know that."

Bill glared. "You say you came to defend this man Vaska. Through no fault of your own, you can't. This idea of yours involves powers way out of your league. You take this on, and you're going to find yourself up against no less than John D. Rockefeller."

"And an international union," she added, derisively.

"So you do understand."

"My husband was killed in the last strike down here."

The mention of her husband startled him. During law school days, he'd heard something about her being a widow. But the news her husband had been killed in the last strike caught him off guard, made him wonder whether the death had some connection with her client. "This strike might kill you. Did you ever think of that?"

"That's absurd. No one would harm a woman."

"It's happened before. It will happen again. You can count on it."

"Undoubtedly, those women were strikers' wives."

"Not women like you."

"Exactly."

He eyed her in exasperation as he took a sip of the bitter coffee. It was cold. The day was not starting out well.

"My father knows the president of the CF&I. And General Chase."

"That connection didn't seem to get you in to see him."

"He was tied up in a meeting."

"Sure he was," he said, sarcastically. "I'm telling you, Alex, those Pinkerton fellows aren't going to check your social connections before they hustle you out of town. Or worse."

She glared at him.

"Your idea doesn't have a prayer," he said. "Even if you got all the background in the world, even if the congressman managed to round up the votes for an investigation, nothing will come of it. The system won't allow it. I know."

"It depends on how you use that system."

As he listened to her words, with their thinly veiled tone of superiority, it dawned on him that Alex MacFarlane regarded this whole thing as a case to be argued in moot court, a theoretical situation without consequences, detached from real people. "If you turned it upside down, it wouldn't change. It's like one of those toys that when you push it over it just pops right up again," he said, ruefully.

She raised an eyebrow.

"Alex, do you seriously believe the majority of the members of Congress, who are in the hip pocket of men like Rockefeller, are going to change anything?"

"Maybe not on the basic issues. At least not at first. But at the very least, public opinion will force the general and the governor to back down on martial law. I'm convinced of it."

"You want to do all this on behalf of Stefan Vaska?"

"That's not enough?"

He shrugged. "It certainly sounds good. In fact, if you were a man, I'd say you were warming up to run for public office."

She gave him a long, cold look as she took a bite of toast.

"Once and for all, you're wasting your time."

She wiped her fingers on her napkin. "All right, then, if you won't give me any names, I guess I'll have to go over to the union headquarters and ask."

"Who?"

She shrugged. "I'll find someone."

"Alex, if you don't quit this right now, there's no way I can guarantee your safety."

"Actually, I don't remember asking for your protection," she said, pushing back her chair and fishing in her pocketbook. "Thirty cents should cover my half of breakfast, including the tip."

"I'll get it."

"I wouldn't think of it." She rose, placed the coins on the table, and left.

He watched her through the plate-glass window, standing in the doorway, buttoning her coat. A group of men walked by her, turned to take a second look. A beautiful woman in high-fashion clothes—probably from Paris—was not an everyday sight in Trinidad. But he doubted she even noticed.

He put down another thirty cents next to the money she'd left and made his way to the door. The Pinkertons watched him go out. The morning air was damp and cold, and he shoved his hands into his pockets. Alex was nowhere in sight.

Chapter Nine

Alex stopped in front of the two-story sandstone building, eyed the sign hung across the entrance: UNITED MINE WORKERS OF AMERICA.

Out of the corner of her eye, she caught a glimpse of someone moving and looked around to see a man stationed in the doorway of the seedy-looking hotel across the street. He wasn't one of the men she'd seen in the cafe, but it was plain he was watching her. Pushing back her fear, she pulled open the door of the union office and stepped inside.

The large room with its high ceiling had the feel of an immense cave. It appeared to be empty. The rancid smell of cheap cigar smoke and old coffee hung in the air. She took a few steps, her heels clicking against the bare wood floor. As her eyes adjusted to the dim light, she saw a man sitting hunched over a desk next to a flight of stairs.

She walked closer and introduced herself. "I'm looking for whomever is in charge of the union."

"And yer business?"

"I need to discuss some matters regarding a client of mine by the name of Stefan Vaska. I know he's a miner, and I presume he belongs to the union."

"Niver heard of 'im."

"Perhaps if you would direct me to the person in charge—"

"That's John Lawson." The man's glance swept from her hat to her shoes. "He ain't here."

"Do you expect him later?"

"Not likely. He's out at the Ludlow camp today."

"Perhaps I can go and see him there."

"Ya won't get through."

Not get through? "I thought I'd hire a car."

"Not a way in the world."

Alex eyed him. "There are no cars for hire in Trinidad?"

"Not if yer goin' to Ludlow or to a coal town with a camp nearby."
He glowered at her. "Besides, the guards will stop ya without the right
identification."

"Guards along a public highway?" she asked, incredulous.

"Ya bet yer sweet life. And they're a mean bunch, the lot of 'em."

After three refusals, Alex decided the disagreeable little man at the
UMWA headquarters had been right about no one wanting to rent a car if
the destination was a union camp. She should have lied when the garage
men asked her where she was headed, but she knew she couldn't carry it
off.

Her search had taken her north along Commercial Street, almost to the
river, which meant she had a long hike back to the hotel. The cold wind
whipped bits of debris around her ankles as she trudged up the block, past
saloons and curio shops. Suddenly, her eye caught a tattered sign propped
in the window of a cheap hotel: STAGE DAILY TO LUDLOW, BERWIND,
TABASCO .25 CENTS.

She paused, reread the sign. The possibility of a stage had never
occurred to her. From its appearance, the sign was old. Still, transportation
was transportation. She went into the hotel to ask. The desk clerk merely
jerked a thumb in the direction of a schedule posted behind him. A stage
was due to leave at noon.

She bought a ticket, went over to the front window, where she could
keep an eye on the street, and sat down on a battered chair to wait.

The only other passenger in the ancient stage was a foreign-looking
woman, no more than a girl, wrapped in a black shawl, a baby in her arms.
Alex and the girl sat across from each other in the stage, avoiding each
other's knees in the small space, and smiled, but neither of them spoke. The
driver climbed up to his perch, snapped the reins across the rumps of the
four-horse team, and they were off.

Once out of the city, the stage careened down the road at top speed, cold
air rushing through the cramped interior. Alex spotted isinglass shades
rolled up tight against the window frames. She reached up and struggled to
loosen the knotted cords that held them in place. They wouldn't budge, and
she finally gave up and sat down. Resigned to a frigid trip, she pulled her
coat collar up over her ears.

Ludlow was seventeen miles north of Trinidad. With luck, she might get
there by two o'clock. Three at the latest. She hunched into her coat.

Eventually, the coach slowed. Alex sat up. The wheels clattered across railroad tracks, and she moved to the window. Ahead was a depot no larger than a tool shed. A sign on its roof read LUDLOW. Next to it was a water tank. Beyond was a meager collection of houses and what looked like a livery stable. She brightened.

But immediately the stage sped up again, leaving Ludlow behind. Leaning out the window, she shouted. "Driver, you missed my stop. Ludlow's where I want to get off."

The coach continued on. Desperate, Alex began to pound on the roof. "Stop. I said stop."

Eyes wide with alarm, the girl clutched her baby tighter.

"Damn it. Stop, I say," Alex screamed.

At last the stage slowed to a halt, and she staggered out.

With one hand clutching her hat against the wind, she peered up at the driver, dressed in a filthy sheepskin coat, his broad-brimmed hat pushed down across his forehead. "My ticket's for Ludlow," she shouted.

"Listen, lady, you need a special pass to stop at Ludlow."

"I thought my ticket—"

"You stop at Ludlow, you gotta show the right pass to the soldier boys. I don't got the right pass, I don't stop."

"But I have to get to the Ludlow camp."

He gave her a dubious look, adjusted the reins in his thickly gloved hands. She decided to tell him her business. "I'm an attorney, and I have to see Mr. Lawson about a man I'm representing."

He seemed unimpressed.

"But since it appears I must walk, the least you can do is to give me directions."

He turned his head and spat. "The camp's back over there to the north. It's those white tents. Ya can see 'em if you look hard."

"Will you be coming back this way later?"

"Not without a pass." He spat again. "Right now, I just wanna get the hell outta here." A moment later the stage started up again, leaving her alone.

Alex stood in the middle of the road and watched in dismay as it disappeared into the mouth of the narrow canyon beyond. She turned, and set off toward the white specks.

The sky was a dirty gray with no sign of the sun. The biting wind plastered her skirt and coat tight against her body; Alex felt her face growing numb. The tiny hamlet of Ludlow was out of sight. Acres of dun-colored grasses stretched in every direction. Strange cacti, their branches twisted and charred-looking, were all that broke the treeless landscape. To her left, an arroyo slashed deep through the barren field. Her head down, she fought against the wind and the fright that knotted her stomach.

Gradually, the specks became shapes of individual tents clustered on the rise like so many soiled white doves huddled against the winter chill. For the first time, she noticed another group of tents no more than a half a mile away. They were brown with the look of the army. Somehow, seeing the tents this close to the union camp didn't surprise her.

As she neared the Ludlow camp, she wondered how it happened to be located where it was. Perhaps a rancher friendly to the union had donated the use of the land. There were so many facets of this strike to investigate.

Just ahead was a tent with an American flag on its roof. The door opened and a man wearing a rough coat and cap came toward her. Unlike the soldiers, he carried no gun.

"Afternoon. May I ask your business, ma'am?"

Strands of hair whipped around her face. "I'm Alexandra MacFarlane. I've come to see Mr. Lawson."

The man frowned.

"MacFarlane," she repeated. Wondering if the tip of her nose was frozen, she eyed the tent. "Could we step inside?"

But he told her to wait, then disappeared into the tent.

She gingerly stamped her wooden feet and looked around her. A telephone wire was strung from the tent to a series of posts set up in the direction of the railroad tracks. A single strand of barbed wire was all that fenced the encampment. Anyone could come in or go out with no trouble at all.

The guard, if that's what he was, reappeared and held open the tent flap.

A Franklin stove sat in the center, and a coal oil lamp hung from the tent's center pole. Sitting behind a makeshift desk of planks set across two sawhorses was a dark-haired man of medium height and build. He was dressed in the simple clothes of a working man and high-topped boots. He looked up, smiled, and rose.

"Mrs. MacFarlane. I got a call from the office you might be coming out."

"Mr. Lawson?" He appeared to be about forty, a nice-looking man, with none of the roughness of manner she'd expected. He didn't look like a socialist.

He smiled as he pulled a camp chair closer to his desk.

"To tell the truth, I'm surprised you made it. This county isn't exactly the safest place for a lady these days. Have a seat."

Alex moved to the stove. "If you don't mind, I'll stand over here for a few moments. My feet are half frozen."

He kept smiling. "I wouldn't wonder. It's cold as the very devil out there."

Rubbing her stiff hands together, Alex watched John Lawson go over and sit down again. The simple act of walking a step or two and taking a seat was done with such economy of movement Alex sensed he was a man who used every moment to his advantage.

"Well, now. What brings you out here by yourself? The militia roam the countryside these days like so many vigilantes. You never know where they'll turn up."

"So I've been told." Despite his friendliness, his pale blue eyes were keen as they sized her up. He seemed intelligent. If he didn't like her purpose for coming, he might throw her out on her ear and she'd be faced with making the cold trip back to town, empty-handed. Unless, of course, she couldn't stop the stage. Then she'd have to walk. The prospect was distinctly unappealing.

"Frankly, Mr. Lawson, I need your help."

"I'll do what I can."

She smiled. "I've been retained to represent a man by the name of Stefan Vaska. I understand that before the strike he worked in one of the mines in Sandoval. At the moment, he's sitting in jail, without charge, though I understand he was arrested for inciting a riot."

"So you're a lawyer."

She nodded, impatient with his apparent attempt to put her off. "Mr. Lawson, I'm here because I believe you're the best person to give me the full particulars of Mr. Vaska's case. Surely, you won't disappoint me."

Chapter Ten

John Lawson surveyed Alex with a deadpan expression. "Vaska, you say? The name doesn't ring a bell."

She drew in her breath sharply, taken completely by surprise. "Of course, it's possible Mr. Vaska might not be a member of the union. But I'm told he was living in the camp outside of Sandoval before his arrest."

"I'm sorry. But with twelve thousand men in the camps—"

"But surely—even with all those men—the union must be aware of anyone picked up."

"Sorry."

"With martial law, my client can be released only with General Chase's permission. But to this point, I haven't been able to talk to the general. In the meantime, I'm trying to familiarize myself with Mr. Vaska's case so that when I finally do see Chase, I'll have the full facts."

"Wish I could help," he said, pushing back his chair and rising. "Too bad you had to make the long trip."

Alex smiled. He wasn't going to get rid of her this easily. "I don't suppose you have some hot coffee?"

John Lawson scowled, obviously embarrassed she'd had to remind him of an ordinary courtesy. "Of course." He stepped to the tent's entrance and held open the flap. "Please, if you'll follow me to the cook tent."

As they set out along the path between two rows of tents, he turned to her. "A woman like yourself, Mrs. MacFarlane, a lawyer from Denver, how is it you're representing a miner?"

Alex eyed him, not sure how to answer his question or even whether she wanted to answer it. She said, "You do believe in due process?"

"Of course."

"Well, so do I. With martial law, it doesn't exist. For my client or anyone else."

John Lawson raised an eyebrow but made no response, as if digesting what she'd said.

Women with shawls clutched around their shoulders hurried past them. They continued walking through the rows of tents, each eight feet square, a stovepipe stuck through the canvas roof. Hundreds of them, home to thousands of men, she guessed, some with families. The rows were divided by wide paths of what once had been grass but was now dirt, beaten hard by thousands of feet.

In the distance were rows of clotheslines. Shirts and pants flapped stiff as cardboard in the icy air. Ahead was a large tent that had the look of a meeting place.

A few yards away, a man emerged from one of the smaller tents, eyed her, gave John Lawson a look that seemed to say, *Don't let these sightseers get you down,* before he disappeared around the corner. A half dozen ragtag children, laughing and calling to each other in several different languages, dashed in front of them, seemingly oblivious to the piercing cold.

"Mr. Lawson, all these people—"

He glanced at her. "Individual rights. That's why all these folks are here."

Alex smiled inwardly at his less-than-direct answer. Two could play the game as well as one. "I thought it was about wages and working conditions."

"Is there a difference?"

She eyed him.

"The guarantees in the Bill of Rights are no different than what the union stands for."

"I see," she said, doubtfully.

"Which is why we've fought for company recognition of the union all these years," he said. "If they don't agree to let the union represent all the men, they can play us one against the other. They'll go on treating us like animals. They'll ignore the safety laws—"

"I thought that had all been corrected since the days when my husband was killed in a cave-in of the mine at Hastings."

"Your husband?"

"Robert MacFarlane. He was an engineer, hired to inspect one of the Victor American mines for a prospective investor."

He pursed his lips, not saying anything.

They walked on for a few yards before she said, "Tell me, Mr. Lawson, do you think the strike will succeed this time?"

"No doubt about it."

The sincerity reflected in his blue eyes was persuasive. Apparently, he believed the union could outlast the nearly unlimited resources of the companies, not to mention the strong public opinion against strikes. "But how?"

"This time we're prepared to wait it out," he said. "The longer we're on strike, the better our position."

"I don't understand."

"First thing, it's winter."

She gave a wry laugh. "I've noticed."

"This country heats its homes and offices and factories with the coal dug in the fields up north. But down here we've got an even better hold."

"How's that?"

"We mine soft coal."

"So?"

"The CF&I is in the steel-making business."

"So?"

"It takes coke to fuel the blast furnaces. Without it, there's no steel. Coke's made by baking the soft coal mined down here in the southern fields. But coke can't be stored. It crumbles. So even though the CF&I knew a strike was on the way, they couldn't do a thing to protect themselves against it."

Alex eyed him, struck by his candor and the cleverness of the plan. They had reached the entrance to the large tent.

"What about the men the companies bring in to replace the strikers?" she asked. "Don't they keep things going?"

"Scabs, we call them," he said. "Most of them never mined coal in their lives, and there're not enough of them to keep the supply up to the demand." He pulled back the tent flap. "Another month, two at the most, and the stockholders will demand the companies settle. This time it'll be on our terms."

Stepping into the large tent, Alex felt the welcome relief of the warm air, smelled the rich aromas of onions, meat, and spices simmering together. The raw planked floor was neatly swept. At one end of the tent were make-shift tables bounded by benches. Women stood nearby at cookstoves, pre-paring the evening meal. One of them was smaller than the others, younger, and quite beautiful, her gleaming black braids pinned in a crown on the top of her head.

Several men, playing cards, were seated around one of the tables. A dark-haired man stood off to one side, watching, a grimy cap pushed back on his head.

"Boys, like you to meet Mrs. MacFarlane," John Lawson said. As he approached the group, he gestured for her to follow him. "She's from

Denver. A lawyer for a man from Sandoval. Vaska's his name. Anyone know him?"

The men stared at her with open curiosity and shook their heads. "This Vaska. He's not one of us," said the man who stood off to one side.

She eyed him, curious. There was something about the quick manner in which he had answered that made her think he was lying.

They went over to the women cooking supper, whose eyes were filled with weariness no amount of sleep could erase. Most of the women nodded politely when John Lawson introduced them. The smaller woman merely wiped her hands on her apron, her mouth tight.

"How about pouring us some coffee?" he asked her.

Without replying, the young woman turned toward the stove, reached for a tin cup with one hand, and with the other, a huge blackened coffeepot. She filled the cup and handed it to Alex. "We have no cream."

Alex smiled. "This will be fine. Thank you."

The young woman's eyes flashed in fury, as if Alex had somehow insulted her. Alex decided not to pursue the matter. She turned back to the men at the table.

"How will you be getting back to Trinidad?" John Lawson asked, taking the other cup of coffee from the young woman.

Alex glanced at him. She had tried not to think about the problem of the return trip. "I came by stage."

"I'm surprised. The last I knew the militia had stopped giving out passes."

"So I discovered." She took a swallow of coffee. "Perhaps I can take the train back."

"Same situation as the stage, I'm afraid. Since the strike, the train doesn't stop at Ludlow either."

"Oh."

"I can arrange a ride for you."

The offer came as a surprise. "Then you have a pass?"

He gave her a crooked grin. "Let's just say, we work around that problem in our own way."

She handed the tin cup to one of the women. She was reluctant to accept any favors from John Lawson. But the stage was no longer a possibility. The train was out. It was too far to walk in this cold through the dark.

"I don't want to inconvenience anyone," she said as they left the tent.

They walked through the early evening dark of winter toward what appeared to be the main entrance of the camp.

"I think you should know there's a risk traveling in a union truck," he said.

She eyed him. "Without wishing to seem ungrateful, Mr. Lawson, I would use another mode of transportation if there were one."

He gave her a little smile.

"So I accept your offer with thanks."

An ancient truck drove up, stopped. A man climbed out. John Lawson went over to him. They spoke for a moment, glanced her way, before Mr. Lawson beckoned for her to get into the truck.

"Dom's a good driver, Mrs. MacFarlane."

"Thank you." She shook his hand, struck by its firm grasp. "Perhaps we'll have a chance to talk further another time."

"Could be."

Alex got in on the passenger side, and Mr. Lawson slammed the door shut. The driver climbed in, shifted gears. A guard pulled back the strand of wire that served as a gate. Alex glanced out the window to see Mr. Lawson, standing by the guard, watching the truck as it rolled past.

Chapter Eleven

Maria Ferrera moved the wooden spoon through the thick stew simmering in the huge cast-iron pot, pleased to see all the chunks of meat among the potatoes and turnips and carrots. At first light, her brother, Dom, had left the camp and bagged three rabbits, a rare treat. Unless a man managed to elude the army guards, who kept a sharp eye out for a lone hunter, meat of any kind was not part of the camp's diet.

As she stirred, her thoughts returned to the woman who had just left, the woman John Lawson had introduced as Mrs. MacFarlane. The slender hands, gloved in fine leather, holding the tin cup of coffee, the gray eyes glancing about her at the sights in the tent, as if it were a zoo, the way she had talked with John Lawson in tones neither too loud nor too soft, words reflecting an education beyond grammar school.

As Maria continued to stir the pot, it dawned on her that Mrs. MacFarlane was the first outside woman to come to this tent camp. She felt a stab of uneasiness. A woman in a mine was bad luck. Yet to imagine Mrs. MacFarlane had somehow brought a curse to the camp was stupid. Maria knew better.

A blast of cold air filled the tent, and Maria turned to see the unmarried men filing in. On most other nights, Dom was in their midst. Since the strike, John Lawson had given him various small jobs that had put him among the group of men who had no families and whom John expected to take the brunt of any battle if serious trouble began. Fiercely proud of being allowed into the group, Dom had taken on some of their nonchalant manner. If necessary, Maria knew, he would go beyond the limits of good sense to prove himself.

Tonight he was making the weekly trip into Trinidad for supplies. So far nothing had happened, but there was always a first time. She tried not to worry.

As she passed among the men with coffee, each of them was generous in praise of the meal. One or two, their eagerness to impress her thinly veiled, joked with her. She always smiled, but she was not interested in any of them. Marriage was not for her.

After the meal, she and the other women who had come to take their turn at the cooking washed the dishes and scrubbed the tables down in preparation for the morning meal. Maria said good night to the men still playing cards and left. Though the hour was early, she was tired, anxious for sleep.

Drawing her shawl around her, she stepped out into the cold and walked along the broad path between the tents. Kerosene lamps lighted a few, but in most the only light was a candle. The figures silhouetted in the faint light bent and moved, as in a magic lantern show she'd seen once, except the shapes were people she knew, people she cared about. She glanced up into the dark sky. There was no moon. The truck would be difficult to see. Dom's trip would go smoothly.

Her thoughts again returned to the woman visitor. What did a woman lawyer do? Where did she live? Denver? New York?

Maria knew about New York. It was the city where they had landed—Papa, Mamma, she, and Dom. Thirteen years ago.

It had begun with the promises printed in the grimy pamphlets passed from hand to hand in the tiny cafe on the town square of Venetico, on the coast west of Messina. There, with a dim view on a clear day of Monte Stromboli's cone rising above the Mediterranean to the north, Papa met his friends, sipped a little Chianti, talked, and dared to dream of a future unlike his father's and his grandfather's.

With money from the sale of their scraps of furniture and the brooch Mamma had inherited from her grandmother, they had set off in the bowels of an ancient steamship for New York. Once there, they found living quarters in unused storage space behind the furnace in the basement of a tenement on the Lower East Side. A single, barred window; ceiling so low, even for a seven-year-old, that if she stretched very tall and stood on tiptoe, she could touch the ceiling with her fingertips. That spring Mamma died. With no money for a proper funeral, she was buried in a pauper's grave.

Papa had packed up and managed to get his small family to the coalfields of Illinois, where he got a job laying track for two dollars a day, seven days a week. But that Christmas the company claimed profits were down and fired the new men. Again, she and Papa wrapped their few belongings in a blanket, Maria took Dom's hand, and they left.

At the railroad station, Papa was standing by a train schedule tacked up next to the ticket window, trying to make it out, when a man wearing a shiny bowler hat and sporty clothes came up to them.

"A fine family you have there, sir," he said, tipping his hat to Papa and smiling broadly at Maria and Dom.

Papa had looked around and smiled at the man in a friendly way.

"If it isn't too personal, sir, it appears you might be needin' some assistance."

Maria stared up at the two gold teeth protruding from the front of his mouth. He moved his tongue, and a toothpick appeared from nowhere.

"We don't need your help. Thank you," she said.

Papa glanced down at her and gently chucked her chin. "Now, *carina*."

Maria continued to glare up at the man.

"If it's work you're after, sir, I've got good news," the man said as he pulled a printed notice out of his pocket and handed it to Papa.

Her father had studied the words for a few minutes before he handed the notice to Maria.

"They're hirin' in Colorado, my friend. A fine place to raise a family. Fresh air. Towering mountains. Top wages. Train fare's included. All you need to do is put your X on the line and you're on the way."

"Don't do it, Papa," Maria hissed.

"How far is this Colorado?" Papa asked.

"Overnight, and you're there." The man kept grinning as he explored his mouth with the toothpick.

Papa took the notice from her and studied it, as if by examining the words long enough, they'd somehow make sense. "Well . . ."

Maria didn't trust the man's cold, bird-like eyes. She knew it was a trick, and she tugged at Papa's sleeve to warn him. "Papa—"

"We must eat," he said to her, a hard edge to his voice that hurt her feelings then but that she later understood. "Give me the paper. I will sign."

A week later, when they stepped off the train at a siding in the middle of nowhere, Papa discovered he had been hired as one of hundreds of scabs to replace miners out on strike.

A man who never took anything from anyone, not even food when his children were close to starving, Papa realized he had another man's job. But it was too late. The paper was signed; the company guards allowed no escape.

He had made the best of it, bettered himself until he was good enough to be assigned his own "room," be paid by the ton, even hire helpers from his earnings. Only four years later something went wrong. A charge went off too soon. Papa and the men with him were blown to bits.

Maria remembered staring at the gaunt women who came to offer their condolences, smelling their fear that maybe tomorrow they would be in her place. When they left, she had decided to wash clothes, to sew, to do anything short of selling her body rather than marry a miner and repeat the cycle.

She taught herself to read better and to do her sums. Because they lived in a coal camp without a school, she began to teach others, at night, around the rickety table Papa had bought from the company store. The quarters she was paid for her teaching, the nickels she earned ironing the superintendent's shirts, plus the five dollars a month Dom earned as a trapper kept food on the table and a roof over their heads.

Now Dom was laying track and had prospects for working as a miner's helper. For now, the union was his life, but she had to help him reach out for something else.

Maria stopped in front of the tent she and Dom shared and went in. Eight feet square, it held a tiny stove, two cots, a table with a washbowl, a chamber pot, and a single chair. It was enough. Maria undressed hurriedly, pulled on a nightdress, and crawled beneath the layer of blankets covering her cot.

As she lay back, she placed her hands over her belly as if she could somehow actually touch the flesh and blood she was certain now was growing within her. From the first moment she'd suspected she was pregnant with Frank Bellamy's child, she'd decided he must never know. If he didn't love his wife, he did love his children, and they needed him. The miners and their families also needed him. The few coal company doctors—who were more like butchers than doctors—had joined the militia. Now Frank was the only doctor for a hundred miles willing to come out to the union camps and care for strikers. She could never let him abandon them or his children to go off with her somewhere.

Her breasts would grow fuller, her waist would thicken. By spring, her pregnancy would become difficult to hide.

She thought about the children who would be waiting for her tomorrow in the cook tent that served as a school after the morning meal. There were the girls whose mothers kept them home from the few company schools to help with the washing and earn a few extra pennies. And there were the boys who had already gone down in the mines. For them, the strike was a wonderful gift of time, proof there truly was some good in everything, no matter how bad it seemed. Now they could go to school and play and be children again. But for how long, no one knew. The strike could be over in a week or could last for months. How many months was the question. She offered a little prayer that she would be able to stay until each child knew at least the ABCs.

Chapter Twelve

Alex sat against the back of the hard, wooden seat of the truck cab, shivering. She glanced at the driver. He had no earflaps on his cap. His jacket looked thin. He wasn't wearing gloves.

He shifted gears, and the truck slowly rolled through the dark along the rutted road. Alex was conscious of something that was not quite right. Several minutes went by before she realized the truck was running without lights.

"Pardon me," she said, peering through the windshield. "How can you see where you're going?"

"Don't worry, missus. I know the way." His voice held the thin bravado of a boy, and she looked at him more carefully. She had thought him a man, but now realized he was probably no more than fifteen.

"I suppose you're avoiding the soldiers."

"Even with lights, they wouldn't find me; they're so stupid."

Alex hoped it was true. The truck lurched and swayed as it rounded a corner. They passed the shadowy form of what looked like a farmhouse. The truck bounced across train tracks, throwing her off the seat so that she hit her head against the roof of the cab. She straightened her hat, tried to laugh. "I guess I should hang on to something."

The boy only shot her a glance. The truck rolled on. The rancid odor of his dried sweat and unwashed clothes filled the cab.

"I must apologize for not having introduced myself," she said finally. "I'm Mrs. MacFarlane."

He glanced at her.

"Mr. Lawson said your name is Dom. He didn't mention your last name, however."

His eyes fixed on the road. "Ferrera," he said.

"I suppose you belong to the union."

"UMWA region 15, local 62." There was the same kind of bluster about the way he said it that she'd picked up before. From a younger boy, it might have been amusing.

She pressed him for more information about himself. "I suppose you worked in one of the mines before the strike."

"At Hastings. That's outside Aguilar. In Number One."

"I see. And your father works there, too, does he?"

"Not no more." Dom adjusted his grip on the steering wheel. "A charge went off too soon, and boom!"

"I'm sorry," was all Alex could think to say.

"It's the way it is sometimes," he said in a flat, resigned tone of an old man.

They bumped slowly along what had to be nothing more than wagon wheel ruts, not talking for a few minutes.

"You have other family?"

"My sister, Maria. She's a teacher in the camp. You mighta seen her when you was in the cook tent."

Alex arched an eyebrow at his reference to her being in the cook tent. As brief as it had been, her visit apparently was common knowledge. She tried to remember whom she'd met in the tent, then thought of the surly young woman who'd handed her the coffee. "Dark hair in a braid on top of her head?"

"That's her."

"She's very pretty."

"Yeah."

Alex eyed the taciturn boy and smiled at his awkward acceptance of her praise. "Dom . . . I hope I may call you Dom."

He shrugged.

"What's it like down in the mines?"

He glanced at her, said he'd gone down in the mines when he was nine. When she didn't reply, he told her about the dark, the sounds, the danger. It was as if he wanted to impress her, and he had.

She tried to imagine the boy-man who sat beside her as a thin little boy of nine when he'd descended into the bowels of the earth, tried to imagine what it would be like to be a child and never see the sun, never feel the wind on your face.

They lapsed into silence again for what must have been several miles. The ride was smoother, and she guessed they'd returned to a regular roadway. Finally, they came to the crest of a small hill. A wide band of lights spread out below. They were close to town, and she gave a silent sigh of relief. As they reached the outskirts, the truck slowed.

They had passed several blocks when out of the corner of her eye, she saw a knot of soldiers lounging around the entrance of a darkened building on the next corner. She tensed, remembered John Lawson's warning about the risk of traveling in a union truck. She saw now there were four men. As the truck approached, they grabbed their rifles. One held up a hand for Dom to stop.

Dom shifted gears, pulled back on the brake.

"What's going on?" she asked, trying for calm.

"It's a patrol."

"What do they want?"

"My pass."

She glanced at him. Beneath his off-hand tone, she caught a hint of fear. A barrel-chested man with a wrestler's thick neck yelled at Dom to get out of the truck. She realized she was holding her breath.

Two of the soldiers walked back toward the truck bed while the big man and a companion waited for Dom to produce the pass. With a bit of show, the boy dug in the pockets of his jacket for what Alex suspected was a non-existent pass.

"Hurry it up."

"I don't find it."

"'Cause you ain't got one."

Dom patted his jacket as if checking for other pockets, obviously stalling for time. "It's here."

A soldier appeared at the passenger door and peered in at her. "Hey, sarge. There's a woman in here."

"Bring her here."

The soldier opened the door and grabbed for her, but she shrugged him away and climbed down. "If you please, I am perfectly capable of managing without help."

She walked around the truck. "Why have we been stopped?" she demanded of the sergeant.

He surveyed her coldly. "Have to check your pass."

Alex felt Dom watching her. She didn't want to endanger him by saying the wrong thing. Drawing herself a little straighter, she glared at the sergeant. "What on earth are you talking about?"

"This union scum ain't got no pass, which means you're under arrest."

"I don't know what you mean."

"With no pass, in this county, you're under arrest."

She gave him a frigid look. "You can't be serious."

"Do ya see me smilin'?"

"This is a mistake."

"You're violatin' the law."

"There's no law about passes."

"There is now."

"Look here, sergeant, you have to take me to General Chase's headquarters at the Columbian Hotel. I know the general personally, as well as his aide, Captain Van Howe. They'll straighten this matter out immediately."

"Says you." He grabbed her arm. "Now, if you know what's good for ya, you'll come quietly."

A soldier shoved Dom, causing him to trip and nearly fall. The lights of an automobile coming across the bridge threw a wide arc of light across the dark street, catching them in its glare. Alex waved and called out to attract the driver's attention.

The automobile—a big touring car—stopped. Someone climbed out and stepped into the light. It was a large man, fat, gray-haired, wearing a dress suit and a silk top hat. She stared at him. He looked familiar somehow.

The man approached, squinting. "Mrs. MacFarlane?"

She looked more closely. "Mr. Baxter?" The man she'd met the day she arrived. "Thank heavens."

Leslie Baxter frowned. "What's going on here?"

"These soldiers—"

Mr. Baxter swung his glance to the sergeant. "Explain yourself."

Before the soldier could answer, she said, "This young man was simply giving me a lift into town, and these men stopped us and demanded to see a pass. They say we're under arrest. The whole thing is preposterous."

"I'm followin' orders," the sergeant growled.

"I mean, there I was out in the middle of nowhere. If it hadn't been for this kind young man . . . I know the county is under martial law, Mr. Baxter, but this . . ."

Leslie Baxter turned toward the sergeant. "You, sir, are doing your duty, for which you are to be commended," he intoned, solemnly. "However, this lovely lady is new to the area with no knowledge of the situation here. I will be happy to escort Mrs. MacFarlane back to her hotel."

She let out her breath, her anxiety subsiding. Still, she couldn't walk away and leave the boy alone. "Please, this young man—Dom—must also be released. He was merely doing me a favor."

"Sergeant, surely, that can be arranged," Mr. Baxter said.

The sergeant's eyes narrowed. He regarded Leslie Baxter as if weighing just how important he was. "What's the name again?"

Mr. Baxter offered Alex his arm. "Leslie Baxter, attorney to the Colorado Fuel and Iron Company."

Dom stared, wide-eyed. Alex almost smiled, enjoying the delicious irony of a company lawyer saving a striker from jail.

She smiled at the boy and thanked him.

The boy tugged respectfully at the bill of his cap. Ill-kempt, probably illiterate, he had a defiant manner she'd sensed in his sister. Yet there was something about him she couldn't dismiss.

Chapter Thirteen

Leslie Baxter accompanied Alex across the hotel lobby toward the front desk. As the clerk handed her the key to her room, she glanced at the clock on the wall behind him and saw it was past ten o'clock.

"A brandy perhaps. After your trying experience," she heard Mr. Baxter say.

She turned, smiled. "Thank you, but I think what I need most is a hot bath and bed."

"Of course." His look was grave. "You do understand, I'm sure. About the circumstances."

"I'm deeply grateful for your help, Mr. Baxter. Without it, I might be sitting in jail. But no, I'm afraid I don't understand what it was all about. Perhaps you will explain later."

"It would be my pleasure."

"Now, if you will excuse me . . ." She turned away and walked up the stairs.

Once inside her room, she went directly to the bathroom and began to fill the tub. Moments later, her clothes strewn across the bed, she pinned the hair off the back of her neck and eased into the steaming water, luxuriated in its warmth as it seeped through her skin.

Lord, never would she have imagined such a day. Managing to get out to the Ludlow camp and back. Actually seeing strikers and their families, which was informative, even somewhat surprising. The soldiers. The narrow escape. The strange boy, Dom. She'd been in the thick of it. She'd been frightened, a little, but it had all been rather exciting, though she wasn't sure she'd travel without a pass again.

Stretching her legs to the end of the tub, she wiggled her toes. Why they weren't frostbitten she had no idea. She squeezed the water through the washcloth and held it to her breasts. She was weary to the bone.

The water slowly cooled, and reluctantly she stood and stepped over the tub's high side and toweled herself dry. Peering into the mirror above the sink, she saw her red, windburned face. She opened the medicine cabinet to find her cold cream, one of those small things she had long depended on. She'd discovered its wonders at the same time she had discovered Robb.

It had been this time of year. She hadn't had time to make the long trip west to Colorado and back to Vassar over Christmas vacation. Her roommate, Cissy MacFarlane, had invited her to spend the holidays with her family in New York.

On that Christmas Eve afternoon, she and Cissy went off to skate in Central Park. When they reappeared through the front door at teatime, Cissy's mother gasped. "Look at you two. Nearly time to bathe and dress, and you look like farmhands with that windburn."

"Mamma, the party's not for another three hours," Cissy said, kissing her mother's cheek fondly.

"Get my cold cream," her mother said, shrugging her daughter off. "Take a hot bath and let it soak in. By some miracle, it may help."

They slathered on the white cream, giggling at the sight of their clown-like faces. It helped. By eight o'clock they were dressed in white gowns of sculptured *peau de soie*, matching slippers, and new white kid gloves. Alex brushed her long hair up into a loose knot at the top of her head. The pearl drop-earrings her father had given her on her eighteenth birthday looked stunning against her ivory skin.

Alex knew no one but her hosts and Cissy. Still, she was excited about the evening. She'd heard about the annual Christmas Eve gala the MacFarlanes held for one hundred of their closest friends. An orchestra had been hired. Every room was decorated with silver-ribboned pine boughs. The entire house was brilliant with candlelight. Champagne would be served.

As she and Cissy descended the curving staircase toward the entrance hall where the MacFarlanes were receiving guests, Alex spied the handsomest man she'd ever seen—dark hair combed back, dark eyebrows over deep-set eyes, high cheekbones. Slim and elegant in his evening suit, he lounged against the door frame with an air of studied boredom as he sipped from a champagne glass. When he saw her coming toward him, he straightened and his gaze moved over her. He smiled as if the sight of her amused him.

"Robb! How wonderful! You said you weren't coming." Cissy ran down the stairs and flung her arms around the man's neck. She twisted around toward Alex. "This is Robb. You know. I've told you all about him. The dearest brother in all the world. And the naughtiest."

Robb laughed and reached up to loosen his sister's hold. "And who, sister mine, is this lovely creature?"

"Oh, you know very well this is Alex. I've written you about her. We share rooms at school. She lives way off in Colorado. You remember."

Never taking his eyes off her, Robb signaled the butler to refill his glass. "Well, hello, Alex-from-Colorado." His deep voice made her shiver with delight.

All pretense of sophistication evaporated as she met his gaze. She couldn't help herself. No wonder Robb MacFarlane was the family favorite. A polo player par excellence, the tales went, a graduate of Harvard and a member, like Teddy Roosevelt, of the school's exclusive Porcellian eating club. He'd gone from engineering school at Cornell to become one of the Rough Riders who had stormed Cuba the year before. Every beautiful girl from Boston to Philadelphia was said to be in love with him. No wonder.

Moments later, they were dancing. At the first intermission, he swept her into the library, closed the door, and kissed her passionately on the lips. There was no stopping him, and she didn't want to, for at that instant she knew this was the man she intended to marry.

How long ago it all was, their meeting, and two years later that single year of marriage. A marriage where romantic notions quickly fell by the wayside, beginning the first night of their honeymoon in Europe.

Their bodies still damp from lovemaking, Robb had climbed out of the ship's bunk, donned his evening suit again, and left—just for a short while, he'd assured her with a kiss—to join a poker game being held in another stateroom. That time he won. More often he lost, which only pushed him on to play again.

They had settled in Denver. Robb claimed that because he was a mining engineer, Denver was a good location. But instead of working, his days were spent playing polo and golf, his nights filled with gambling. The bill collectors hounded her even as Robb begged for more credit from wealthy friends, but whenever she mentioned going back to her old job at the newspaper, Robb flew into a rage. During the long, lonely days, she often stared into the mirror, wondering if she was the cause of the problem. Then came the offer from a friend of her father's for Robb to inspect several mines.

She'd insisted he face up to his responsibilities. He balked. In the end, it was the pay—enough to write off some of the debts he'd been hounded about—that persuaded him to take the job. She'd seen him off on the train in the morning. Two weeks later, he was dead.

There'd been tears and guilt, but with her father's help, the wounds gradually healed over, and she settled for the life she had found.

But in the last few days, in this strange place, it was as if she'd pulled open a door and crossed a threshold. What had started as a relatively simple matter of getting a client out of jail had become a major challenge. She was filled with a sense of purpose she hadn't felt for years, maybe never.

Alex put on her dressing gown and slippers and went to the window. The street below was seething with restless men. She thought of the soldiers. Across the street, a man stood in the shadows of a doorway, and she wondered if it was the same Pinkerton man she'd seen earlier that morning.

Today John Lawson had given her some union cant, though there'd been a thread of sincerity running through it she hadn't expected. When Dom had been stopped, she'd encountered, firsthand, the arbitrary, arrogant intimidation of citizens under the guise of martial law. Put together, she had the germ of a case for the investigation she'd present to Ed. But before she forgot the details—whom she'd talked to, what they'd told her, her general impressions—she wanted to write them down. Sitting at the desk, she reached into the drawer and rummaged for pen and paper, eager to begin.

Alex had finished only a page when she realized how hungry she was; she hadn't eaten since morning. She called downstairs, but the dining room was closed. The desk clerk asked if soup and rolls would be acceptable. She told him to send up a tray, along with a glass of red wine, as soon as possible. Though it wasn't the steak and fresh vegetables she'd had in mind, it would have to do. As she waited for the food to arrive, she continued to write.

Finally, there was a brisk knock on the door. She let the bellboy in, making space on the desk for the tray. The soup was barley, and its rich aroma made her mouth water.

When she handed the boy a tip, he reached into his jacket, produced two pieces of mail, and put them on the desk next to the tray.

As the door closed behind him, she sat down at the desk and spread the napkin across her lap, took a sip of wine, eyeing the two envelopes. The handwriting on one was her father's. The other was a telegram. She picked it up and worked open the flap.

It was from Margaret Keating, saying she had taken the liberty of opening her husband's mail. He was expected back Christmas Eve. Could Alex come to share their Christmas dinner? Grinning, Alex pressed the telegram to her breasts. The invitation was exactly what she'd hoped for.

With soaring spirits, she took another sip of wine, then spooned the thick soup, savoring the taste and the feel of its warmth when she swallowed. It wasn't until she'd finished eating that she opened her father's letter.

Sliding out the heavy sheet of stationery, she realized she had half expected to smell a hint of the cologne her father always patted on his face after shaving. But unfolding it, she saw the letter was typewritten on office letterhead with his secretary's initials at the bottom.

> Dear Alexandra,
> I received your telegram telling of your arrival. I need not elaborate on my displeasure. By now I am certain you have assessed the impossibility of the situation. Telegraph the time of your return, and I will have Jim pick you up with the car at the station.
> Your father, Jonathan Russell

She looked up from the letter, picturing him with hands clasped behind his back as he stared out his office window and dictated to his faithful secretary. Alex loved him. He loved her, in his way. It didn't surprise her that he still disapproved of her decision. If he knew of the danger, he'd be down on the next train.

She had no notion what new obstacles she'd encounter. At the moment, she didn't care. She could tackle anything. At long last, she was really alive, doing something of consequence.

She removed the tray from the desk and pulled out another sheet of hotel stationery. She had to respond to Margaret Keating's invitation. With no delays, the letter should arrive the day after tomorrow. As Alex picked up the pen, she tried to recall today's date. Christmas was in four days. Or was it five? She'd lost count. A letter took too much time. She opened the single drawer again and reached for a pad of telegram forms. If she missed seeing Ed while he was in Pueblo, her chances for the investigation might be lost.

Chapter Fourteen

The next morning, Alex rose up on her elbows and squinted out at the feathery snow drifting past the window. Before she did anything else, she had to answer her father's letter. She had no intention of mentioning her plan, such as it was. He'd only raise objections. She simply wanted him to know he shouldn't count on her immediate return.

She threw back the bed covers, got up, and put on her dressing gown. She wanted to get him out of her system. Sitting down at the desk, she wrote:

> Dear Father,
> Work will keep me here until after Christmas. I am well and hope you are the same. I'll write more soon.
> > Hurriedly, your loving daughter, Alexandra

She addressed the envelope, slipped the single sheet inside, and sealed it shut.

She sat back, her thoughts returning to the people she'd seen in the union camp. Where had they come from? Was the life of mining coal, even before the strike, better than the ones they'd left behind? She visualized the rows of tents she'd seen at the Ludlow camp, the orderliness of it all, like a village planned down to the last detail of street signs. There was nothing casual about its arrangement.

John Lawson had indicated that this time the union was prepared to outlast the companies, implying careful planning and preparation. The location probably had been chosen with care. But had the land itself been purchased or leased? In either case, the arrangement had, undoubtedly, been handled well before the strike, for a strike which encompassed every coalfield in the state didn't just happen. But purchased or leased from whom?

Hands and face washed, Alex put on her French blue wool challis blouse and gray twill skirt, brushed her hair into place, and pinned on her hat. Throwing her coat over one arm, she picked up the telegram and letter she intended to leave at the front desk and went downstairs for a quick breakfast. Before the light snow turned into a real winter storm, she was anxious to get to the courthouse to begin a title search of the land occupied by the union camps.

As she took her customary seat by the window, Leslie Baxter came striding toward her. After last night, she realized he was exactly the person to give her the companies' view of the strike. The courthouse could wait.

"Good morning, Mrs. MacFarlane," he said, regarding her seriously. "I trust you have recovered from your unfortunate experience last evening."

"I'm quite well. Again, thank you."

"I was glad to be of assistance."

"Please. Won't you join me for a moment?"

"My pleasure." He lowered his bulk into the flimsy chair opposite her.

"I don't believe I mentioned it before, but I'm here in Trinidad to represent a miner accused of inciting a riot," she said.

"Well, now. An attorney." His smile was thin.

Alex pushed aside her annoyance at the implication of his comment. "My client tried to save my late husband in a mining accident some years ago."

"Ah," he intoned, solemnly. "Then that explains it."

"I beg your pardon?"

"The tie with your late husband. Of course. What with the incident last evening, I couldn't imagine how you would be mixed up with one of those strikers like that boy."

She smiled ruefully at his relief at discovering her mission was legitimate after all. She sensed he also expected to hear a full account of whatever she had done earlier in the day that would have brought her into contact with Dom and his truck. He would be disappointed. "I have learned, of course, that with martial law, civilian representation is temporarily at a standstill."

"Indeed."

"So until matters are resolved, I must remain in Trinidad longer than I had originally intended. Of course, while I'm here, I want to familiarize myself with the situation in which the alleged incident took place."

"Naturally."

She gave him her most winning smile. "Since you're the counsel for CF&I, I was hoping you might provide me with some insight into the strike."

"Gladly." He beckoned to the waiter. "Please, what may I order you for breakfast?"

"That's most kind, Mr. Baxter. Thank you. Coffee and toast should be fine."

"You're certain? Doesn't sound like enough to keep a bird alive."

They exchanged smiles, Leslie Baxter gave their orders, and the waiter disappeared. "Now, where was I? Ah, yes. The strike."

She nodded.

"First, it is part of an international conspiracy to subvert our capitalistic system. These union types—Lawson and his ilk—are nothing but socialists."

She was tempted to pass on her impressions of John Lawson but decided against it.

"The Greeks are the worst."

The accusation was new to her. "I'm not sure . . ."

"Some of them are veterans of the Balkan Wars. They're as cruel and ruthless a bunch as the world has ever seen."

Alex thought of the dark-haired, rather menacing-looking man who had been so quick to deny Stefan Vaska belonged to the union and wondered if he was Greek.

"Second, the strike is a clear violation of the Fourteenth Amendment, which protects the right to purchase or sell labor. Time after time, the Supreme Court has upheld the rights of states to impose protection for the general welfare."

"Which explains the militia?"

"Exactly."

"But what about the local peacekeeping officials? The sheriff? The Trinidad police?"

"They were helpless, dear lady. Terror stricken. Order had to be restored."

"I see."

"Las Animas and Huerfano Counties were on the brink of anarchy until the governor called in the Guard."

"And martial law?"

"Unfortunate, but necessary."

Alex traced a finger along the crease in the tablecloth as she tried to sort out this view of the strike so unlike Bill Henderson's. "But back to the companies' position on the strike."

"Indeed." Baxter went on, talking of a state's rights to protect itself against workers who attempted any violation of liberty of contract. She decided not to mention recent court decisions that recognized restraints on that liberty.

"Would you also comment on accusations that the companies ignored existing state laws, such as those requiring the eight-hour day?" she asked. "And those requiring safety measures?"

"Balderdash! All of it! In the first place, the CF&I voluntarily instituted the eight-hour day last April. Due, I might add, to the far-reaching leadership of Mr. Welborn."

"Isn't he the president of CF&I?"

"You know him?"

The few times she'd met Jesse Welborn, she'd found him a self-satisfied bore. "Not well. We've met only at large social functions."

He idly fingered his watch chain. "In any case, what the union also fails to acknowledge is that CF&I already eliminated payment of wages in scrip in every one of its mines."

"Then why . . ."

The waiter placed their breakfasts before them. Snapping open the snowy napkin and tucking it under his chin, Leslie Baxter attacked the ham and eggs on his plate with gusto. After a few moments, he paused. "As to safety regulations, there again CF&I is a leader."

He leaned forward, his fork and knife poised on either side of his plate of food. "Every man who goes down into a coal mine knows the best coal is high. Sometimes a room will be forty feet high."

"Good heavens, I had no idea," Alex murmured.

"For safety's sake, those rooms must be timbered. But are they?"

She waited.

Leslie Baxter stopped in the middle of cutting a piece of ham, fixed her with a look of disgust. "No, ma'am. Not a timber in sight. And why? Because the men don't get paid for timbering. So they don't do it. Oh, they know they're risking their lives, but they do nothing to protect themselves." He pushed the ham into his mouth, chewed, and swallowed before he continued.

"The fact is, Mrs. MacFarlane, Lawson rants about wages and hours and safety, when it's all a smoke screen for the real issue."

"Which is?"

"The closed shop. That's what the union wants. That's all it wants. Here and everywhere else across the country. Which I assure you, they will never get. Never." His voice was hard. "You cannot rob a man of his freedom to work where he wants, and you cannot prevent a company from hiring whom it wishes. That is the American way."

She remembered John Lawson had talked about the need for a closed shop. The issue was one she and her father had discussed often. Though she understood why it was vital to a union if it was to have the power to bargain effectively with management, she agreed with Leslie Baxter. Both workers and companies had to have freedom of choice.

He continued. "The irony is that two-thirds of the men who were working in the mines down here when the UMW called the strike weren't even members. They wanted no part of the union."

"Two-thirds?" She made a mental note of the figure, though it was hard to believe. "How do you explain all the tent colonies filled with miners?"

Mr. Baxter narrowed his eyes. "Fear."

"Of what?"

"Fear of the union hoodlums—union organizers, they call them—who will stop at nothing to shut down the mines. Kill, maim, terrorize. Men become members to save their families, dear lady."

Alex thought of John Lawson and the other men she'd met. Had they killed as Mr. Baxter claimed?

Leslie Baxter took a gulp of coffee. "This strike has been in the planning for months. Years, in fact. As I said, it's part of a national conspiracy."

She was intrigued.

"Take their tents. They're on land that was leased months before the strike."

"Leased, you say? That's interesting, because I'd wondered about that."

"Of course, we weren't aware of it until the strike was called and up went tents brought in from the West Virginia strike. When we checked into it, we found out about the leased land." He poured some cream in his coffee and glanced at her. "They also feed the poor devils, dole out twelve dollars a month."

"To all twenty thousand people?" she asked, amazed.

"Actually, on that point there seems to be some serious division of opinion. I'm told only the card-carrying members and their families are so lucky."

"But still," she marveled. "That's a great deal of money."

"Which, I can assure you, doesn't come solely from the dues of local union members. This strike is the creature of the leaders in Chicago." He frowned. "But let me return to the matter of the camps, why they're located where they are."

"Please do."

"Every one of the five union camps was placed in the direct line of transportation between Trinidad and a nearby coal camp for the sole purpose of illegal picketing."

"But picketing is legal."

"Not if it obstructs the entrance and exit to the workplace or incites disturbance."

Alex had to agree.

"Every time we send a truck with men to replace the strikers, it goes past a union camp. The same thing always happens. Some men, but mostly women—women are the most vicious—even children—can you imagine, children? They line up, shouting the most horrible epithets and throwing rocks."

"Rocks?"

"The strikers' weapons have been confiscated, thank the Lord."

She took another sip of coffee. "But I've also heard company guards are responsible for some of the violence."

His look was sharp. "Unfortunately, on a few occasions, that's true. But in all cases, for self-protection."

"I see."

He pushed his empty plate away, regarding her intently as he pulled the napkin from under his chin. "But now, you must tell me, Mrs. MacFarlane, in the few days you've been here, you must have formed some impressions of all this."

Alex studied his seemingly genial expression. She was glad she'd had the opportunity to discuss the strike with someone besides Bill. But if Leslie Baxter wanted some reassurance that she was sympathetic to the companies' stand, she wasn't ready to give it, and she told him so.

Hurrying through the swirling snow toward the courthouse, Alex reviewed the conversation. Baxter had painted a picture of the mines, principally those owned by the CF&I, as responsible to their workers and of a self-serving, scheming union. He had exuded confidence about the companies' position. If John Lawson thought the strike had the companies worried, Alex knew now he was sadly mistaken.

So it was tempting to believe Baxter's attitude was a sign that the companies were in such a strong position they could easily outlast any strike. Yet given John Lawson's determination, they might be in for a surprise. Conceivably, the strike—and martial law—could go on for months, perhaps a year or more.

She strode up the hill, flakes sticking to her lashes, her breath coming fast with the steep climb. The courthouse was ahead. The sight of it reminded her of the governor and his part in all this mess. It seemed obvious he was more interested in protecting his political future than in abiding by the law. Clearly, national exposure was the only force strong enough to make him call off General Chase and the militia.

Yet even Ed Keating, who loved an uphill battle more than anyone she knew, might not want to go along. He might tell her the status quo was too powerful to overcome, that it would take a miracle to get the votes. He could be right. But why should that stop them? Ed was a good Irish Catholic who believed in miracles. When she saw him, she'd remind him of that.

Chapter Fifteen

Bill Henderson glanced up from the pile of papers on his desk, not really surprised to see Judge Southard standing in the open doorway, a cigar in one hand, a broad smile fixed on his face, his eyes sharp as a coyote's on the hunt. Uninvited, he came in and sat down.

"I thought I'd come by and see how you were getting along." The judge crossed his legs and leaned back, puffed on a good Cuban cigar Bill would have given his eyeteeth for.

"As well as can be expected."

"There are some who say because of this strike Trinidad's very survival—correction, Las Animas County's survival—is at risk."

"I'm one of them."

The judge eyed him through a veil of cigar smoke, ignoring his comment. "Of course, the health of the coal industry is key. Wouldn't you agree?"

"It's a factor, yes." *Whatever it is you're driving at, spit it out, you old bastard.* "Thus it follows that it's vital for us to do whatever it takes to guarantee the smooth delivery of coal during the strike."

"Whatever it takes?" Bill shook his head.

The older man's smile faded. His eyes narrowed. "Counselor, I thought you and I had agreed how important it was for you, as an elected county official, to protect the greater good."

"I don't know about agreed, your honor, but you're right that we talked about this before."

The judge uncrossed his legs. "What do you know about this woman who just came to town? MacFarlane, I believe."

"She's a classmate from law school days."

Judge Southard clamped down on his cigar. "Don't give me that crap."

Bill regarded the judge with disgust.

"I happen to know she comes from Denver. Her father is Jonathan Russell, the principal of Russell and Associate, a firm that represents some of the biggest banks in this whole damn region."

"As usual, your sources are impeccable, your honor."

The judge glared. "If we were in court, I'd cite you for contempt."

"No offense intended, your honor."

"Get rid of her."

"I take it you mean Mrs. MacFarlane."

"Goddamn it, who else would I mean?"

Bill studied the judge for a moment. The man was little more than a two-bit shyster with the power to make life miserable for others. As long as it was between the judge and him, Bill was willing to put up with it, to bide his time. For Southard and his cronies to hone in on Alex MacFarlane, a misguided but innocent bystander, was something else again. He stood up, went over to open the door.

"I gather my time is up." Judge Southard's mouth twisted into a half-smile.

Bill held the door, and the judge rose from his chair, carefully placed his bowler on his head. "Whether you like it or not, counselor, you are still part of the team that keeps this county running."

The door closed, Bill slammed a fist against the thin wall. He was sick of Southard, sick of the entire godforsaken place. What in the hell had ever made him think he could take the stink out of the county's political sewer?

He went back to his desk, sat down. The fury he felt was an old friend. Growing up, rage at life's injustices had been as much a part of the family diet as the beans he and his father had eaten three times a day. It had settled on him in earnest when he was eleven.

That year had been dry. June was usually as wet a month as there is on the western slope of the Rockies. But it hadn't rained once. Even the water in the sloughs and reservoirs around the Morris ranch, the biggest in the county, evaporated before the first crop of alfalfa flowered out. Meager spring runoff emptying into the thirsty streams was all that kept the wells and the cattle going. A few places, like theirs, were lucky to have a spring up in the high country.

One night, the chores done and the daylight long gone, he and his father sat by the stove silently eating at the rough wood table, the pot of beans between them, the lantern overhead shedding the only light in the cabin.

Suddenly, spoon in mid-air, his father said with a chuckle, "Hey, I just thought. For once, it's old Morris instead of us that's over a barrel."

"What d'ya mean?" Bill had asked.

"It's simple. Those reservoirs of his are as dried up as an old maid's cunt. Lord amighty! Won't be long before he'll be over here, hat in hand, beggin' for some of our creek water."

But Alton Morris didn't have to beg. A week later his cattle simply pushed through Henderson's fence on the hill above Lost Lake Creek. Bill's father went to Lenny Bickle, the justice of the peace, to raise a stink. Bickle sent out a call for Morris to come in and explain himself.

It was Morris's attorney who appeared at Bickle's Hardware, where court was held. A man with soft hands and clean fingernails, full of grave looks, using the smooth legal prose that no one—including Lenny Bickle—understood, he completely turned the tables on Will Henderson.

The condition of the Henderson fences clearly violated the range law, which required a man to make provisions for keeping other men's cattle off his property. A fence in disrepair was the same as no fence at all. Mr. Morris, not the defendant, was the aggrieved party. Lenny Bickle wound up agreeing, said he was forced to slap a fine on Will.

The law and his friend Lenny Bickle had let him down, but Will Henderson hadn't given up. Rifle in hand, he managed to get past the wrought iron fence and Morris's strongmen to confront him in the front parlor of his fancy brick house. He was thrown out almost immediately, but, by God, he had made his point. Or so he'd stoutly maintained to Bill when he came home that day.

But the next morning, a decaying skunk floated in their well. When Bill rode up into summer pasture, he came across some of their calves, their bellies slit, their guts putrid and purple, pecked at by the crows. This time his father didn't bother riding into town to see Lenny Bickle. The message was clear: no one can fight and beat the men who can afford to hire smooth-talking lawyers.

That's the way it went. One incident after another. By the time Bill was seventeen, the homestead his father had claimed and worked for twenty years had been whittled to half its original hundred and sixty acres. The property had been sold to pay property taxes or lost as a result of so-called legal boundary disputes.

That April, on a day still cold enough for patches of snow to pillow the base of the pine trees, they were castrating young bulls. After two false starts, Bill finally worked up his nerve to tell his father he'd decided to try to get into the state university the next September. Because he'd never been able to stay in school long enough to earn a high school diploma, he might have to take some kind of a test to be admitted to college. But he was pretty sure he'd make it. Once there, he'd work his way through. After that he'd go to law school. By Jesus, with a lawyer in the family, nobody would ever again take unfair advantage of a Henderson.

The big man had listened carefully, not saying anything, only staring at him, dark eyes smoldering beneath bushy black eyebrows. That night when Bill lay on the verge of sleep, his father had climbed up to the tiny loft room and said, "I want no lawyer in this house."

He'd peered at his father as he stood outlined by the faint light from the kitchen below, thinking how he loved the man, for all his stubborn pride, how eventually his father would thank him.

"Hear me?" his father said again.

"I hear you," he'd replied, and his father had disappeared down the ladder.

Gazing through the book-sized window at the sliver of moon, Bill had decided that with or without his father's permission, he had to go.

He came home from college the next summer to help bring in the hay. He was four years from law school, but it didn't make any difference. True to his word, his father had asked whether he was still set on law school. When he said he was, his father told him to get out, and Bill had left.

Time went on. Bill's fervor to become the little man's legal voice never cooled. It was the winter of his last year in law school when his father collapsed in the south pasture, pulling a calf. Bill went home to bury him. There was no funeral. The homestead had been sold for back taxes.

At the edge of his thoughts, Bill heard the door open, and he looked up. Alex walked in. He stood up.

"Good morning," she said, briskly, all business. "I don't mean to interrupt, but I was on my way to the county clerk's office, and I thought I'd stop off to let you know I contacted John Lawson out at the Ludlow camp."

"Ludlow? What in God's name were you doing there?"

"Well, I found out it was John Lawson I should see. A strange little man at the union headquarters told me he was at the Ludlow camp. So that's where I went."

"How'd you get there?"

"I took the stage."

"The stage?" he asked, incredulous. "Were you stopped by guards?"

She looked around the office impatiently. "You don't mind if I sit down?"

"No. Of course not. Have a seat."

She gave him a stiff smile as she perched on the edge of the chair. "No, I was not stopped by guards. And, actually, I found Mr. Lawson quite interesting."

He nodded. Lawson was a good man, honest, tough—a union man first, last, and always.

"I've decided I rather like him. Though he's—devious."

Bill tried to picture her out at the Ludlow camp, talking to a union leader. He almost smiled at the thought of the miners' reaction to a woman like Alex MacFarlane.

"He claimed he doesn't know Stefan Vaska."

"Could be true."

"He showed me around the camp a bit. He was polite enough, but it was plain he considered me a nuisance. Until . . ." She raised an eyebrow. "Well, after a while I had the strangest feeling he'd decided that what he told me about the strike might be passed on to other people, beyond Trinidad."

"The man's not stupid."

"What he told me most certainly wasn't the story I heard from Leslie Baxter at breakfast this morning."

He straightened. "Leslie Baxter's in town?"

"He came in on the same train from Denver as I did," she said. "Anyway, it was Mr. Baxter who saved me and a young man—a member of the union—from being carted off to jail."

"You and a striker were going to jail?" He shook his head in amazement as Alex told him the rest of the story. "You were damn lucky."

She cocked her head, her expression thoughtful. "I guess I was."

He leaned his elbows on the desk, resting his chin in his hands as he gazed at her and tried to make sense of the news about Baxter. "I don't get it."

"Get what?"

"About Baxter being here. He doesn't generally show up unless there's a crisis."

"Maybe there's going to be a settlement," she suggested.

"I doubt it. But something's going on. The question is, what?"

"I'll go over to his office, wherever that is, and ask him," she said.

He laughed at the absurdity of her suggestion.

"What's funny?" she bridled. "Leslie Baxter and I get on very well."

"Well enough for him to tell you of the possible terms of the strike settlement?"

She frowned and rose. "Say what you want, my talks with John Lawson and Leslie Baxter were most enlightening. Now I need to do a title search."

"What for?"

"Mr. Baxter told me the land being used by the union camps was leased. The question is, who are the owners? I presume they're union sympathizers. Or at least not unwilling to take union money."

"So you find out; what does that prove?"

"I'm not sure at the moment."

He took in a deep breath, already tired of it. Yet he had to admire her tenacity. The woman was like a bulldog. "Well, if you're determined to go to all that trouble, Dick Bryant's the clerk."

"Thanks." She started out through the door and stopped. "But maybe before I do that, before the snow gets any worse, it occurs to me I should go out to Sandoval. It might be important to know who saw Stefan Vaska at the post office that day and try to discover who accused him of inciting a riot."

"Oh, for God's sake." He leaned back, banging the back of the chair against the wall.

"I was wondering if you have an automobile?" she asked, apparently oblivious of his reaction.

Alex MacFarlane was like no one he'd ever encountered. "I suppose you want me to drive you out there."

"Well, since you're the district attorney, you must have a pass." Her tone was bright, confident.

He sighed, straightened.

She smiled. "You see, I have learned about how one must have a pass."

"Good for you." He desperately wanted to stay clear of her and her schemes, but somehow he felt responsible for her. A lone woman of her ilk in the midst of this tinderbox was no joke. Reaching for his coat and hat, he said, annoyed, "Okay. You win. We better get going before the snow gets any worse."

Their breath fogged into the cold air as Bill steered the Ford south toward Sandoval. The snow was coming down harder than back in town. Driving on the rutted roads might turn treacherous. Fortunately, the trip was not more than ten miles, more or less.

Alex glanced at him. "I appreciate your doing this. I didn't know for certain you had a car, but I hoped."

"Bought it secondhand last summer. A Ford's not much for looks, but it holds the road." Bill liked automobiles. He liked the speed. He was intrigued by anything mechanical. Treat it right, it worked. Plus, it didn't talk back. Some day he'd buy a Stutz Bearcat like he'd seen in Pueblo last year—yellow, with wire wheels and a three-speed gearbox connected to a differential on the rear axle.

Alex turned her gaze toward the treeless countryside, pristine in its blanket of snow. "It's so barren."

"It's cow country. Coalfields notwithstanding."

Alex hugged her arms for warmth and leaned back, studying him. "I do seem to remember hearing you grew up on a ranch. I suppose you miss it."

He glanced at her, surprised she knew anything about him. "I had to sell it for taxes after my dad died."

"I didn't know. I'm sorry." Alex traced a finger over the frosted door window. "Is your mother still living?"

He'd given up thinking about his mother years ago. For him, she'd never existed. "She went back East to visit her aunt one summer. I was about three, I guess. She never came back."

"Growing up without her must have been hard," Alex said.

Bill maneuvered the car around a bend in the road, remembering the stories he'd made up about how his mother was a famous vaudeville star who toured the world. No one bought it. But each time he told the story, it came closer to the truth, until he almost believed it himself.

"My mother died when I was a senior in college," she said. "It was April. I remember because the fruit trees were in blossom, and I didn't see how there could be so much loveliness and sadness at one time."

Bill didn't know how to respond. Personal confessions made him uncomfortable.

"Everyone said she was a great beauty. Not a Sargent-portrait kind of beauty. More vibrant. Even flamboyant. It was her coloring. Her hair was redder than mine. And she had this marvelous carriage. She moved with such—what's the word? Panache."

Her wistful smile reminded him of a little girl's.

"There was nothing she couldn't do. She painted watercolors. She wrote marvelous poetry no one could understand. She had a villa on the Mediterranean, where she held a salon, as the French call it, attended by every literary figure who counted."

"Not someone you'd find around here," Bill said, sardonically, struck by the fairy tale quality of the life she was describing. The real world was something else, something he was sure Alex knew little about.

"Sometimes now I look back, and it's like a dream. I spent two summers with her over there. It was marvelous."

He glanced over at her.

"Of course, Father grumped around about her staying over there," she said, smiling at the memory. "He adored her."

Bill had met Jonathan Russell at a meeting of the Bar Association once. He couldn't picture the thin-lipped man adoring anyone.

The snow was heavier now, forcing him to lean over the steering wheel for a better view. Alex didn't say anything more, maybe sensing his need to concentrate. Suddenly, he saw the truck. "Hey, now. What do we have here?"

"What's the matter?" Alex asked.

"Guards."

"Where? I can't see a thing out there."

"Just ahead. They must have been sitting in that truck that's parked by the side of the road."

Alex squinted out into the snow-filled air at the dim figures in army issue coats, stiff-brimmed hats pulled down low to shield their faces from the weather, rifles in their gloved hands. "My God, it's like last night all over again."

Bill gave her a sidelong glance and kept the car going at a steady pace. As they came closer, the men cocked their weapons. He thought of Alex's tale of Mr. Baxter coming to the rescue last night. Today the good counselor was nowhere in sight. Bill would have to depend on his pass.

Slowing the car to a stop, Bill lowered his window as the men approached. They were hard, dangerous looking, and Bill heard Alex catch in her breath. He'd thought about bringing his pistol but at the last minute decided against it. It was a toss-up. You brought it, giving you a chance to hold your own in a bad situation, but with the good possibility you'd be thrown in jail for possession. Still, a lot of people—including strikers—managed to stash a weapon of some kind.

Two of the men leaned down and peered into the car. The other man stood behind them with arms crossed—a head taller, wide shouldered. Though he could see no insignia, Bill guessed he was an officer.

"State your name and business," demanded one of enlisted men with a heavy black beard frosted white with snow, his breath strong with whiskey.

"We're on our way to Sandoval," Bill said, trying to stay easy, resting his elbow on the windowsill.

"Is that a fact?" said the man, grim faced.

"I have a pass." He began to pull open his overcoat to get out his wallet.

"Hands where I can see 'em, mister."

"I was getting my pass."

"What's the name again?"

"Bill Henderson, county D.A."

"The man himself," came a hard voice from the snow-filled air.

Bill squinted to see who had spoken. Karl Linderfelt—Lieutenant Linderfelt—one of the cruelest sons of bitches he'd ever had the misfortune to know. Instantly, he felt a surge of fear.

"The lady is Mrs. MacFarlane," Bill added. "We're on our way to Sandoval."

The enlisted man raised his glove to smear aside the mucous hanging from his nostrils. "And your business?"

"Just a visit."

"Don't shit me, mister."

"I repeat. Just a visit. Soldier." With his elbow still on the windowsill, he shifted gears with his other hand. "Now if you don't mind, the lady's getting cold."

Alex attempted a smile. "We won't be staying long."

Linderfelt leered at her, exposing a mouth full of perfectly even ivory teeth.

"We need to be back in Trinidad by mid-afternoon," she added.

The guards exchanged lewd glances. "We'll ride with ya," said the bearded one.

Linderfelt stepped forward. "Wrong, boys. You ride on the running board. I'll get in with the lady."

For a split second, Bill almost said, "The hell you will." But he thought better of it. They had guns. He didn't. And with all that liquor in them, there was no saying what they'd do. Two of the men stepped up onto the running board, using one hand to grab a hold inside the car, leaving the other to hold their rifles. Karl Linderfelt went around to the passenger side and pushed in beside Alex.

Bill eased the car forward, slowly accelerating until the snow flew up around them. Alex moved closer to him as Linderfelt draped his arm around her shoulders and pressed his leg against hers. Bill forced himself to hang on to the steering wheel.

Approaching the town, even Bill's fear couldn't push aside the sense of depression that always settled over him when he visited Sandoval. Maneuvering the car through the wire gate and down the main street, it occurred to him that it was no different than any of the coal towns—if that's what they were. One small weather-beaten board house after another, each no bigger than a single room, stovepipes poking through leaky roofs—testimonies to some men's indifference to other men's right to a decent life.

Ahead, Bill saw the two-story sandstone building that served as a combination general store and post office and pulled in. The sign over the entrance said COLORADO SUPPLY COMPANY, HENRY LAMM, MGR. The wind had let up, and an American flag hung unmoving from the nearby flagpole. Standing in the protection of the roof's overhang were several men hunched in their coats, rifles cradled in folded arms. Without any comment, the two guards stepped off the running board and joined them.

Bill set the brake, and Linderfelt pushed open the door. "Well, sweetheart," he said to Alex. "You behave yourself now."

Alex didn't respond. Glancing at the men standing around the door, Bill decided they looked like trouble.

Linderfelt chucked Alex roughly under her chin, climbed out, and went over to the men under the eaves.

"I didn't realize," she said, under her breath, as if she were talking to herself.

"Well, we got here. The next problem is getting back," he said. "I'd advise you to make this short."

She regarded him gravely for a moment, and they got out. Walking past a grinning Linderfelt and the other men gathered on either side of the entrance, they went inside.

Chapter Sixteen

As Alex walked into the dark store, Bill behind her, she was struck by the acrid smell of pickle brine. A potbellied stove surrounded by unoccupied chairs stood in the center of the room. Except for a scattering of cans, the shelves were empty. On the wall behind one section of the counter was a honeycomb of cubbyholes with pieces of mail sticking out from many of them.

A pasty-faced man with the jowls of a bulldog, nearly as wide as he was tall, appeared from the rear of the store. His dark button eyes surveyed them.

"Mr. Lamm, good to see you," Bill said, extending his hand. "Bill Henderson, district attorney."

"Henderson?" The man moved closer. "Oh, ye-ah. Didn't reckanize you at first, the day bein' so dark and all."

"Let me introduce Mrs. MacFarlane. She's a colleague, an attorney from Denver."

Lamm kept his eyes on Bill.

"I had a few questions about—" Alex began.

The man gave her a cold look. "The strike's been bringin' curiosity-seekers down here right regular," he said, dryly.

"Wouldn't be surprised," Bill said in an easy way as he glanced about him. "Looks like business is a little slow."

"Don't get me goin' on that one, Henderson. Fact is, I said to the judge the other day when I was in town, I said, 'Judge, your martial law ain't worth a damn. Do I see the strike over? Nosireesir. Those bandits are twistin' our tails, and we're goin' broke.' "

"It's hard times, that's for sure," Bill agreed, scowling sympathetically.

As she stood next to Bill, it seemed as if he were playing a part in a play. He was like a chameleon, able to change his colors when the situation demanded it. But her own impatience pushed her forward. "Mr. Lamm, I was wondering if—"

Bill interrupted. "Have things been pretty quiet so far?"

"So-so," Mr. Lamm said. "Except for that row about the mail a few weeks back."

"What happened?" Alex cut in.

Lamm glared at her. "You Denver people wouldn't understand. This rabble thinking they have a right to the world. Comin' here from God knows where, takin' white men's jobs in the mines and then big as brass sayin' they want their mail." He spun his glance to Bill. "I tell you, Henderson, it's un-American."

Bill looked appropriately glum. "So there was trouble about some men picking up their mail?"

"I thought sure you knew. Seems like the sheriff stuck 'em all in jail."

Bill gave a rueful half-smile. "This martial law makes it tough even for a D.A. to know what's going on."

"I guess that's so," Lamm conceded. "It was a Saturday. I was busy. Though, God knows, not like before the strike. Here comes this pockmarked sonofa . . ." He glanced at Alex. "This thug. Surly so-and-so. He comes right in and says he wants his mail."

"Were there other people in the store?" Alex asked.

Henry Lamm shot her a hard look, dug a finger in one of his ears to explore its depths. "Like I said. The place was full."

Bill smiled. "A half dozen men or so, you'd say."

The man's eyes suddenly flashed. "What the hell do you care, Henderson?"

"I was wondering . . ." she began, wanting to ask whether there had been others who'd asked for the mail, but stopped when she caught Bill's dark look.

"These days you hear all these stories," Bill explained, resuming that slow way of speaking.

The door opened. Linderfelt and the men who had been standing outside filed in, rifles in hand. Lamm gave them a wave and invited them to sit down by the stove. As they shook the snow from their coats and hats, they grinned at her, and the terror she'd felt in the car returned.

"Stories, hell," Mr. Lamm was saying. "I'll tell you the truth of it. This fella—the one who was hollerin' for his mail—the union put him up to it. That's a fact."

"But you gave him his mail?" Alex asked.

Without looking at her, he said, "I told him to go to hell. That's when he started at me. Said it was his right. Then these boys here . . ." He glanced at the men warming themselves around the stove. "Well, they took care of things."

Alex inwardly shuddered at the thought of what "taking care of things" might mean. Because Stefan Vaska had the audacity to believe it was his legal right to collect mail sent through the U.S. mails, he had ended up in jail without benefit of due process. The outrage of it infuriated her.

"I tell you, Henderson, I'm sick of it," continued Henry Lamm.

Buttoning up his coat, Bill nodded. "That goes twice with me."

Lamm looked from Alex to Bill. "What'd you say you come out here for?"

Bill grinned. "Oh, just for a visit. To give Mrs. MacFarlane a look at the countryside, you might say."

"Helluva day for it," Lamm said, squinting at Alex.

"Isn't it though," she agreed with forced cheerfulness. "So, before the storm gets any worse, we better be on our way back to town." She had began to pull on her gloves when out of the corner of her eye, she saw the two guards say something to Linderfelt. Taking Bill's arm, she said, "I want to thank you for your time, Mr. Lamm."

As the two men moved toward her, one of them said, "Like the story about the sonofabitch bellowin' about his goddamn mail, did ya, lady?"

The stink of the man nearly made her gag.

"Ya shoulda seen what he looked like when we got through with him. Face all pulpy, like jelly." He grinned, revealing a gaping hole where his front teeth should have been.

"Back off, soldier," Bill said, in an even tone.

"Back off yerself. I'm talkin' to the lady here." The man attempted to take her other arm.

"Get your hands off her," Bill said.

The man looked around at Linderfelt and the other men. "Hey boys! How's about us havin' some fun?"

Linderfelt grinned, and two men pushed out of their chairs. "Forget it," Bill said, his tone steel hard as he tightened his grip on her arm and began to guide her toward the door. "Mrs. MacFarlane and I are leaving. Alone."

The man reached out to seize her, and in that instant Bill snatched the rifle from his grasp and thrust the barrel against his chest. "I said alone. I mean alone." He threw a glance at Linderfelt and the others. "If any of you so much as make a move to stop us, I'll blow your heads off." He jabbed the barrel into the man's belly for emphasis.

"Sorry for the ruckus, Mr. Lamm," Bill said, his manner suddenly relaxed again as he and Alex stood at the door now.

The fat man, his face mottled and red, nodded.

"The soldier's rifle'll be at the sheriff's office."

Alex's entire body began to shake as she sat inside the car while Bill cranked up the engine. The rifle was leaning against the fender. In between glances at the store's entrance, he eyed the sky as if to survey the weather. His craggy face held a grim but assured look, as if whatever came his way at this moment, he could handle it. All afternoon, she'd sensed he was in home territory. He might not know all the men by name, but he knew their type and how to deal with them. If it weren't for him, she most certainly would have been raped.

For the first time, she understood the danger he talked about. She had been foolish to place him in a position where he'd been forced to defend her as well as himself. Gradually, her thudding heart slowed. Her terror subsided.

In spite of everything, the trip hadn't been wasted. From Henry Lamm's report, Vaska's attempt to get his mail had been just that: an honest attempt to claim what was rightfully his. If anyone had incited a riot, it had been Lamm.

Bill brushed the snow off the car and climbed in, laying the rifle carefully on the back seat.

"I want to thank you," she said.

He glanced at her. "For what?"

"In the store, if you—"

"They're a bad bunch," he said. "Dangerous as hell."

Seeing the thrust of his chin and hearing the anger in his voice, she wanted to defend her insistence on making the trip. But Bill was so pigheaded, he'd only lash out at her. "Will the road be okay?"

"It doesn't look good."

"I'd really like to get back. This place . . ." She gave an inadvertent shudder.

He shifted into reverse and eased the car out into the center of the street. "We may have to hole up for awhile."

"Not here?" she asked, suddenly panicked.

"Relax. There's no hotel."

She felt a surge of relief. "Which means that getting back surely is the best course."

"Do you have any idea how stupid it was to come out here in the first place?"

"You brought me here," she snapped, knowing he was right.

Once they left Sandoval, the wind picked up, slanting the snow against the windshield. In the growing darkness, it was impossible to see more than a few feet ahead. The snow obscured the view, eliminated any tracks to guide their way. Drifts were building up. They were going at a crawl, nearly stopping sometimes, finally going on. Suddenly, the car veered off to the side. With a lurch, it came to a stop and settled off to the side of the road.

Alex and Bill exchanged glances. "I'll go take a look," he said, struggling to open the door.

"Maybe we can push it clear," she said.

He sent her a doubtful look, and they both climbed out.

The wheels on the left side of the car were buried halfway down the ditch beside the road.

"Move over behind the wheel and steer. I'll push," he directed.

But the car didn't move. Alex climbed out. "How far is it to Trinidad?"

"I suppose you're planning to walk," he said, brushing the snow from his coat.

"Well, we've come aways. Surely, it couldn't be too far."

Bill looked around him. "I'd judge it's about half a mile to the Nevils."

"The Nevils?"

"Friends of mine. Their ranch is just over there." He pointed into the swirling snow.

"I don't know how you can tell. It's impossible to see. I say we follow the road and—"

He yanked open the car door, pulled out the rifle, retrieved her purse, and handed it to her. "In case you don't know, a blizzard in these parts is no joke."

"I realize that."

"We can hole up in the car till this is over. If it doesn't get too cold, we'll at least be out of the wind. Or we can go to the Nevils."

"Bill . . ." She squinted at him through the snow.

"Which is it?" he demanded.

"I . . ."

"Come on." He started off. After a few steps, he stopped and looked back at her. "I said to come on, and stay right behind me. If we use our heads, we'll make it."

They began to walk alongside a barbed wire fence. The snow was drifting up at every post so that some steps were knee deep, but a few feet farther the snow barely covered their shoe tops. The air was a screen of white flakes, the size of quarters now. She stumbled and dropped behind so she couldn't see him. Panicked, she made a desperate effort to catch up again.

Snow had worked beneath her coat collar, and she could feel the melt seeping through her dress. She was exhausted. Her toes were numb. She longed to stop and rest. She felt as if she'd been walking for days. The world was a blur of white. Then she saw something. Squinting through the snow, she saw lights. She hoped they were the right ones.

Chapter Seventeen

Bill pounded at the back door, called out. Finally, Juanita, wearing an apron over her skirt and a man's old sweater, pulled open the door and peered out at them through the curtain of snow. She was aiming a revolver in their direction.

"Juanita, for God's sake put down the pistol. It's me. Bill Henderson."

"Billie?" she asked, doubtfully, pronouncing his name with the soft inflection of her native Spanish. "Come where I can see."

Bill took Alex by the elbow, and they stepped closer. "I like a cautious woman, but we're freezing to death."

Juanita stepped aside and motioned for them to come in. "Forgive me. You never know these days.

Bill and Alex stomped the snow from their shoes and stepped into a small room the size of a large closet. On one wall were shelves filled with jars and bottles of various shapes. On the other a variety of coats and hats hung from pegs. Beneath them was a line of boots. The smells of leather, wet wool, and carbolic acid used to doctor animals instantly made him feel at home.

"Juanita, this is Mrs. Alex MacFarlane. We drove out to Sandoval, but the snow got so bad we couldn't make it back to town."

"You should be ashamed, Billie Henderson. Taking this girl out in a blizzard. Here, let me help you." She frowned at Alex and began to unbutton her coat. "You need to get out of those wet clothes. I will get you hot water to warm your feet."

Placing the rifle in the corner next to the coatrack, Bill put his arm around the older woman. "You're a sight for sore eyes."

The older woman leaned against him. "It is good you are here." She gave him a weak smile. "But now, Mrs. MacFarlane, you must come with me and get out of those clothes." She guided Alex through the small house toward the lone bedroom.

Bill stepped back onto the porch, shed his clothes, and donned Charlie's slicker, which he found among the collection of coats hanging from pegs on the wall by the door. "Juanita, how about getting me some clothes?" he asked when she returned to the kitchen.

Surveying his bare legs and feet sticking out from beneath her husband's coat, she burst out laughing.

"Clothes. That's what I need," he pleaded good-naturedly.

"Sure, sure," she said, chuckling and shaking her head.

The Nevils were as close to family as Bill had. He ached for them and the tragedy of Rogerio's death. More like a son than a nephew, the boy had been their life before he'd been killed by company guards. The goddamn strike was a cancer not even a rancher and his family could escape.

Warm and dry again, dressed in some of Charlie's old clothes, Bill stood at the kitchen window and peered out into the darkness. "I think I'll go out and give Charlie a hand."

"You'll do no such thing," Juanita Nevil said, handing him one of two jelly glasses whose bottoms held what appeared to be whiskey. "Drink this."

Alex came into the kitchen, dressed in a pair of overalls, cuffs rolled up, a wool shirt, and a pair of thick socks. Her face was still pink from the cold, her hair tied back with a piece of ribbon. She looked like a schoolgirl. She glanced down at her clothes in an embarrassed way, then smiled at Juanita. "Thank you."

"Too big, but they will do." She handed Alex the other glass of whiskey.

A sudden blast of frigid air filled the room, and a door slammed. "Nita, who in the hell . . ." came Charlie's familiar deep voice from the porch before the man himself appeared. Six and a half feet tall, with a ruddy complexion and a thick head of graying blond hair, he loomed in the doorway like a giant bear and stared at Bill and Alex.

"Well, if this don't beat all." He grinned. "Lookee who's come in out of a goddamn blizzard. Old Billie Henderson hisself. Jee-sus."

"Charlie Nevil, don't you dare come into my kitchen with your boots on," Juanita said.

"A regular bully, that's what the woman is," Charlie said, regarding his wife affectionately. He had started to unbutton his sheepskin coat when he noticed Alex. "And who's this pretty lady?"

"How do you do." Alex went over and shook Charlie's hand. The act struck Bill as something only a man would do. "I'm Alex MacFarlane."

"Mrs. MacFarlane's an attorney from Denver," Bill said. "She's here on business."

Charlie eyed her curiously as he shrugged out of his coat.

"She decided she had to get to Sandoval this afternoon," Bill said, dryly.

Alex gave him a frosty glance. "We were on our way back to Trinidad and got stuck."

At dinner, Bill and Charlie talked about the price of beef and whether there would be enough water next summer to fill the stock ponds. The conversation slowly petered out as if to make way for what Bill knew had to be said.

Looking at Charlie, he said, "You know you have my condolences."

Juanita glanced down at her lap. "Sometimes I think Rogerio is just out in the barn. That he will come in when it gets dark."

Charlie reached out to put a hand on his wife's arm. "The boy was like a son."

Juanita glanced at Alex. "Rogerio was my brother's boy. We raised him since his mother died. He was our heart. A month ago, two company guards from Sandoval came into our yard and shot him in the back."

"I rode in for the sheriff," Charlie said. "But he said it was out of his hands."

Juanita swung her glance toward Bill. "The shootings must stop."

"They will."

"When?" she demanded.

Bill couldn't look her in the eyes.

"I had to write to my brother and tell him of the death of his son, little more than a boy." Juanita's dark eyes filled with tears. "Mother of God. It is more than the heart can bear—to tell him what really happened."

"It's all right, mother," Charlie said quietly.

"Tell me, Billie. You are a man of education, of importance. A district attorney." Juanita leaned forward, her strong hands roughened from years of work, clutched together. "How is it possible for me to say to my brother his son was blown open like a butchered animal?"

The wet snow slapped against the windows. Here, in the warm shelter of their small kitchen, the least he could do was to offer Juanita and Charlie some word of comfort, but there was nothing adequate to say.

Chapter Eighteen

Alex took her turn at a trip to the outhouse, clutching the rope Charlie had stretched from the house to prevent anyone from getting lost in the blinding snow.

Juanita decided she and Alex should sleep in the bedroom. The men were to sleep on makeshift mattresses of blankets around the Franklin stove in the front room.

Alex pulled on a flannel nightdress, which Juanita had put out for her, and slid under the quilts on the double bed. A few minutes later, already dressed for bed, Juanita came in and quietly closed the door. "I must apologize."

"It's I who should apologize," Alex said.

"No, no. We speak only of our own troubles. You have come all the way from Denver."

"Please, it's quite all right."

Juanita began to take the pins out of her blue-black hair, coiled at the nape of her neck, and it fell to her waist like a black satin scarf. "Tell me of yourself. Your husband is a lawyer like Billie?"

"My husband was killed in a mining accident during the last strike here. He was a mining engineer."

"Ah," Juanita said sadly. "And your children?"

The question had been asked by well-meaning people, usually other women, many times before. By now she no longer felt compelled to explain her answer. "There are no children."

She smiled. "But you and Billie?"

"No, no. It's nothing like that. Bill and I met in law school. I came here to defend a miner, and Bill has been—most helpful."

Juanita climbed into bed. "But you are friends?"

Alex wasn't certain how to answer. "Acquaintances."

The older woman chuckled softly. "I could see it back in the kitchen."

Alex chose not to speculate about what Juanita had seen. If Mrs. Nevil imagined some kind of romantic alliance between her and Bill, she was no different than the Denver dowagers who had begun their matchmaking barely a year after Robb had died. Apparently, it was inconceivable to the world that a woman might be able to exist without benefit of a husband.

Alex smiled. "You and Mr. Nevil—Charlie—how did you meet?"

"Ah," Juanita sighed and arranged the pillow behind her back. "I was sixteen. My father had a small place east of Trinidad. It was his habit to hire on extra hands when it was time to brand. Charlie was one of them. I was up at the house with Mamá. It was time for dinner. The meal was spread out on the porch table for the men, and here Charlie comes up from the barn with Papá.

"Tall and thin as a not-ripe string bean, that slow way he has of walking, that smile. Oh, Mother of God, that smile. It shone on me and I was a cooked goose." Juanita laughed. "I didn't know about cooked gooses till later. But I was a cooked goose."

Alex smiled, an unexpected sense of peace and well-being inside her as she hugged her knees beneath the covers and waited to hear the rest of their story.

"But from the first moment, Mamá knew. I could tell she didn't approve," Juanita said. "Gringos and Mexicanos do not mix, she said. Mamá was a woman of strong opinions, I can tell you. So Charlie moved on."

"You were already in love?"

"Love. Yes. As young as I was, I knew I could not live my life without him," Juanita said. "I would be half a person with no Charlie. So one day I met him in town, and we took a buggy to Raton, where a priest married us. It was years before Mamá would talk to us."

It all sounded so romantic. Alex had known passion. In the early days of her marriage, she had been barely able to wait for Robb's return home, when they would lie in bed, consumed with each other's bodies. But she had never experienced love so deep that she felt incomplete without it. She envied Juanita.

"Nita," boomed a deep voice from the other room. "Are you ladies ever goin' to pack it in?"

Juanita winked at Alex. "You don't like bedtime stories, Charlie Nevil?"

"I like my sleep, woman. That's what I like."

His wife smiled, blew out the lamp on the dresser, and climbed into the other side of the bed. For a few moments, the only sounds were the creaking of the house and the heavy breathing of the men in the other room. Cautiously, Alex stretched her feet down the cold sheets to the end of the bed.

The aroma of coffee stirred her senses, and Alex opened her eyes to blackness. At first, she thought it was the middle of the night. Then, hearing the quiet opening and closing of doors, she knew it must be early morning. Very early morning.

She curled into a ball, listening to the sounds and treasuring the warmth of the bed. Only then did she realize Juanita was no longer beside her.

Reluctantly, she got out of bed, felt her way to the door, and opened it. The light from the kitchen partially illuminated the front room. There was no sign of either man. The house was quiet.

She lit the lamp in the bedroom and put on the clothes she'd worn the night before. When she picked up the pitcher to pour some water into the washbasin, a shard of ice fell out. She decided a quick once-over of her face and neck would be the most washing she'd do this morning. Glancing in the mirror, she combed her fingers through her hair. It would have to do. She wanted to find Bill and the others.

In the kitchen, the table was set with four places. The coffeepot simmered on the back burner. Alex noticed a bowl covered with a dish towel on the drain board of the sink. Curious, she lifted it and saw a mound of dough. Everything appeared to be in readiness for breakfast, except the people to eat it.

She peered out the windows of the back porch for a sign of life. The snow had stopped falling, and through the clear early morning darkness, yellow patches of light from the barn fell across the blanket of snow covering the yard. She chose one of the old coats on the rack by the door, donned a pair of boots from a group lined up beneath the coats, and went outside.

The dark made it difficult to see the way. A path, just a footstep wide, had been beaten down in the snow. The cold nearly sucked her breath away. She felt her ears and face numb. Gratefully, she pulled open the barn door and stepped inside.

The air was warm and full of the smell of animals. Along one side, two cows stood munching hay. She walked closer and discovered Juanita, balanced on a one-legged stool, her strong hands pulling down rhythmically on the teats of a honey-colored cow.

"Ah. Good morning," she said, smiling gravely as she looked up over her shoulder at Alex. "You slept well?"

Alex laughed. "I'd say so, being the last one up. Now tell me what can I do to help."

"You can take in the milk pails," she said as she stood up and handed Alex a bucket full of milk. Behind her was another.

"Carry them both at the same time," Juanita instructed. "They balance better that way. Put them on the table on the back porch next to the separator. I'll be in after I gather the eggs."

Alex eyed the buckets uncertainly for a moment before she picked them up and nearly stumbled with their unexpected weight. Cautiously, she walked to the door and pushed at it with one foot. It was closed tight. Juanita had disappeared. There was nothing to do but put down the pails.

With the utmost care, she lowered them onto the hard-packed dirt floor and pushed open the door. She stuck out one foot to keep the wind from slamming it shut, reached over to pick up the heavy pails. The path was icy and narrower than she remembered. Once she tripped, and the warm milk splashed across her hands. By the time she reached the back porch, she was shaking with the exertion.

After a few minutes, Juanita came in with a basket half full of eggs. "Will you separate the milk?" she asked as she picked up a strange-looking contraption and took it into the kitchen.

"I . . ."

"That's all right. I will do it."

Alex stood beside her, watching her work for a few minutes before Juanita glanced up and said, "You could roll out the biscuits. The rolling pin is in the top drawer of the cupboard. The dough is over there."

Alex went over to the bowl, lifted the cloth, and stared down at the smooth white ball.

"Juanita, I'm afraid . . ." Alex looked over her shoulder at her. "The truth is, I haven't the faintest idea what do. I've never cooked anything. Unless brewing tea counts."

"You have never cooked at all?" Juanita asked, obviously incredulous.

Alex shook her head. When she and Robb had set up housekeeping in their little house on Washington Street, a hired girl had done the cooking and the chores. After that came a succession of her father's cooks.

Juanita's eyes sparked with amusement. "I will show you."

Lightly flouring the breadboard, the rolling pin, and her hands, Juanita proceeded with the sureness and speed of long practice. "It is easy, no? You can try it when you go back to Denver."

Alex smiled, her mind lingering on what Juanita had just said about going back to Denver.

"You live by yourself?" Juanita asked, expertly pressing out biscuits.

"When my husband died, I moved back home with my father."

"He took care of you then," Juanita observed, gently.

Her father had taken care of her, but without her, he would never have survived his wife's death. They had come to depend on each other.

"Actually, it was a mutual arrangement. I managed his household, and I worked with him in the law firm." It occurred to her that she had used the past tense.

"But how hard to be a widow so young," Juanita said, placing the last of the biscuits on the baking sheet.

"I'm thirty-three."

Juanita gave a little shrug. "Young enough to marry again, to have a family."

"I don't think so."

Juanita reached out to place a hand on her shoulder. "Forgive me. I speak out of turn. There is still the bacon to fry and the eggs to cook."

Bill and Charlie finally came in, deep in a discussion about how to treat something called scours. Alex helped Juanita serve the food. The men continued talking, pausing only to ask for something more.

She was beginning to feel at ease with the Nevils. They seemed to accept her presence. Still, she was anxious to get back to Trinidad to pack. Tomorrow was Christmas. She planned to take the early train to Pueblo for her visit with the Keatings.

After the third cup of coffee, Alex suggested it seemed a good time to try to dig out the car and get back to town. But Bill and Charlie decided against the idea, stating it would be better to wait until the sun melted some of the snow. They went outside again, and Juanita turned to preparations for the noon meal. Alex did what she could, but she was frustrated and impatient to get back to Trinidad.

It was well after lunch when they finally began the trip back to the car. Alex and Bill rode double on the broad back of one of Charlie's work horses. Charlie was on a paint.

It was slow going across the snow-covered fields. When Bill started to dismount at the first gate, Charlie waved to him to stay put and got down to do the job. Without speaking, the two men seemed to understand each other. Alex found herself envying the closeness between them.

The afternoon sunlight had turned the landscape into a world shimmering like diamonds, nearly blinding her with its brilliance. She ducked her head behind the shadow of Bill's back for relief, conscious of how broad and solid it was. Occasionally, inadvertently, her head touched against it, but he seemed not to notice.

Finally, they spotted a large hump of snow, a bit of the hood showing through. Climbing down from the horses, the three of them began to shovel. The work was exasperatingly slow. They decided to hitch up the work horse to the length of chain Bill kept in the car. It was more than an hour before the car was out of the ditch, fully upright.

"You'll never make it," Charlie declared, surveying the drifted road.

Alex suspected he was right, but Bill argued the point until Charlie convinced him to let the old mare finish the job and pull the car at least to the first reasonably clear stretch of road.

The trip was made with little conversation between them. By the time they finally stepped inside the hotel, it was after five o'clock. As they walked across the lobby, Alex heard the sound of men singing a Christmas carol in the smoking lounge. "Good Lord. I guess I lost track of time," Bill said.

"Tomorrow is Christmas. I've got to catch the early train for Pueblo."

"You haven't changed your mind then?"

She smiled. "I have to go. Otherwise Ed and I won't really have a chance to work out the details."

He regarded her in a strange way. "I guess not."

The caroling stopped and a half dozen men strolled out of the lounge and went into the bar. Without the usual throng of officers, the lobby was oddly quiet. Perhaps they'd gone home for the holiday.

Alex glanced at the staircase, then back at Bill. "Well, I suppose I should go up and pack a few things for the trip."

They looked at each other.

"Listen, I was just thinking," he said. "If you don't have other plans, how about dinner tonight?"

"That would be nice," she said, surprised by how pleased she was with the unexpected invitation.

"Can't tell what will be open," he said.

"It doesn't matter." She was glad she wouldn't spend Christmas Eve by herself. "There's always the hotel."

"Sure." He smiled. "Seven o'clock okay?"

"I'll meet you in the lobby."

Chapter Nineteen

Alex turned on the lights in her room. The closest thing to a dinner dress she'd brought was the cranberry silk dress. The color was becoming and fit the season. She took it out of the wardrobe and laid it across the bed. Glancing at her watch, she was trying to decide if she had enough time for a real soak in the tub when the telephone rang. She ran into the sitting room.

"Alex? It's me, Bill. Say, about dinner . . ."

The receiver at her ear, she glanced at the window, darkened by the winter night, sensing he was about to cancel their dinner date. She slowly let out her breath.

"The superintendent of Cokedale is giving a last-minute dinner party for some visiting dignitaries who just arrived in town. All the local officials are supposed to attend. I'll have to renege on dinner."

"It's quite all right," she said, reaching for a light tone to hide her disappointment.

"I'm sorry. I really am."

"Bill, I understand." She placed the receiver back on its hook.

She went back into the bedroom. Sweeping the dress off the bed, she returned it to the wardrobe and turned to stare about the room, resentful of how let down she felt. She'd believed his fury over martial law. Apparently, she'd been duped. Why else was he now so willing to heed the bidding of the very men he claimed to loathe?

She picked up the book she'd brought and settled in one of the overstuffed chairs in the sitting room, determined to push aside her disappointment. She opened it to the page marked by a slip of paper, began to read, then realized she'd forgotten the gist of the last chapter.

She looked up. All she could think about was Bill and the party. She shrugged. It was probably just as well. Tomorrow's train to Pueblo left at eight o'clock. She'd be smart to get to bed early. She put the book down on the end table. Somehow she wasn't in a mood to read. She might as well go downstairs for supper.

In the dining room, a lone waiter eyed her sleepily as she took her usual place. Muted sounds of rough laughter and men singing came from the saloon next door. Gazing out the window through the veil of snow at the street lamps, she felt utterly alone.

Once Christmas Eve had been her family's time for a gala celebration with friends, the one time in the year she and her father could count on her mother being home. Emily Russell loved giving parties, extravagant affairs with marvelous decorations, exotic food, music. Everyone in town coveted an invitation to dinner at the Russells' on Christmas Eve.

The first year after her mother's death, Alex tried to carry on the tradition. In retrospect, she realized how foolish she'd been. Her father never came down from his bedroom, and the guests went home early. The next year, she limited herself to buying a tree and decorating it with the balls and bright trinkets her mother had collected, which proved no more successful.

The third year, Phyllis and Ben Thomas, her family's closest friends, suggested she and her father join them and their children and grandchildren for wassail and cookies. Her father reluctantly agreed. In time, this simple celebration became routine.

Generally, they were home by six-thirty. Cook saw to it a light supper was served on trays in the library, where after dessert they opened their few presents in front of a roaring fire. She usually gave her father a rare book. Last year, he had given her the jeweled lapel watch.

For thirteen years—interrupted only by the single year of her marriage—they had clung to each other. Though they never spoke of it, each was grateful for the other's company as they went through the motions of Christmas, glad when the holidays were over.

The waiter finally took her order. Roast chicken, which was dry and tasteless. With little appetite, she skipped dessert and went upstairs. By now, her father was undoubtedly home from the Thomases'. She placed a call. It took several minutes before the connection was made.

"Alexandra? The Thomases wondered where you were," he said before she could say hello.

"I hope you explained," she said, trying to keep a light tone.

"Cook ruined the roast tonight," he said.

"You must speak to her, Father." Alex sucked in her breath, fighting against the guilt he demanded she feel. "I'm going to visit Ed Keating and his wife tomorrow. You remember the congressman."

"That nincompoop!"

"Father—" She stopped. The space between them was too vast to bridge. "Merry Christmas, Father."

She waited, but when he didn't reply, she hung the receiver carefully back on its hook.

In the silence of the small sitting room, she stared at the telephone, overwhelmed by her frustration and loneliness. Her father was her flesh and blood. The only family she had. Instead of giving her the small bit of comfort she had yearned for, he had reminded her of how she had failed him.

The routine was so familiar. It would continue for as long as she allowed it to. Between them was his belief that she owed him unswerving obedience. He seemed oblivious of the fact that she was a woman of means with a substantial inheritance from her mother's estate and her own earnings as her father's law partner.

Fuming, she went into the bedroom, then remembered she hadn't bathed. She undressed, went into the bathroom, and turned on the water. As she wrapped a towel, turban-style, around her head to protect her hair, she felt an unexpected sense of determination come over her. She shut off the water when the tub was only half full. In a matter of five minutes she had washed and toweled herself dry. She took her nightgown off the hook on the back of the door and slipped it on.

As she put on her dressing gown and tied it, she decided that living in Denver with her father again would prevent her from ever getting any recognition on her own. She didn't think she'd go back East either. She'd live in the West. It really didn't matter where, as long as she could see the mountains.

She might open a small office in a town about the size of Trinidad, though perhaps in the northern part of the state. She'd buy a cottage within easy walking distance. She'd never handle real estate transactions again if she could help it.

Back in the bedroom she took her slippers out of the wardrobe. As she stuck her feet into them, the decisiveness slipped a notch. With all her plans for setting up her own practice, what was she really after? Recognition, of course. Everyone yearned to be appreciated. She was no different. But it was more than that.

She turned off the light and went into the sitting room. At the window, she leaned her forehead against the cold pane, idly watching two drunks shuffle slowly through the snow blanketing the deserted street. A great wave of loneliness spread over her again.

If only . . . She thought of Juanita Nevil's tale about falling in love with her husband. Watching the two of them, their easy way with each other, had made her realize how large the hole was in her life.

She took in a deep breath, pulled down the window shade, and forced her thoughts back to the dinner party going on somewhere on the hill beyond, undoubtedly in the best part of town. Bill had explained that his presence was mandatory, which seemed plausible. After all, he was the district attorney, restricted by certain obligations. Yet, from the little she knew about him, he struck her as too stubborn to automatically comply with directives. Something was going on. She felt it in her bones.

Chapter Twenty

Bill made his way up the snowy hill, the tops of his overshoes flapping around his calves. When he'd gone back to his rooming house and found Judge Southard's clerk waiting with the invitation to the Trumbulls', he'd been tempted to say he was busy. But a sixth sense had stopped him. Whatever had triggered a last-minute affair important enough for the judge to require his attendance, it was worth knowing about, firsthand.

He felt bad about canceling his dinner with Alex. He was surprised how much he enjoyed her company. Maybe it was because she was the only person in town he could really talk to these days.

Just ahead, on the south side of Chestnut and Second Streets, stood the Trumbull's imposing gray stone house. Surrounding the broad lawn was a high wrought-iron fence. Faint strains of a cello drifted into the night. As he approached, the massive oak door decorated with a Christmas wreath swung open to reveal a young Spanish-American woman wearing a stiffly starched cap and apron over a black dress.

"*Buenas noches,*" he said.

With a deferential smile, she took his coat.

At the far end of the spacious wood-paneled entryway was a broad staircase, its banisters trimmed with ropes of pine and red velveteen ribbon. From a room beyond came voices and subdued laughter. The cello was now more distinct, but not loud enough to interrupt conversation.

Evelyn Trumbull appeared. No more than five feet tall, stout with carefully waved gray hair, she wore an evening gown the color of pea soup. A walnut-sized diamond pendant on a substantial gold chain lay in the crevice between her large breasts. "Good of you to come, Mr. Henderson," she said as he approached. "Mr. Baxter told me he wanted to talk to you the moment you arrived. But come in and meet everyone first."

There were about fifteen men and several women in the room. General Chase in full-dress military uniform, Leslie Baxter, the mayor, and the publisher of the *Chronicle* stood off to themselves next to the fireplace. With them was a man with washed-out blue eyes whom Bill recognized as Jesse Welborn, the president of CF&I. Whatever the reason for this meeting—and that's what it was—it must be important for the likes of Welborn to be present.

Introductions were made, and punch was passed by the maid who had met Bill at the front door. He felt out of place at such parties. He didn't give a damn about appearances or about the people who did. The conversation was stiff, carefully guarded. After awhile, Leslie Baxter appeared at his elbow and motioned for him to join him in the hall.

"A festive occasion, wouldn't you say?" Baxter asked amiably. Bill cocked his head, waiting.

"I know our good hostess, Mrs. Trumbull, will miss our presence, so I'll get right to the point."

"Good."

For a moment, Leslie Baxter studied the punch glass he held in his hands; then he looked up and said, "When I arrived several days ago, I had occasion to meet a Mrs. MacFarlane. Charming lady. Later I was able to help her out of an awkward situation she'd gotten herself into. The next day, we talked over breakfast. From what she tells me, she is in Trinidad to represent a miner presently in custody."

"True."

"And as she freely admits, present circumstances preclude any service she can render her client."

"Also true." He heard the cynical tone of his voice.

"Thus, it seems only sensible that until the strike is settled, she would be wise to return to Denver."

"What's your point, Baxter?"

Leslie Baxter smiled. "Only that I'm returning to Denver tomorrow and that I'd consider it a privilege to serve as Mrs. MacFarlane's escort."

Bill folded his arms across his chest. "You want me to tell her to go home. Is that it?"

"We're concerned for her safety."

Bill rocked back on his heels, struck by the intriguing realization that no matter how far-fetched and ill-defined Alex's ploys were, they must already be worrying the CF&I. "I'll tell you something, Baxter. Mrs. MacFarlane is a woman with a mind of her own. She pretty well does what she wants. She certainly doesn't listen to me. If you want her to leave town, you better tell her yourself."

The lace-covered dining table was set with sparkling crystal and gleaming silver. Overhead was an imposing brass chandelier. Gold-rimmed china bowls filled with mock turtle soup were placed before them and the table talk turned to Christmas plans. Parties, receptions, trips to Denver. It was as if the strike and martial law didn't exist.

The soup bowls were removed, and Bill's dinner companion, the wife of the newspaper publisher, began to complain about women who came from the camps to her back door with their children, begging for work. A woman across the table declared the strikers and their ragtag families were a nuisance.

The voices took on an ugly tone. The slight twinge behind Bill's eyes had turned into a full-fledged headache. At this rate, the dinner would be interminable.

The pantry door swung open, and the maid entered, bearing a standing rib roast on a silver platter. All eyes turned to Malcolm Trumbull as he stood to carve. The maid passed tiny roasted potatoes, peas, and crescent rolls.

Wine was poured, and Jesse Welborn raised his glass. "If I may—"

All eyes turned toward him.

"Let me offer a toast to our kind hosts, to a merry Christmas and happy new year. And to peace."

As Bill took a sip of the Bordeaux, savoring its smoothness and flavor, he knew the peace Jesse Welborn spoke of had no relation to the peace included tonight in the prayers of the thousands of men and women huddled in the camps.

The ladies having retired to the living room for coffee, Jesse Welborn stood with his back to the library fireplace, an after-dinner brandy in one hand, a cigar in the other, looking like a general who had gathered his officers around him the night before a major battle.

Bill decided the analogy wasn't too far off the mark. The Colorado Fuel and Iron was the biggest company in the southern Colorado coalfields, and Jesse Welborn was its president. As to a battle tomorrow, that might also be possible.

"Gentlemen, I'm happy to announce the strike will soon be at an end," Welborn said.

The men seated around the room exchanged glances and smiled gravely. Lounging by the window at the far end of the room, Bill puffed at the Cuban cigar he'd taken from the humidor on the mantel, careful to disguise any sign of his eagerness to hear what else Welborn might say.

Welborn obviously had left the comfort of the company boardroom in Denver to travel to Trinidad for a reason that would affect every man in the room. They were in it together. That's why the judge had made sure he was invited. Whatever the conspiracy, and he was certain it was a conspiracy, he was about to be a part of it.

"Upon review of the company books for the final quarter of the year, it is clear the strike is seriously affecting profits," Welborn continued. "Our sources tell us the UMWA will be out of funds to support the strike in a matter of months. Unfortunately, we cannot wait that long. Our grave responsibility, not only to our stockholders but to the public, does not permit that. However, as long as coal production returns to normal, we can outwait the union for as long as it takes."

Heads nodded.

"As you know, it's been our practice to bring in miners to replace the strikers. To date, that has been a relatively small number. Now we must get the mines up to full force."

Welborn paused to take a sip of brandy.

"Mr. Fred Gates, our manager, tells me we've opened an employment office in Joplin, Missouri," he said, "and that we have had excellent response."

"Splendid," Malcolm Trumbull intoned solemnly.

Jesse Welborn turned to Chase. "General, if you would please, describe the role of the militia."

"My pleasure," Chase said, raising his bulk off the couch. "The minute the train carrying the workers crosses the Kansas border, we'll take over and make certain that not a man gets off before the final destination."

"What's the bait?" asked the publisher of the *Chronicle*.

Leslie Baxter, who was sitting back in a large leather chair, flicked his cigar ash into the nearby spittoon. "Why, sir, they are being given an opportunity. Specifically, twenty acres of prime land."

"As a give-away or . . ." the sheriff started to ask.

"To be paid for in monthly installments," replied Baxter, smiling broadly.

Those poor sons of bitches, Bill thought. The ploy of offering land, one used in other coalfields before, was designed to saddle a man with installments large enough to eat up his wages for worthless land—not a drop of water, all sand and cactus. Shit. He'd had enough. He stubbed out his cigar in a glass ashtray, took a deep breath. "These men in Missouri—they were aware of the strike when they signed up?"

All eyes turned toward him. He'd disobeyed the judge's orders to keep his mouth shut and go along, no questions asked. In doing so, he'd stepped over the line into the enemy camp. He could feel his heart pounding at the realization of what he'd done. They might send goons to get him back in line, but it was too late.

Leslie Baxter smiled. "Actually, Mr. Henderson, what we're offering these men—"

"The law says that before men sign up to work during a strike, they must be apprised of that fact."

"Of course." Baxter swirled his brandy slowly. "When they get here, they'll be fully informed."

Judge Southard rose, glancing around at Bill, then back at Jesse Welborn. "As you may recall from earlier introductions, Mr. Henderson is our esteemed one-term district attorney."

Bill eyed him. What the hell difference did a political future mean if he'd sold his soul to get it?

Jesse Welborn's icy blue eyes studied him.

"He is also a great student of the law." Southard's tone dripped with quiet sarcasm.

Welborn squinted, regarding Bill even more closely.

Do that, Bill thought. *Give me a good look. I'm one of those strange birds who believes it's law, not politics and money, that should run this land.*

"Maybe you can tell me, Mr. Welborn, when you decided to bring men from Missouri, did you consider the question of the National Guard's involvement going beyond their jurisdiction, which is limited to the boundaries of Las Animas and Huerfano Counties?"

Jesse Welborn shot a glance at Mr. Baxter, who said, "We did."

"Any other concerns, Mr. Henderson?" Welborn asked, coolly.

"Actually, yes. When is this trainload of men arriving?"

Welborn's look was cold. "In the next few days, I believe."

Chapter Twenty-One

A whistle blasted in the clear air of Christmas morning, and the engine of the train bound for Pueblo came rolling into sight just as Bill parked the Tin Lizzie by the depot. Only a handful of passengers stood waiting, and he spotted Alex easily. Taking the steps two at a time up to the platform, he called out to her. His voice was drowned by the squeal of brakes and whoosh of steam.

He hurried down the platform and called to her again. She finally saw him.

"I almost missed you."

She smiled. "Good morning."

"I learned something you and Mr. Keating should know." He saw the confused look on Alex's face and realized she hadn't heard what he'd said. "Let's get away from this racket." He guided her around the corner of the station house.

"I'm sorry about breaking our date."

"It's all right. I'm sure it couldn't be helped." Her tone was matter-of-fact. For some reason, he wasn't surprised. Alex MacFarlane wasn't the whining type.

"At the dinner last night, Jesse Welborn announced they were hauling in a whole trainload of scabs."

She cupped her hand to one ear.

"They're bringing men in from Kansas under false pretenses," he shouted. "They have no idea they'll be working in a strike area."

"Hasn't that happened before?"

"Sure. But this time national guardsmen will be posted at all the train exits to make sure the men don't get off before they arrive."

She didn't react to what he'd said. Maybe she hadn't heard. Steam rushed out from beneath the waiting cars.

"I'm afraid they're boarding," she said.

He let go of her arm, and she ran toward the nearest car and got on.

As the train moved slowly down the tracks, he walked along the platform toward where he'd parked his car. What good would it do for Alex to tell the congressman about the scabs? There was nothing new about using the military against some citizens for the financial benefit of others. Hell, that was what martial law was all about in the coal counties.

Back in the car, he felt strangely let down. Thinking that a good cup of coffee might raise his spirits, he headed for the Newhart Cafe. But when he pulled up, the shade in the front window was drawn. CLOSED FOR CHRISTMAS, a sign said. He glanced up and down Main Street. The usual Pinkerton boys hunched in strategic doorways, some maybe with orders to keep their eyes on him now. Otherwise, the sidewalks were deserted.

Christmas was for families. That was the truth of it. But for him, growing up, the work had gone on like every other day. He parked in the vacant lot behind Mrs. Willard's boardinghouse, got out, climbed the steps to the closed-in back porch, and went inside.

The kitchen was dark, the stove cold. No sign of the hired girl who did the cooking. The front hall was quiet. He peered into the parlor where Mrs. Willard had put up a little tree and decorated it with strings of popcorn. At the moment, it looked as forlorn and lonesome as he felt.

Climbing the stairs to the second floor, he automatically went down the hall and opened the door to his room. As district attorney, he was given the premier location at the front of the house.

He walked over to the window and stared out at the houses across the street—modest homes, a mixture of one and two stories, with neat yards. In one of them, a swing dangled from the branch of a cottonwood, forgotten for the day.

He glanced about him. The bed was made. His clothes were hanging in the wardrobe or stacked in the drawers of the chiffonier. Everything in its place. A picture of a dark landscape Mrs. Willard had bought at the county fair last year hung above the bed. Aside from the books on the table by the bed that he'd borrowed from the library last week, there was no hint of who lived there or the kind of person he was.

He picked up the book on the top of the pile and sat down in the rocker next to the window. The grandfather clock in the downstairs front hall chimed nine o'clock. He was hungry, and lunch was three hours away. Then he remembered Mrs. Willard's policy of not serving meals on Christmas Day. The two other roomers who remained at the boardinghouse had said they'd be having dinner with friends.

He turned to the first page. It was a Sherlock Holmes tale, the kind of book he liked to take his mind off the mess at the office. For several

minutes, his eyes traveled down the pages, but he couldn't seem to concentrate on their meaning, and finally he rested the open book on his
lap.

He thought of Alex. She was well on her way to Pueblo by now. It
seemed a fool thing to do, going all that way for one day, and on Christmas
at that. He wondered what time the train would get in, took out his watch,
snapped it open.

The gold watch had been a gift from Judge Broadhurst. The face was
ivory, the filigreed hands as fine as spider's silk. On the inside of the casing
lid was the inscription: TO WILLIAM H. HENDERSON FROM HILMAN
BROADHURST, U.S. DISTRICT COURT, 1908.

Judge Broadhurst had invited him to his home on Capitol Hill to celebrate the last night of his clerkship. Mrs. Broadhurst was a gracious hostess
who did her best to put him at ease. Though a clerkship in the Broadhurst
court was an honor reserved for the top man in the graduating class, social
graces were not a requirement, and Bill found himself watching which fork
to use for which dish. If Mrs. Broadhurst noticed his clumsiness, she didn't
let on. It was the first time he had ever tasted beef Wellington.

Bill admired Judge Broadhurst. He had learned a great deal in his service. But the research and writing didn't satisfy his urge to get into the fray.
When his year was up, he was ready to move on. He felt hamstrung.

The other young clerks in the office hadn't helped matters. They were
from families like the MacFarlanes. They belonged to all the right clubs
and lived in houses big enough for three families with room left over. After
the office closed, they ate at the popular restaurants, often at the Brown Palace Hotel just a few blocks up the street from the courthouse.

The law for them was a family tradition, not a passion. He guessed it
wouldn't be long before each of them would be a junior partner in a presti-
gious firm somewhere in the country, marry a rich man's daughter, have a
few kids, die never knowing the true purpose of the law.

So he kept his distance, did his job, and looked for the right opportunity.
His search lead him to Sims and Charlton in Pueblo. The firm specialized
in trial work; its reputation was legendary. For years, the newspapers had
been filled with accounts of the trials in which they were pitted against big
business and big money in representing clients no other attorney would
touch. To handle cases like that was his dream.

Even at the time, he had known it was a long shot to go down there out
of the blue and ask for a job. When he'd mentioned his intentions to Judge
Broadhurst, the judge had raised his eyebrows, but he had wished him luck.

Arriving in Pueblo, Bill had asked the stationmaster for directions, and after several wrong turns, he found the small office on the second floor of an aging building near the courthouse. When he entered and found no sign of a clerk or secretary, he'd thought nothing of it. After calling out a hello, a voice told him to come on back, and he was greeted by a man who turned out to be Mr. Sims himself.

Seated behind a large pine desk cluttered with papers, Jack Sims was a man of average height, lean as a strip of beef jerky. Only a fringe of gray hair remained on his otherwise bald head. Bright eyes peered out from folds of aging skin.

Bill introduced himself and stated the purpose of his call. Mr. Sims asked him to have a seat.

"We've cut back, Mr. Henderson," the elderly man said, as he tipped back tentatively in an ancient swivel chair. "Fact is, we haven't had a client walk in here for several months."

Bill tried to smile. The man's statement confused him.

"I'd like to take you on. My guess is that with you coming from Hil Broadhurst's shop, you're a crackerjack. Right?"

Bill leaned forward in his chair, his soft-brimmed hat dangling from his hands. "I can do the work. Yes, sir. But, you see, I've heard about the firm, what you've done over the years—"

Jack Sims held up an arthritic hand. "Let me guess. You want to save the sonsabitches over there at the CF&I steel mill, the men getting their hands and legs chopped off by machinery, their lungs seared. The Mexicans getting cheated out of their land down in the San Luis Valley. Prostitutes cut up by their pimps. Not a one your average all-American people the CF&I sells its steel to. But I ask you: who's average? Anyway, the way I look at it, we're all Americans."

"Who deserve the same protection under the law."

"Couldn't have said it better myself. I can see you share our views."

"I'll admit to a limited amount of trial experience, Mr. Sims, but I'm a fast learner. I'm sure I could represent the firm well."

Jack Sims had studied him curiously for several minutes before he said, "It's damned foolishness, but I'll talk to Sid. Come back tomorrow."

The partners decided to hire him, and at first Bill was ecstatic. Then he realized Mr. Sims had not exaggerated about the firm having no clients—at least not the kind Bill had hoped to serve. But he had moved to Pueblo and cut the ties he had in Denver. He decided to stick around, for he had developed a thorough liking for his bosses.

The word spread among Jack Sims and Sid Charlton's friends that a sharp young lawyer from Denver had joined them. Clients appeared, but the work was confined to title searches, real estate closings, and probate work. Not a single client looking for redress from personal injury at the steel plant or the smelters, not a victim of a land swindle, not a person wrongly accused.

Mr. Sims and Mr. Charlton—who was a head taller than his partner, not a pound heavier, and looked to be in his eighties—let Bill take over the work. They often complimented him. He was busy. Still, he had the strange feeling he was a front man at a carnival show.

One day Bill's curiosity became too much for him.

Tapping on the door of the office the partners shared, Bill poked his head in and asked if he could speak to them for a minute.

They put down their newspapers and invited him to come in. "Bill, boy, you're drawing them in like flies," observed Sid Charlton in that cracked kind of voice he had.

"Mr. Sims. Mr. Charlton. Since I joined your firm a month ago, the work I've done is largely—"

"Boring as hell," Jack Sims observed. "But you've done us a service."

"How's that, sir?"

"The truth is that until you came along we were on our uppers. But now, thanks to you, we can pay a few bills," Mr. Sims said.

"But—"

"I know. You're thinking of all those headlines. Well, I'll tell you, press clippings don't bring in big fees," Mr. Sims said. "Anyway, awhile back we about stopped taking any more business."

His partner nodded. "You see, Sid and I decided we'd had enough of these poor so-and-sos coming in here with injuries that prevented them from ever working again. None of whom we could represent. Oh, our criminal cases—we batted a thousand on those. But personal injury? We'd lose every time at the trial court level. The few we took up to the court of appeals met the same fate. Every damn time the lower court's judgment was upheld." He stood up and began to pace.

"The law of contributory negligence and assumption of risk is nearly impossible to overcome," he said. "Add in juries sympathetic with management, and our clients, or others like them, don't have a prayer."

Bill looked from one man to the other.

"We know somewhere out there is a first-rate, humdinger of a plaintiff with evidence so indisputable and ironclad any jury and even the good judges of our court of appeals would have to find for the plaintiff. There can't be a crack. Not even a hairline." He peered at Bill. "Are you following?"

"Yessir."

"While we're waiting for this man who is the father of a half dozen children under the age of seven and paralyzed by a faulty hoist or some such, we're hunting up some sponsors for a workmen's compensation law. One with teeth in it," Sid Charlton said. "I don't have to tell you legislators with that kind of intestinal fortitude are a rare breed in this state."

"Our fellow attorneys-at-law believe we have retired," Mr. Sims said, his rheumy eyes dancing. "Let them, if it saves them anxiety. In the meantime, we're cataloging the cases we've handled. Every one of them. On the lightning principle."

"Sir?"

"You know, one man struck by lightning isn't news. A town burned to the ground by it gets the public's attention. In short, one way or another, we're out to get us that workmen's compensation law."

"But what about the other trial work you do?"

"Did. Past tense. It needed doing. We never doubted that. But . . ." Jack Sims stuck his hands in his trouser pockets. "Well, Sid and I are to that point in life when we can see the end of the road. We talked it over and decided to clear the decks and concentrate on reform legislation. Personal injury seems to fit the bill. Ever consider the problems inherent in the law of negligence when it comes to prosecuting a claim for the working man?"

"How do you mean?" Bill asked.

"Why, it's enough to make a man living in a free country like ours ashamed. Let me quote from the statutes. 'Duty of the master.' Master? And 'servant's assumption of risk.' Servants? I thought we emancipated the slaves. It's legal language that's guided a helluva lot of legislation and judicial decisions. As far as I'm concerned, until that kind of language and what's behind it changes, our hands are tied and any expectations of redress our clients might have are doomed."

"So you're drafting legislation?" Bill asked, regarding each man with deepened respect.

"And buttonholing some people. But it'll take time."

Bill went back to his desk to continue reviewing a client's will. But that night, sitting cross-legged on his narrow bed in a shabby boardinghouse off Union Street, softly strumming the guitar he'd bought at a pawn shop, he decided that, unlike the two old men, he wasn't ready yet to devote his life to a losing cause, no matter how noble. He had a fire in his belly that only action could quench. He decided to go to Trinidad.

Bill sighed at the memory of how naive he'd been, stuck the watch back in his pocket, and rose. He thought of Alex again, and of the wise, old men with their plans to get legislation through. The lightning principle, they'd called it. It suddenly occurred to him Alex was after the same thing.

Chapter Twenty-Two

Maria Ferrera stood in front of the cook tent, her breath fogging in the cold morning air, and distributed the last of the hard candy someone sympathetic to the union had donated for Christmas to the eager children dancing around her. In her dreams last night, she had crept from tent to tent, like Santa Claus, leaving toys, wool mittens and caps, new shoes.

Two toddlers clung to her skirts, searching her apron pockets for more. With a heavy heart, feeling the tears form in her eyes, she bent down, kissed their heads, and shooed them away with pretended playfulness.

She pulled in a deep breath to steady herself, went inside to look for Dom. Rumors had been flying around the camp all day about a trainload of scabs being sent from either Kansas or Illinois, depending on whom you talked to. Tempers had been strained to the limit even before the news. To keep them under control was going to be difficult, even for John Lawson.

He'd called a meeting of the men several hours ago. Maria was sure it would be over by now. As she stepped into the tent, she saw the men were still gathered around John, seated at one of the tables. Louie Tikas, John's chief lieutenant, who was next to him, was talking with his usual passion about guns. A pox on him. There was a murmur of voices as his words were translated for those who spoke little or no English. Someone reminded him all hell would break loose if the army caught them with weapons. Louie didn't care.

Maria stood by the entrance and surveyed the crowd. Young men stood at the edges, frowning, but eager for action. Dom was whispering to the man next to him. He gestured as he spoke, and his intensity frightened her.

The usual method to protest the use of scabs was throwing rocks. It was the only tactic left to them, short of all-out war. The talk returned to guns. "This new bunch might really break the strike," one man said. John heard everyone out, always waiting for the translations. Maria marveled at his patience, at how he was able to keep them together.

She thought of the women, waiting in the tents for word of the meeting. They were a tough lot, tougher and meaner than the men. Maybe it was the pent-up anger and frustration. She'd heard stories of Indian women who had skinned their captives alive, cut off the eyelids of girls who were prisoners. She'd seen women in the camps give birth on a filthy pallet on the floor in a house with no heat and get up to care for the other children the same day. She and other women had fought off company guards who tried to rape them. Women dealt with life from the moment it appeared in their wombs till they laid out the dead. Their courage seldom failed.

Up to now, violence among men was all anyone in the outside world knew of the strike. What if the women and children, with no guns, showed another side of the picture to the people of Trinidad? Then, surely, they would understand the people in these camps were no different than anyone else, wanting nothing more than the chance for a better life, fairly earned.

Guns had never worked. Women and children might. The idea excited her. But it wouldn't be right to express herself before the men. She would talk to John Lawson after the meeting. She stepped outside to wait.

Finally, the door to the cook tent opened, and men streamed out into the cold. The conversations in a babble of languages were angry. Obviously, nothing had been solved.

When John Lawson and Louie finally appeared, she approached them, told them she had a suggestion to offer.

"We must use the women and children."

Louie nodded. "Those kids have good aim."

"I don't mean throwing stones like before"

John Lawson and Louie regarded her with more interest.

"It is important people see that the strike and the union is more than men who want more money."

"I don't want to risk any more lives than we have to," John said.

"Life is a risk."

His blue eyes darkened as he studied her, as if weighing what she had said. "All right. Walk along with me back to the headquarters tent. You can explain as we go."

Chapter Twenty-Three

A small Christmas tree decorated with glass balls stood on a round table in one corner of Ed Keating's modest front room. From the kitchen came the aroma of roasting chicken. He settled back in the walnut-framed rocker placed before the fireplace, glad to be home. Perched on the footstool next to him, Alex was describing the situation in Trinidad.

When he'd received her letter, he was astonished she was down there, flabbergasted to learn how deeply she seemed to be involved. He'd seen her only occasionally since she'd left her reporting job at the *News*. Somehow he'd thought she'd resigned herself to her father's law practice and the Denver social scene.

Now here she sat facing him, full of determined hope. An advocate for an outsider's cause.

"It's go-for-broke in this strike, Alex. I could see it last October."

His wife Margaret refilled their coffee cups, offered them some fruitcake, and took a chair by one of the two parlor windows to resume her reading in the waning afternoon light. He wished the two of them could have enjoyed the day alone, but the strike was obviously shifting into another gear. Something had to be done. Thank God his wife was a woman of unending patience.

"This business of the trainload of scabs you talk about proves how high the stakes are."

"If it's true," Alex said.

"Oh, it's probably true."

"Ed, I know the companies have a right to bring in men to replace the strikers, but if they bring in an entire trainload of new miners under false pretenses as Bill says . . ."

Ed nodded. "Let's get back to the idea of an investigation."

"You do think it's the way to go, don't you?"

"It has merits. Particularly now with a real possibility of an extended strike." He paused. He didn't want to lead her on with false hopes. "The

Democrats may have control of the Rules Committee now, but that doesn't mean getting a vote through for a congressional investigation is any easier. Certainly, not one to investigate a strike. Several of the most powerful members come from districts controlled by mining interests."

She stood. "I see the problem."

"I thought you would." He finished his coffee and studied her for a moment. Alex was a knockout and as smart as they came. Women had the vote in Colorado and soon might have it on the national level. Alex should hold state office.

"You ever think of running for the Colorado Senate?" he asked her.

She smiled. "Oh, Ed."

"I'm serious. You have a feel for politics. You've worked in two campaigns I know of. It's a good time for Democrats."

She laughed. "Can't you just hear my father?"

Jonathan Russell was one of those men who spent their lives wishing their daughters were sons. Alex's husband had waltzed around, racking up debts. Alex deserved better. The saving grace was she had only her father to contend with now, which God knows was enough.

"Even so, I'll admit the idea has crossed my mind a time or two." Her eyes sparkled. "But you've changed the subject, Mr. Congressman."

He smiled.

"I need your help, Ed. You're the only one I can go to. Those counties are in your district."

"I know."

"You said the idea has merit."

He nodded and smiled. It was Christmas Day, not a time to diminish hopes. "I'm just a lowly freshman, Alex."

"When did anything like that ever stop you?"

He chuckled.

She drew a sheaf of notes out of her handbag. "See these? I've begun to snoop around. I've talked to the union man, John Lawson, and to Leslie Baxter, the CF&I attorney. Both would make good witnesses."

"What a prince of a fellow old Baxter is," Ed couldn't help adding with a good dose of sarcasm. "But two witnesses are only a beginning. For a hearing to be effective, you're going to have to find a dozen on either side of the fence."

"How about the business with the new scabs?"

"That could be used—*if* there is a hearing."

She eyed him with a look that told him she was not about to give up on the idea. "Do you think Bill Henderson was exaggerating?"

"Who knows? I could ask some of my old railroad pals. If anyone knows, they will." Growing up in Denver's rough fifth district, supporting his mother since he was twelve, he'd learned the necessities of survival. Though he'd worked his way up to editor for the *News* and now served in Congress, he hadn't lost touch with the boys.

"If it's true, how will the strikers react?"

"They'll be mad as hell, that's for sure," he said, picturing their fury, then catching himself as he realized how he'd taken the bait she'd offered him. He never could resist a good story, and she knew it. "Maybe I'll drive down to a saloon I know and ask around. By the time dinner's ready, I'll be back."

The instant he returned, Alex was beside him. "Well? What did you find out?"

"Patience, my girl. First things first," he said and went to the breakfront, where Margaret kept the decanter of sherry. His delay of Christmas dinner had probably stretched even Margaret's infinite patience with him. It was time to make a few amends.

Pouring a thimble of the amber liquid into the rose quartz glasses his wife saved for special occasions, he gave one to Margaret and another to Alex. Raising his own glass, he gave a toast to Christmas.

"Now let's go in," Margaret said. "Gertie's put the dishes on the table. I'm starved."

The three took their seats, and Ed hungrily eyed the steaming dishes of mashed potatoes, green beans, and beets set around the roasted chicken. After dinner, they were to go to a party given by old friends. Alex had accepted the invitation to spend the night in the guest room.

As the Parker House rolls were passed around, Alex asked, "Now will you tell us what you found out?"

He gave her a sardonic smile. "About what you suspected." Breaking open a roll, he filled the interior with butter. "They hired men in Missouri, promised them land and double wages."

Her eyebrows shot up. "I hadn't heard about the double wages."

"It's an old trick. They'll never see a penny of it," Ed said.

"And they're not aware of the strike?"

"Nope."

"How many are there?"

"A trainload, like you said." He glanced around the table for the choke-berry jam. "Pass the jam, will you, Margaret? A roll without jam is like a pretty girl who hasn't been kissed."

Smiling at his old joke, his wife obliged.

"How many men would that be?" Alex asked.

"Hard to say. Three, four, maybe five hundred. Sealed in. They're to be unloaded at a couple of spots and trucked to the coal camps. That's all anyone knows. So far."

"Does the union know?"

"The word's out."

"Leslie Baxter told me the union's guns had been confiscated."

"Some, yes. Not all. I suspect they've smuggled in a good many more."

"Even if they had some guns, would they have enough to go up against the militia?"

"I doubt it. But they could still kill lots of people."

Alex paused in the midst of cutting a piece of chicken. "The papers will cover it."

"Without a doubt. There'll be the usual stuff about the strikers raising Cain, the militia valiantly protecting the helpless new miners. Not a thing will come out about the sealed cars."

Alex put down her fork and knife. "Ed—"

"I wish it wasn't true, but there's no way I can pull it off." He always liked a good fight, but even using every political maneuver he knew, the odds of getting a resolution were such a long shot that no betting man would touch it.

"Isn't there anything you could do?"

"I'll be going back to Washington next week. I could try to get in to see the president."

"Can the president call for an investigation?"

"He has his ways."

Chapter Twenty-Four

The sun was setting the next day when Alex stepped off the train at the Trinidad depot. To her surprise, she saw Bill coming toward her.

"How was the trip?" he asked, as he took her bag.

"Fine." She regarded him curiously. "How did you know when I was getting back?"

"I guessed," he said, walking beside her.

"You were right about the trainload of scabs," she said. "Ed Keating asked some railroad men he knew."

"What was the congressman's reaction?"

She frowned. "Guarded. Not encouraging. Though he did say he'd talk to the president."

"So it's a matter of wait and see."

"I suppose it is." All the way back to Trinidad, she'd tried to convince herself the meeting with Ed had been a success even as she'd known he had never encouraged her in any way. His offer to see the president was little more than a courtesy, for old times' sake. Still, she had to hope.

As they neared the Ford, Alex noticed a thin, narrow-shouldered man standing in the shadows of a small brick building next to the depot. She looked more closely and realized it was the boy, Dom. He beckoned to her with a slight movement of his head. How had he known she'd be at the depot? The union must have spies like the coal companies. Somehow she wasn't surprised.

Alex touched Bill's arm. "I see someone who wants to talk to me. It won't take a minute."

As she neared the building, Dom stepped back inside, and she followed. The room was musty; wooden cartons and barrels were stacked against the walls. There was no one else around.

Immediately, his voice low, he said, "Mr. Lawson says to tell you about the march tomorrow."

"March? What march?"

"Down Main." His dark eyes darted toward the door. "In the morning."

"Who's marching? Does it have something to do with the scabs the companies are bringing in?"

His face was a blank as he stepped back outside. "I gotta go."

"Wait—"

He paused for an instant.

"Tell Mr. Lawson—" She glanced at Bill Henderson waiting for her by his automobile. A march down Main Street was something a district attorney was likely to know about. Yet maybe not, not any more. She looked back at Dom. "Just tell him I appreciate the information."

The next morning, Alex stood at the window of her sitting room and gazed at the street below. It was a few minutes after nine. Off to her right, a band of shabbily dressed women and children turned the corner at Commercial and headed east down Main. Her interest piqued, Alex opened the window, leaned out. Was this the march Dom had told her about? A small woman, carrying an American flag, was in the lead. Judging by the vigor of her stride, she was young. Her hair beneath a serviceable black hat was dark. Alex peered at her more carefully and realized she'd seen her before, that she was the woman in the cook tent at the Ludlow camp. Maria. Dom Ferrera's sister.

Behind Maria came more women, more children. All of them were singing with gusto—the high, shrill voices of the children lifting into the cold air.

> The union forever, hurrah! boys, hurrah!
> Down with the militia, up with the law;
> For we're coming Colorado, we're coming all the way,
> Shouting the battle cry of union.

Alex scanned the line of marchers, then glanced up and down the street. There was no sign of the militia. A traffic policeman stood outside the bank across the street and watched, his club behind his back.

Some of the women wore hats and dark-colored skirts and coats, all out of fashion, probably donated by a church. Most clutched shawls with one hand and a child with the other. Occasionally, a women raised her fist and shouted some slogan. Several boys waved small American flags. Here and there, a child broke into a skip.

The group moved quietly forward. A few early shoppers had come out of the stores to see what was going on.

Alex was too curious to stay where she was. She hurriedly pinned on her hat, took up her coat, and went downstairs. As she stepped out the front door, she noticed, off to her left, a line of cavalry. In the center of the line was General Chase on a handsome black mount. Apprehensive, she decided to get a closer look.

She walked faster, almost running down one block to the next, past the people lining the curb. As she was about to cross the street, a flash, a movement of some kind caught her eye, and she saw sabers being drawn out of their scabbards, then held at the ready by Chase and his cavalry. Behind the horses, infantry soldiers filled the street. Alex caught in her breath. A current of dread pulsed through her.

The marchers had stopped, but now they pressed forward again toward the cavalry. General Chase sat looking at the advancing women for a moment before he spurred his horse toward them. Then, as if he had changed his mind, he suddenly wheeled his horse to ride back toward his men.

Maria, at the front of the marchers, ran up to him. When Chase saw her, he yelled at her to get back, kicked out at her. His boot caught her in the breast. Maria staggered, clutched herself. In that instant, the marchers surged forward.

A woman shouted something. One of the cavalry officers rode up to Chase. Whether he intended to talk to the general or protect him, Alex couldn't tell, but the action seemed to frighten the general's horse; it reared, throwing Chase to the ground.

Women and children ran toward him, laughing raucously at the sight of the stout man on his back. Red-faced with fury, the general struggled to his feet and yelled, "Ride them down. I say, ride the women down."

Spurring their mounts, the cavalry plunged forward. Sabers slashed down into the crowd. Screams filled the air. The women turned to run back down the street.

A toddler, bloodied, his clothes torn, crying for his mother, fell to the ground. Alex gasped in horror and ran into the street, scooped him up in her arms. At the sound of hoof beats clattering over the brick street, she looked over her shoulder and saw a rider lean from his horse and smash a boy in the face with his fist. Women and children ran in every direction.

Alex dashed down the street, her heart pounding, the child clutched against her breasts, the only thought in her head to reach the safety of the hotel. It was as if the entire world had exploded. Everything looked strange.

Confused, she wasn't sure where she was, but as she ran through the fleeing marchers, she realized her cheeks were wet with tears.

Suddenly, hands gripped her arms. "Alex. God, but I'm glad I found you."

She looked up and realized it was Bill. "I have to get the child inside."

"Come on. In here," he said, leading her into a nearby store and guiding her to a chair by the entrance.

The child's eyes were wide with terror. He fought to free himself from her grasp, but she held tight. Finally, his screams waned until they slowly subsided to an exhausted whimper. "There, there, little one," she crooned. "It's all right. We'll find your mother."

"I don't know what luck you'll have," Bill said, "Chase'll probably jail as many of the women as his boys can get their hands on."

"It's the general who should be in jail," she said through clenched teeth as she tried to soothe the child.

"Alex, that was a union demonstration out there."

She looked up at him, appalled, yet in that instant knowing he was right. "Damn them. Damn Chase. How could they do this to women and children? Is there nothing sacred in this insane war?"

Bill placed a hand gently on her shoulder, but she shrugged it away. Her anger was beyond the reach of a comforting touch. She stood, unsteady for an instant, the child in her arms. "I'm going to the jail."

"Don't."

She glared at him.

"If you show up there, they'll take you in."

"They wouldn't dare."

"You know they will."

Alex staggered up the hill toward the courthouse, the child in her arms, the sidewalks littered with debris—pieces of coats, a hat, a child's shoe, the American flag, its staff broken off. Just ahead, she spied a soiled hair ribbon lying light as a feather on a melting snow drift. She prayed its owner was safe.

The little boy was asleep, a dead weight in her arms.

The only children she had known were those of her friends. Occasionally, she had been invited to an elaborate birthday with gaily colored balloons and little cakes with pink icing. The children were chubby with round cheeks, bright eyes, and neatly bobbed hair. The boys in velveteen suits, the girls in beautifully smocked dresses of the finest cotton, gleaming patent leather shoes on their little feet.

This little boy in her arms was bones and angles with sallow skin, in pants and a coat, gray with washing, several sizes too small. She stopped and gently brushed a strand of tangled black hair off his forehead.

As she neared the front doors of the courthouse, she became aware of a great pandemonium seeping out into the cold air. The noise grew louder the closer she came. She stepped inside, stunned by the sound of women's high-pitched shouts and crude curses—protests—so loud she wanted to hold her hands over her ears.

The child in her arms stirred, opened his eyes. Bill appeared. She realized he had followed her.

"Alex, give Chase's goons a chance to cool off."

"I can handle this myself."

"No, you can't."

She looked into his eyes dark with worry, then down at the child. She had no wish to risk his life.

"All right. Then you go down there and find out if a woman has a child missing."

Bill nodded, went down the stairs toward the jail. As she waited for him to return, Alex held the child to her, the women's angry voices vibrating in her head. The outrage of what was occurring around her was beyond all understanding.

A few moments later, Bill reappeared, shaking his head. "No one knows a thing."

Alex realized her teeth were chattering. "I need to get the child to the hospital."

"They might not treat him."

She gazed at the child's scraped knees. "He could have something more serious the matter with him than it appears."

"And then what?"

"Then I want you to drive us out to Ludlow."

He frowned. "What makes you think the child's mother is out there?"

"She might not be. But John Lawson is there. He'll find her. And if he doesn't, I'm going to raise bloody hell."

Alex insisted Bill wait in the car while she took the child into St. Joseph Hospital. A sister in a white nursing habit who sat at the front desk said the doctor was busy. Alex remained firm. The nurse rose, leaving her to stand in the middle of the entryway, and disappeared down a hall. Finally, Alex sat down on one of the straight-backed chairs lined up against one wall. Thankfully, the child had fallen back to sleep.

An hour went by. Alex rose and went to the front desk presided over by a nun she hadn't seen before.

"Yes?"

"I've been waiting for a doctor to see this child."

The nun eyed the little boy in a not unkindly way. "I'm afraid there's nothing we can do just now."

"But the child's knees are cut. There might be—"

"I'm sorry. There are so many patients today."

It was nearly five o'clock, dusk, when Bill steered the Ford up the rutted road toward the Ludlow camp. Alex's exhaustion had not softened her anger. Two guards were stationed at the makeshift gate. When she got out of the car, one of them tried to take the child from her. She pushed him away and demanded to see John Lawson.

Bill climbed out and gave the men a hard, even look. "I'd go find him if I were you, boys. The lady means business."

The men studied him for an instant, as if deciding whether it was worth making a fight out of the matter, glanced at each other, then shrugged, indicating with a wave she and Bill should follow them.

Just as they approached the tent with the American flag flying from its roof, the flap was folded back and Maria Ferrera stepped out.

Alex almost gasped. From the moment the melee had broken out, she had presumed Maria, the woman who had led the march, would be the one person the militia would hold. Yet here she was, safe and sound.

"Roberto?" Maria called the instant she saw the little boy in Alex's arms. "Is that you?"

The child reached out a hand toward Maria and Alex let him down.

"Where did you find him?" Maria asked, as the child toddled toward her and clung to her skirts.

Alex regarded her with astonishment. "On Main Street. Where else?"

"His father is like a wild man to know if Roberto is safe. Thank you for bringing him back."

Alex was incredulous. The young woman acted as if the child had merely been lost. Was she so accustomed to death that what had happened during the march was commonplace? Or was anything, even risking a child's life, worth proving the union's point—whatever that was? "The child was nearly killed."

Maria looked at Alex, her dark eyes nearly black. "I had hoped such a thing wouldn't happen."

"But you knew it might, didn't you?"

Maria raised an eyebrow, glanced at Bill, then back at Alex. "Come. We will get something to eat and talk."

"Thank you, but this is not a social call."

Maria gently picked up the child. Her eyes flashed. "You are not willing to listen then?"

"Listen to what?" Alex glanced away, disgusted, furious, then looked back. "You people are no better than the companies, than the militia."

"We are women who demand a better life for our children."

"So you just follow union orders. Is that it?"

"The march was my idea."

Alex stared at her, unbelieving. She felt someone behind her. She glanced over her shoulder, saw John Lawson, arms folded, listening. "Is it true?"

"Absolutely."

She swung back to Maria. "Then you ought to be ashamed."

"And you? What are you? A coward who sits in your fine, warm house, looking the other way while thousands go hungry." The younger woman's eyes burned with fury. "If you know so much about us, then why are you so angry? Maybe it is because you are wrong."

On the way back to Trinidad, Alex gazed out the passenger window of Bill's automobile, not speaking. The image of Maria consumed her thoughts. With the child in her arms, she had been as beautiful and compelling as a Madonna in a Rembrandt painting. Yet her eyes had held a fire no painter could capture. She had challenged Alex as surely as if she had flung down a gauntlet.

Chapter Twenty-Five

As Bill steered the Ford back across the bridge into town, Alex knew what she had to do. She asked him to stop by the telegraph office before he let her off at the hotel.

"What's up?"

She smiled in spite of her exhaustion. "You know perfectly well what's up. That march today is exactly the ammunition Ed Keating needs, and I'm going to see he gets it. Tonight."

Inside the office, Alex felt the telegrapher's doubtful stare as she scribbled the message on the lined buff-colored pad.

CONGRESSMAN EDWARD KEATING, HOUSE OFFICE BUILDING, WASHINGTON, D.C.

UNION WOMEN AND CHILDREN MARCH IN PROTEST. CHASE ORDERS CAVALRY RUN THEM DOWN. SEVERE INJURY DONE. WOMEN AND CHILDREN NOW IN CUSTODY WITHOUT CHARGE. THE BALL IN YOUR COURT.

ALEX

She tore the sheet off the pad and handed it to the telegrapher. "How much will that be?"

The squat man read the message and eyed her curiously. "You sure you want to send this, ma'am?"

"I am."

He studied the telegram again.

"If I counted correctly, I believe it's twenty-nine words, not counting the address," she said.

He nodded. "Two dollars and sixteen cents."

She reached into her purse and gave him the money. "I'll wait while you send it." Then, thinking the telegram might somehow go astray, she watched him tap it out and asked for a copy. When he came back, he grudgingly handed her a copy of the message. Now she would just have to wait.

The shrill ring of the telephone roused Alex from sleep. It rang again, and she opened her eyes to the darkened room. Fumbling for her dressing gown, she threw back the blankets and groped her way out into the sitting room toward the telephone.

"Mrs. MacFarlane?"

"Yes," she answered, her voice husky with sleep.

"You have a call from Congressman Keating," the operator's voice said.

"Thank you." Alex sat down.

The line crackled. There was a pause. "Alex?"

"Ed?"

"Sorry about the hour, but I thought you'd be interested in this morning's headlines. Some of the boys phoned them in to me." Ed's voice was faint.

"I can barely hear you," she said, the weight of sleep gone.

"This better?"

The voice was clearer.

"Fine."

"Well, listen to this one in the *Post*, of all places. 'General Orders Women Trampled.'"

She couldn't believe it. A headline like that from a paper never known for its support of the union. "Any others?"

"How about the *Chieftain*? 'Czar Terrorizes Helpless Women.'"

Alex raised an eyebrow, astounded. The *Chieftain* was a Pueblo paper, located not a mile from the steel mills, always a friend to its owners.

"Any eastern papers?" she asked, hopefully.

The line crackled.

"Would the *New York Mirror* suit you?"

She laughed.

"Let's see. Here it is. 'Unarmed Women Mowed Down.'"

"What about the stories?"

"Short but sweet. The boys are clamoring for more. I suspect by the end of the day the train in from Denver will be full of reporters.

Alex took a deep breath, still not quite able to believe what she was hearing. "Is there any doubt about what has to be done?" She decided not to mention the investigation over the telephone.

Ed Keating laughed. "Not a doubt in the world."

"Does that mean—"

"I'm hanging up now," Ed cut in. "But I want you to keep me informed."

"You can count on it," Alex said, feeling her heart race. "Good-bye. And thank you."

Alex replaced the receiver on the hook and stared out the window. Morning newspapers across the country were carrying stories about the march and the strike that had precipitated it. Instead of the usual slant, favoring the coal companies, they had focused on women and children as hapless victims, caught in the middle of a great power struggle. Though it was true, the real issue was who and what had placed them there. She thought of Maria, a source Alex now knew she must tap.

At the very least, she hoped the storm of public opinion would force Chase to release his prisoners, including Stefan Vaska. It wasn't enough now. But it was a start. It was time to pay him a visit.

Phil Van Howe regarded her with eyes bloodshot from what she hoped was a lack of sleep. "General Chase is not seeing anyone."

"Don't you think that's unwise? Given the circumstances?" she asked, calmly.

"Please, have a seat," Phil said, obviously agitated.

"Thank you, I'll remain standing. I want to see General Chase."

"Alex, for the life of me, I don't understand all this. You know better than most what we're up against here. General Chase is only doing what the governor asked him to do."

Alex gave him a level look. "Are you telling me the governor ordered Elmer Chase to ride down helpless women and children?"

"The governor ordered General Chase to maintain order. He had no other choice."

"Oh, come now. I was there. I saw what happened. Those women and children were walking down the street without weapons, and Elmer Chase ordered the cavalry, swords drawn, to ride them down."

"You're mistaken."

"You know perfectly well I am not mistaken. Furthermore, there were a hundred witnesses who would testify to the truth. I want to see General Chase. Now."

Phil gazed at her for an instant. "All right. Wait here. I'll ask him if he'll see you."

For several minutes, the low voices of arguing men came through the door that separated the sitting room where she waited from the bedroom beyond. Finally, the door opened and General Chase appeared.

"I'm a busy man, Mrs. MacFarlane," he said, brusquely, dispensing with the usual social proprieties. "What exactly is your problem?"

"The problem, as you put it, is not mine. It is yours, General."

He glared.

"Your treatment of the women and children who marched yesterday was inexcusable. From this morning's newspapers, it would appear the nation agrees with that assessment."

His eyes cold, Elmer Chase folded his arms across his chest, looking like one of those windup toy soldiers. There was a time when she would have laughed at the sight of him.

"You must release the prisoners at once," she said.

"The disposition of prisoners is none of your business," he snapped.

"Technically, you're correct. Under martial law, you have complete power. But morally and ethically, the prisoners' treatment is indeed my business and everyone else's who cares about upholding the law and human rights."

"I agreed to see you out of courtesy, but I refuse to tolerate your implications."

"I imply nothing. I am saying in plain English, General Chase, that you have violated every code of decency."

"How dare you," he said, red-faced in his fury. "The governor of this great state gave me a job to do, and I am doing it. Until I arrived, two counties were in chaos. Those are the facts."

"And Las Animas and Huerfano Counties are not in chaos now?"

"My men are carrying out their orders."

"Your men are primarily company guards and Pinkerton detectives of the lowest sort."

"You, Mrs. MacFarlane, are a union sympathizer. I've known that ever since you set foot in this town."

"That is a lie," she said, coldly. "I ask again. Are you or are you not going to release the women?"

"I have absolutely nothing more to say." He turned toward the suite's bedroom.

"Are you?" she repeated.

He suddenly wheeled and roared, "If you were something beside an infernal busybody and a socialist bent on causing trouble, you would know that at this moment there isn't a single prisoner in custody. Including your client, Vaska. Now get out.

"And hear this, you with all your friends in high places," he added. "From this moment on, you no longer have my protection. Any more trouble, and I'll have *you* locked up."

Chapter Twenty-Six

Bill had a hard time hearing the judge over the excited din in the Newhart Cafe.

"Look at this," the judge snapped, flinging a copy of the *Pueblo Chieftain* down on the table. "That MacFarlane woman's to blame for this."

Bill picked up the paper and gazed at the inch-high headlines, suppressing a grin. "Well, now." Alex's telegram had hit pay dirt.

The judge glared at him. "How long have you known the woman was up to this?"

"Chase only mowed down those kids yesterday, Judge." He signaled to the waitress.

The judge sat down and leaned across the small table, his face distorted with rage, only inches from Bill's. "Did you understand my instructions about her or did you not?" he asked in a low voice.

The waitress came up to the table. "Can I get you gents some breakfast?"

Bill smiled at her. "A cup of coffee should do it. The judge has another table."

Southard rose. "What she did forced Chase to clear the jail."

"Well, I'll be damned." If Chase had cleared the jail, Stefan Vaska had been released.

"You deny any knowledge of what the MacFarlane woman did?" Southard demanded as the waitress put a cup of coffee on the table.

"No comment," Bill said as he reached for the sugar bowl.

On the way back to the office, Bill speculated about how Southard had connected Alex with the headlines. Knowing the way this town worked, he was reasonably sure a telegrapher had passed the news on to Southard or one of his boys.

He didn't believe it had been Alex's intention, but the union was certain to see the headlines as a boon to its cause. He wondered about her reaction to Vaska's release, whether she'd go back to Denver now.

With the release of the prisoners, the courthouse was unusually quiet as he went up the stairs. Down the hall, he could see light shining through the frosted panel of his office door, and he realized he'd forgotten to lock up.

He opened the door to see Alex studying the contents of the bookcase. She looked around at him with tired eyes and said, "I hope you don't mind my just walking in."

"Nope." He hung up his coat and hat.

"Stefan Vaska's been released." There was a flat quality to her voice.

"I know."

"I thought he might have gone back to the union camp near Sandoval."

"Why would he?"

She seemed not to have heard. "I have to find out if he's all right. Besides, it's important he doesn't leave. I want him to testify later. And once martial law is lifted, I want to clear his name." Alex was almost babbling.

"Are you okay?" he asked her.

She tried to smile. "Just a little tired."

Bill pulled out a chair. "Sit down."

She shook her head. "I'm fine."

"I know you won't want to hear this," he said as gently as he could. "But first, I heard the strikebreakers being shipped in had arrived on schedule."

She shook her head slowly.

"And about the congressional investigation—"

"What about it?"

"There isn't any, Alex. It's not even in the works."

"It's coming. I know it is."

"As for Vaska, there never were any formal charges filed against him. He's a free man. He's probably well down the road."

"Bill, the minute his sister finds out he's been released, she'll want to know how he is. Besides, Stefan Vaska is a victim. His testimony is vital."

"Helpful, maybe. Vital, no."

The old spark reappeared in her eyes. "I disagree."

He shrugged.

"Anyway . . ." She paused, pretending to examine the title of a book for a moment before she glanced at him again. "I think it would be a good idea if I left town for a few days."

Bill tensed. "Did Chase threaten you?"

"In a way—" She pulled in her breath. "Yes, he did."

"Sonofa—"

"I thought maybe if I went out to the Nevils . . . It's near the Sandoval camp. I know I would be imposing, but . . ."

Seeing her trying to hang on to her courage even as she teetered on the brink of exhaustion, he knew this was a woman he could love. Whatever he might have thought about her motivations was wrong. "They won't mind," he said. "Go pack a few things. We probably ought to wait a few hours before we head out. Just send up a few prayers we can get through."

A light appeared in the porch. The door opened, revealing Charlie's big frame. Bill was not surprised to find him holding a rifle.

"Hey, there, Charlie. It's me, Bill. And Alex."

Charlie stepped down into the yard. His hair was tousled, and he wore a thick blanket-like robe over his trousers. "What in the Sam Hill are you doin' out here this time of night?"

"Don't know if you've heard, but all hell's let loose in town," Bill said, slapping his arms against each other for warmth. It had to be at least zero.

"I was hoping it would be all right to stay with you for a day or so," Alex said.

The smaller figure of Juanita appeared.

"What is going on here?" Juanita reached out and took Alex by the hand. "You and Billie come inside."

Warmed with two cups of coffee and persuaded Alex would be safe, Bill finally went out to start the car. The engine would be cold, and he jacked the left rear wheel up to keep from cranking the whole transmission and being run over. He realized Alex was behind him. He turned to her. "Charlie'll keep his eyes out, but I wouldn't stray too far from the house."

She didn't reply.

He could feel more than see her eyes. "Be careful."

"You, too."

Bill got in and closed the door. As he drove out of the yard, he glanced in the rearview mirror and saw the now-familiar slim figure going back inside. Alex MacFarlane, he realized, had become a part of his life.

Chapter Twenty-Seven

Alex spent the next day doing what she could to help Juanita with her chores. As they worked—Juanita churning the butter, Alex washing the separator and the breakfast dishes—Juanita seemed lost in another world, weighed down by sadness. She spoke only when Alex asked her a question.

It was mid-morning when Charlie came back inside and set his rifle near the back door. As the three of them sat at the kitchen table, sipping coffee, he reported on the progress of a calf he was nursing back to health. Juanita listened with her usual courtesy, made a few comments, then lapsed back into silence.

Alex wished she were invisible, wished she hadn't come. Clearly, she was intruding. Regardless of her own fears, she'd been a thoughtless fool to invite herself.

The demands of the day's routine went on—preparing the noon meal of meat and potatoes and pickled fruit, later coring the apples and rolling out the dough for the crust of a pie. Now and then, Alex was drawn to the window, uncertain what she expected to see. Only the raucous screech of huge crows poised on the corral fence posts interrupted the quiet. Nothing but cattle moved across the white fields.

She'd been in Las Animas County for only a week. Yet in that short time the strike had taken hold of her, insidiously, until she was as afraid as everyone else. She loathed the strike, loathed the companies and the union leaders that fostered it.

The purpose that had brought her had transformed into something entirely different. She had no reason to stay now that Stefan Vaska had been released. She should leave, get on with her life, but she couldn't, at least not yet.

The light was fading when she went to the window again. As she peered out, she felt Juanita behind her. "You are looking for Billie?"

She shook her head.

124

"Charlie is out there. You do not have to worry."

Alex smiled, grateful for the woman's quiet courage. Alex probably had placed the Nevils in danger, and she hadn't meant to.

"It would do you good to go outside."

"You need help," Alex protested.

"I'm going out to milk. Why don't you go see if Charlie could use a hand?"

Standing at the back door, dressed in a pair of Charlie's coveralls, an old jacket and hat of his, and a pair of boots, Alex could see Charlie transferring hay from the stack in the middle of the field just beyond the barn onto the flatbed wagon. Buttoning her coat and pulling on a pair of heavy work gloves, she went across the yard, climbed the corral fence, and walked across the field toward the wagon. The cold, dry air was bracing. It made her feel wonderfully alive. Charlie leaned on the handle of a pitchfork, watching her as she approached.

"Jump on," Charlie called, giving a wave. "I'm headin' over to the south pasture first."

As she climbed up, she saw the rifle in its scabbard hanging from one of the wagon posts. Charlie slapped the reins against the rump of the same sturdy mare she and Bill had ridden to retrieve the car only days before.

At the fence, she climbed down and opened the gate. The horse and wagon moved through, and she dragged the wire fence back in place and worked the loop down over the fence post.

Anticipating the hay, the cattle moved toward them. Instructing Alex to throw out the hay as they went, Charlie guided the wagon in a wide circle around the snow-skimmed field.

Charlie clucked the horse to go on, and they moved through another fence and into another field. The process was repeated. When she looked around to get her bearings, Alex saw the Nevils' small house framed by the peach-colored sky. Dark was no more than a half hour away, when it would be hard to see what she was doing when she closed the gates.

Charlie laughed, perhaps catching her anxious looks toward the house. "Don't worry. Old Bess here could find her way back home blindfolded."

"That's what Juanita said about you the first night Bill and I came here." Alex hung on to one of the wagon posts, letting her legs absorb the shock of the bumps, as Charlie guided the empty wagon across the field.

"You kinda cotton on to Bill, do ya?"

She glanced at him.

"Known him a good while, I guess."

"Well, we met when we were in law school," she said. "But we haven't seen each other for quite awhile. Six or seven years, at least."

The horse stopped, and Alex knew it was time for her to open a gate.

Charlie began to wrap the reins around the brake, but she glanced around. "No, I can get it."

He shrugged and smiled. "Suit yourself."

Once back on the wagon, she waited for the next question she knew was coming. She suspected that, in his book, a woman had no business on the loose, that a romantic attachment would somehow make it all right.

"Nita and I think a good deal of Bill. In some ways, you could say he comes close to taking the place of the son we lost."

Juanita had not told her of a child dying. It was horrible enough their nephew had been killed.

"I'm sorry. I mean about your losing a child."

They rode on in silence for awhile.

"Funny thing about death. The years cover it up some, but it's always there."

"I know," she said. For an instant, she wondered if she had said the words aloud.

"Nita said your husband was killed in one of the cave-ins back in '03. Around here, I think she said."

"In one of the Hastings' mines."

"She said it had something to do with why you came down here," Charlie said.

"My client—Stefan Vaska is his name—tried to save my husband. I never did know all the particulars about my husband's accident. But from what I do know, Vaska was working in the same area of the mine where my husband was checking the timbers or some such. He was a mining engineer."

"That's what I heard," Charlie said.

Alex stared across the field at the lights of the house, suddenly struck by how often she'd been using Robb to justify her presence here. "Stefan Vaska was only a boy then. Seventeen or so. He'd just come to this country. Couldn't read or write—even speak English, for that matter. He tried to pull my husband clear from the debris but couldn't."

The horse stopped again. Automatically now, she jumped down from the wagon and opened the gate. When she climbed back up, she said, "It was my fault."

"What was?"

They had reached the yard behind the barn.

"I talked him into taking the job. He didn't want to go, but I made such a scene about his gambling debts . . ."

Charlie didn't say anything as he climbed off and began to unhitch Old Bess. After he had worked off the harness, he handed it to her as if it were a familiar routine. "Over the years, I've discovered something about beating yourself."

The harness in her hands, she stood without moving, held in place by the words.

"See, I let Johnnie, our boy, he was four . . . I let him come along when I went fishing one day. I wasn't paying attention like I should. I don't know how it happened. Don't to this day. He drowned because I wasn't watching. But all the sorries in the world don't bring him back, and that's the truth of it. I bring it up because I thought you should know."

He took the oil lamp hanging by the door, lit it, and led the horse into the barn. From a bin by one of the stalls, he scooped out some oats, tossed them into a bucket, and put it down before the horse. "I'd guess this old mare is about as spoiled a horse as you'll find west of the Mississippi."

She smiled, her mind still on what he'd said about sorries, knowing he was right.

"The harness goes over there on that peg, if you're wonderin'," Charlie said.

She went over to hang it up, then came over to Charlie, who was standing in the threshold of the barn. Not speaking for a few minutes, they looked out at the winter evening.

"So you see, Alex, there's no sense to tryin' to redo the past. No matter which way you twist it or work it around, it sticks right where it should. In the past. Let it be. It's hard a thing to do, but you get used to it as the years go by."

She barely knew him, yet she'd opened her heart to him as she had with no one else, even her father. She slipped a hand through his arm and hugged it to her. "Juanita is a very lucky woman."

He gave a chuckle and picked up the rifle he had leaned against the door. "That's just what I keep tellin' her."

The sound of Charlie snoring came through the closed bedroom door. Otherwise the house—full of its sadness—was quiet as Alex lay on her makeshift mattress of old coats and blankets, with more blankets over her. The embers of the dying fire in the stove glowed orange through the grill-work of the small door, flaring occasionally to cast eerie shapes onto the opposite wall.

She had imposed on the Nevils' hospitality enough. Tomorrow she had to get in touch with Stefan Vaska. Bill had warned her against going, and her own fear had held her back. But with all her talk, she'd done very little for Stefan Vaska.

She liked to think his release was due to her, but it wasn't really. An investigation would expose why he and the others had been held illegally in the first place. For now, the least she could do—if not for him, for his sister—was to find him.

Charlie glanced at her as he steered the buckboard closer to the Sandoval union camp. She could tell by the set of his jaw that the four or five shabbily dressed men who emerged from one of the tents to watch their approach worried him. Instantly, she wished she hadn't asked him to drive her here.

"Can you shoot?" he asked.

"My father used to take me skeet shooting. That's all."

"That'll do." He pulled back on the reins. "I'm goin' up to the welcoming committee that's standin' there and tell 'em what you're after. The rifle's under the seat." He glanced at her, smiling, but the flat look in his eyes told her he was in earnest.

"They don't appear to have any guns," she said.

"But somebody else we can't see might. It never hurts to be prepared." He set the brake and handed her the reins.

Charlie climbed down, ambled up to the men. "Hey, there," he called to them amiably.

They eyed him suspiciously.

"Say, the lady here is lookin' for a fellah named Vaska. Stefan Vaska. Seems he was livin' here in the camp before he was arrested a couple of weeks ago. Now the lady's been told this Vaska's out of jail."

No one replied.

"She was wonderin' if he's back here in the camp."

One of the men, badly stooped, stepped forward. He had the hard look of a man accustomed to danger. "Stefan Vaska ain't here," he said with a thick accent.

"You know him then." Charlie's tone was still friendly.

"I tell you he ain't here," the man repeated.

Charlie nodded, slowly letting his glance move from one man to the next. "Okay. But say—" He rubbed a gloved hand across his chin as if in thought. "You don't know where the lady could find him, do ya?"

"Ludlow, maybe. Forbes." The hunched man shrugged.

The others turned back to the tent.

"You sure you can't tell us where to find Stefan Vaska?" Charlie asked the stooped man.

"Stefan Vaska's a goddamn fucking sonofabitch," he said, matter-of-factly. Then he walked away.

Charlie looked back at Alex, raised an eyebrow, returned to the buckboard. He climbed up, took the reins from her, and released the brake. "Well, now, I'd say your Stefan Vaska isn't a very popular fellah," he observed as he slapped the reins against the mare's rump. They started off.

"Apparently not."

Charlie reached under the seat and pulled out the rifle, handed it to her. "Here. Till we get out of range of the camp, you keep an eye on it. Just in case."

Alex held the rifle uneasily as the buckboard rolled away from the camp. When the cluster of tents was out of sight, Alex turned and handed the rifle back to Charlie.

"What went on back there?"

He glanced at her. "I'd guess, whether it's true or not, they think your Mr. Vaska did a sight more than go into Sandoval for his mail."

"But what?"

"Hard tellin'." He called for the mare to "giddup," and as they rode across the prairie, Alex tried to imagine what Vaska could have done to cause those men to hate him so much.

Alex had just put the last of the supper dishes away in the cupboard when the sound of a car's engine cut through the evening quiet. Charlie went to the window, cupping his hands around his eyes to peer out into the darkness. "It's Billie."

A moment later, the back door opened, boots stomped to rid themselves of snow, and Bill stepped into the kitchen. Her spirits soared at the sight of him. Standing in the shadows was a man barely five feet tall, with what seemed an abnormally large head and a wizened face.

"Everyone—I'd like you to meet Lee Casey, reporter for the *Emporia Gazette*." Bill turned to the elf-like man. "Lee, this is Mrs. MacFarlane."

"The Emporia, Kansas, *Gazette*?" she asked in amazement as she shook the man's hand.

"None other."

"But how on earth—"

"I'll explain after the introductions," Bill said, turning to the Nevils.

"Here, both of you, sit down," Juanita said, hurriedly brushing the crumbs off the oilcloth covering the kitchen table. "I will bring you some supper. If I know Billie, he hasn't eaten since he left here."

"You're sure we're not imposin'?" the small man asked with a thick brogue.

"Billie brings you, you are welcome," Juanita said, pulling up another chair to the table and indicating where Bill and Lee Casey should sit.

Charlie held up his cup for Alex to fill with coffee and asked, "What brings a fellah from Kansas way out here?"

"It was this lady here. Mrs. MacFarlane." He glanced at Alex, giving her a puckish grin.

"The town's been crawling with reporters the last day or so," Bill said. "Lee was the only one who came looking for me."

Juanita added some kindling to the stove and stirred the remains of the stew still in a large pot on the back burner. Alex poured coffee.

"Sure and why not? The district attorney's got his side of the story to tell." He laughed, looking around as if to see that each person appreciated his small joke.

"I suppose the other reporters didn't see the sense of it, what with martial law and the general bein' in charge," he said. "But I said to m'self, the general wasn't the man who let the cat out of the bag, now was he? Best talk to the man or—" He turned to Alex. "Or to the fair lady who did.

"So through the good graces of Mr. Henderson, here I am." He pulled out the chair next to him. "I'd be pleased if you'd sit down, Mrs. MacFarlane, and tell me how you see things down here."

Alex regarded the little man with dancing brown eyes. "You must know Bill White." Bill White, she'd called him, as casually as if they were old friends. Actually, she'd met the illustrious William Allen White—editor and owner of the *Gazette*—only once the previous summer at former President Roosevelt's Long Island home. She'd liked him, admired his keen sense of what lay behind the headlines.

Juanita placed plates of stew before Bill and Lee Casey. "More coffee?"

"If it's no trouble. Please," said Mr. Casey, glancing up at Juanita. He turned back to Alex. "Mr. White's a credit to us all. As fine a newspaperman as you can find, though he's a good deal higher on life's ladder than yours truly."

She laughed, elated with the coincidence of this leprechaun bringing her a connection with a nationally known journalist. He was like a gift from God, a bonus she hadn't counted on.

"Tell me, Mr. Casey, did you interview General Chase?" she asked.

"Lee, if you please."

She smiled. "All right. Lee."

"I couldn't get near the rascal. A Captain Van Howe talked to some of us. About the army protectin' the health and safety of the town."

"Did someone ask him why slashing women and children with sabers and kicking them in the head was necessary to protect the citizenry?" she asked as she took the heavy coffeepot from Juanita and filled the cups.

Lee eyed her. "Seems those were all lies. Or so said the captain."

She swung around and put the pot back on the stove with such fury it nearly tipped over. The rage she'd felt the morning of the march returned full force. "I saw it. At least fifty, maybe a hundred, other people saw it. It happened. Believe me."

"And now what?" asked Lee. He pushed back his plate, fished a pad from one pocket, a pencil from another.

"Anything's possible," Bill said. "The bear's been poked, as the saying goes, and you never know when he'll bolt the cage."

The reporter eyed him quizzically. "Which bear are you referrin' to? The union or the companies?"

"Both."

Alex gazed at Bill, considering his answer. "You know, I've had this feeling—about the strike, I mean. Like something is about to happen."

"Could be," he said.

Lee looked up from his writing.

"All the signs seem to indicate the strike's about at the end of the line. And it's not all because of the scabs."

"What do you mean?" she asked, pausing in the midst of clearing the plates.

"Well, when I went over to talk to Lawson, he was tight-lipped. Wouldn't say a word. Then last night, when I poked around town, I picked up talk that the boys on the national level see the strike one way, Lawson another. It's no secret the dissension has always been there, but now with the strike not going as well as they thought and with the drain on the UMWA treasury, it's even worse."

"Does anyone know how much money we're talking about here?" Lee asked.

Alex had put the plates in the sink. She turned around. "Mr. Baxter told me the strike is costing the union fifty thousand dollars a month."

Lee whistled softly.

She scooped hot water out of the stove's reservoir into the kettle and poured it into the dishpan, swished the soap in the wire holder through it, and placed the dishes in it to soak.

As she sat down again at the kitchen table, she stole a glance at Charlie and Juanita. Their eyes were heavy.

"Maybe the companies are just planting rumors," Alex suggested.

"Oh, the dissension is real. I'm sure of it," Bill said. "Though the companies undoubtedly are making the most of it."

"Lord save us, it's always the same. The money dries up, the children go hungry, the men are forced to go back to work." The little man shook his head.

"And probably at lower wages than they got in September," Bill said.

The absurdity of it all appalled her. "So, in essence, the entire strike will have been an exercise in futility."

"Not for the companies," Lee observed caustically.

"The top echelon of the union in Chicago will probably pull out its support. The strike always was a calculated risk," Bill said. "Now that it's going badly, why bet on a dead horse?"

Lee eyed Bill, then Alex. "If this one fails, what's the chance they'll try another?"

Bill cocked his head. "Hard to say. They struck ten years ago."

Alex rose, unable to sit still any longer, and began to pace. She was impatient to get where she would have a better sense of what was going on. "Lee, how long do you think Chase and the women's march will be news?"

The little man shrugged. "A day, maybe two. By then the appetite for another good scandal or murderous rampage will be up. You know how it is."

Alex glanced at Bill. "What do you think?"

"It's hard to say. Lee's probably right. But let me look around, check the rumor mill first before you try going back to town."

Chapter Twenty-Eight

Bill picked Alex up at the Nevils' two days later and drove her back to the hotel. As she walked past the usual crowd in the lobby who seemed to spend their days sitting in the overstuffed chairs, Alex sensed a different tone to most conversations. They were more animated, with a hard, almost self-satisfied edge. She wondered what it meant.

At the front desk, she asked for her key. The clerk reddened, asked her to wait a moment while he spoke to the assistant manager. He disappeared through the door to an office behind the desk. A moment later a small man with narrow shoulders and dark hair slicked tight against his head appeared.

"Ah, Mrs. MacFarlane. It seems we have a problem."

"Oh?"

"Yes. Well, you see, we thought you had gone back to Denver."

"I beg your pardon."

"So when we found some of your personal effects still in your room—"

"I told the desk clerk before I left that I would be back in a few days."

He gave her a vacuous smile. "In any case, we rented your suite."

She stared at him, dumbfounded. "I had paid in advance, for two weeks."

"Of course the hotel will see you receive a full refund."

Alex regarded the man with impatience. "You don't seem to understand. I am not leaving Trinidad. I do not want my money returned. I want my suite."

"I'm afraid that's impossible. As I say, it's been rented."

The buzz of conversation across the lobby had stilled. She glanced behind her, meeting the gaze of the men in the chairs. In that instant, she was certain this was General Chase's doing. Her heart was pounding in her fury over the audacity of his interference, even as she knew it shouldn't surprise her. She turned back to the assistant manager. "Then give me another one."

133

"The general and his staff have those accommodations."

"A room then."

"I'm sorry." His tone was cool.

"If you don't have something on Main Street, a room facing Commercial will do."

"We're full up."

She eyed the officious man with contempt. "You have not one single room available? Is that what you are telling me?"

"Correct."

"And where, may I ask, are my belongings?"

"We put them in storage."

"I see." Her mind raced, frantically thinking what to do. She could continue to make a fuss, but sensed it wouldn't do any good. There were other hotels, the kind frequented by traveling salesmen. She'd seen them on her walks around town. She doubted any of them had private baths. As a woman by herself, sharing the bathroom with other guests on the floor or even the entire hotel would be awkward. Perhaps a boardinghouse. But which one and where? Bill was the only person she could think to ask.

"In that case, I will make other arrangements. I will telephone you shortly to tell you where to deliver my luggage."

He nodded solemnly.

She turned, forcing herself to meet the amused stares of the men in the lobby as she made her way to the entrance. Just as the bellboy reached to open the door, Leslie Baxter entered.

Seeing her, he doffed his bowler, gave a slight bow. "Ah, Mrs. MacFarlane. What a delightful surprise. I thought you had returned to Denver."

"Did you?"

"With General Chase's release of the prisoners and your need to represent your client gone, we naturally thought you'd gone home."

"Actually, I've been thinking of locating out of Denver for some time." Alex felt her heart race as she spun the half-truth. Leaving Denver was a certainty; where she would move was not.

"Is that so?" Mr. Baxter's eyes widened.

"In fact, I'm delighted we ran into each other," she gushed. "I was just thinking you would be the person to ask for advice."

The eyes above his smile narrowed, grew wary.

"You must know everyone in town."

"Well, not everyone."

"But, surely, you would know the best person to consult about purchasing a house."

His smile disappeared. "I thought you and your father were in practice together."

"Indeed we are. But since I've been in Trinidad, I've found it a fascinating place. The Spanish heritage adds a wonderful flavor. Wouldn't you agree?"

He only stared at her.

"It occurred to me that once the strike is settled, with the return to normal commerce, Trinidad would be an excellent choice for setting up a branch office." She gazed at him, eyes wide, praying they didn't give away her lie.

He nodded gravely. "I should think it would be an excellent spot. Yes, indeed."

She placed a gloved hand on his arm. "We must talk again."

"Of course."

Alex stepped outside, adjusting her coat collar, letting herself calm a moment as she recalled Leslie Baxter's discomfort at her fabricated story about staying in Trinidad. Within the hour, it would be known by every coal company man and General Chase.

His shock, she decided, was actually a compliment. Her initial indignation at being thrown out of her rooms had cooled. That pleased her, too. Yet she was puzzled. If the strike was teetering on its last legs, why did the company care if she stayed or left?

She strode up the hill toward the courthouse, struggling to make sense of it. What did they fear? Then it hit her. The investigation. Through the political grapevine, they knew about Ed Keating's attempts to see the president. She grinned. She had hit a nerve.

Chapter Twenty-Nine

Alex walked past Bill into the boardinghouse and instantly smelled the marvelous aroma of something baking, something with apples.

She glanced about the spacious entryway. A whatnot and a grandfather clock in a walnut case stood against the wall to her left. Next to it was an umbrella stand that held only a walking stick. The front parlor was just beyond. To her right was the staircase. The sunshine had turned the etched glass pane above the window into a rainbow of colors. Directly in front of her, down a hall, she could see a kitchen.

When she'd asked Bill about a boardinghouse, he'd suggested the one where he lived. She'd objected. It might not look right. He'd ignored her, said he didn't like the implications of her ouster from the hotel. Besides, he was sure Mrs. Willard would be insulted if she found out Alex had chosen another place than hers.

Alex had never been in a boardinghouse, but standing in this hallway she felt as if she'd returned to the comfortable and inviting living quarters where she had stayed her freshman year at Vassar.

A large-framed woman, wearing a patterned housedress, appeared at the top of the stairs and peered over the banister at them. "Mr. Henderson, I thought that might be you." She came down, smoothing her gray hair.

Bill introduced her to Alex.

"You poor lady," Mrs. Willard said, smiling sympathetically. "When Mr. Henderson telephoned to say you'd been thrown out of the hotel, I couldn't believe it at first."

"You're most kind to make room for me," Alex said.

"I'm afraid the room's awfully small. My sister stays there when she comes for a visit. The rest of the time, it's mostly a storeroom."

"Anything is fine. Believe me, I'm grateful to have a place to rest my head."

"You're welcome for as long as you care to stay. The bathroom's upstairs at the end of the hall. Supper's at six o'clock."

The oval oak dining table was covered with a bright yellow cloth, a nickel-plated lazy Susan holding a variety of condiments in the center. Mrs. Willard's other roomers filed in and introduced themselves as they took their seats.

Miss Runyon, broad-shouldered, with a ruddy complexion, reddish-brown hair streaked with gray and direct green eyes, explained that she taught English at the high school. Jim Lotman, slender, unassuming in manner, was a teller at the First National Bank. He'd moved to Trinidad from Lafayette, Louisiana, where he'd grown up. His speech still held a bit of a Cajun lilt. Jeremiah Evans, stout, with a round face, was the assistant manager of the Arkansas Valley Feed Store.

The hired girl spread platters of pot roast, mashed potatoes and gravy, green beans, and biscuits before them. Mrs. Willard served apple strudel with whipped cream for dessert. Alex relished every mouthful.

When Bill explained the reason for Alex's move from the hotel, everyone took turns recounting experiences connected with the strike. Small insults by drunken soldiers, streets and sidewalks crowded with ugly-looking strangers. The strike had invaded their lives. They didn't like it and blamed the union for their discomfort.

As she listened to these seemingly decent people, it occurred to Alex that the strike and martial law were not disasters but annoyances for them, experiences that had touched their lives but not their hearts.

If the congressional investigation did materialize, would the findings reveal anything that might change their minds? She wasn't sure. She hoped the ordinary citizens living in Denver or Chicago or New York who followed the newspaper accounts might see something different.

After supper, Mrs. Willard explained it was the custom to adjourn to the parlor. The furniture was dark walnut, as substantial looking as its owner. Books were stacked in neat piles on a table in one corner. An upright player piano sat against one wall. The brocade-like material covering the horsehair sofa and matching chair beside it was slightly worn, and the maroon velour drapes were faded. But like the rest of the house, the room offered comfort. It had been a long time since Alex had felt so at ease.

Bill disappeared, then returned with a guitar. Alex had never thought of his playing an instrument. She knew he'd grown up on a ranch. Other than that, he was just a lawyer she'd gone to school with, his private life a blank. The unexpected discovery that he played the guitar delighted her.

A lively discussion began over the evening's music selections. An Irish tune or a hymn, a music hall hit or a patriotic ditty? Bill sat on the floor, cross-legged, the guitar in his lap, and began to strum. Alex found room on the sofa beside Miss Runyon, who assumed the role of conductor.

Singing had not been something Alex and her father had done. She'd never been in a choir, not even in college. Her voice was thin. Tonight it didn't matter. Bill's rich baritone was enough.

When the clock struck ten and everyone rose and said their good nights, she was sorry to see it all come to an end.

Alex lay on the narrow bed, weary of trying to get to sleep. Finally, she sat up, groped her way to the light knob by the door, and turned it. Blinking in the light, she reached across the narrow space between the bed and the dresser for her watch. It was only one-thirty. She'd been awake for three hours.

She had a faint urge to urinate but ignored it. Finding her way up the stairs and down the hall to the bathroom in the dark at this hour, she'd be liable to wake half the house.

She pushed back the blankets, swung her feet over the edge of the bed, felt for her slippers. She wished she had something to read and remembered the books in the parlor. She put on her dressing gown and opened the door of the tiny room. The kitchen was to her right. The light was on. Curious, she walked down the hall and peeked in.

Bill was sitting at the kitchen table, bathrobe over his pajamas, barefoot, reading a newspaper, a half-finished glass of milk by his elbow. When she came in, he glanced up, a surprised look on his face. He stood.

"I wondered who was up," she said, smiling.

"I couldn't sleep." He pulled out the chair across the table. "Want a glass of milk? Tastes pretty good."

She sat on the edge of the chair, intending to only stay a moment or two. "No, thanks."

He sat down again, held up the newspaper. "I was checking the *Denver Post* to see what they were carrying about the strike. Couldn't find a thing."

She gazed at the back of his hands, noticing how dark and thick the hairs were, the way the ligaments running from his fingers stood out. Conscious she was staring, she glanced up at his face again. "I suppose the march is old news by now."

He put down the paper and smiled at her expectantly, as if waiting for her to continue.

"I never realized you played the guitar."

"I don't—very well. I was going to give it to Rogerio."

"Have you always played?"

He swallowed the last of the milk. "Took it up when I was working for a firm in Pueblo. There wasn't much else to do after hours."

She tilted her head, absently twisting the ties of her dressing gown as she gazed at him. Something inside her stirred. "You never mentioned you lived in Pueblo."

"I worked for two old men as smart as the Lord makes 'em. They were the ones who got me interested in workmen's compensation."

She leaned forward, resting her elbows on the table, and noticed a hairline scar in the cleft of his chin. "So you never married?"

He laughed, lacing his hands behind his head as he leaned back, balancing the chair on its back legs. "What brought that to mind?"

She shrugged, feeling herself color, realizing the question must have been in her mind for some time. "I don't know. We were talking about what you'd done, where you'd lived."

"No, I've never been married."

"Did you ever think of it?" It suddenly seemed important to know.

"Once or twice, I guess. But a man needs roots and money to marry."

"I thought marriage was about love." Had she said the words out loud or to herself?

Bill regarded her oddly, straightened his chair so it sat squarely on all four legs. "I know it's none of my business—"

Their gazes held.

"That's all right," she said, anticipating his question. "I did love my husband. Or thought I did. I was young and naive."

"How long were you married?"

"A year."

"I'm sorry." His eyes were warm with feeling.

"Don't be. It was long ago. Sometimes I wonder if it wasn't just a dream."

Bill got up, took his empty glass to the sink, rinsed it out, and came back to the table.

The undercurrent of feeling floating between them made her uneasy.

He looked over at her. "I owe you an apology, Alex."

"For what?"

"I've misjudged you."

"And I you." She stood, smiling, pushed her chair back under the table. Her head told her to leave and go back to her room.

He pushed to his feet. "Alex—"

She stepped backward toward the door. "It's late."

"I think I understand now why you came down here."

"Why I came and why I've stayed aren't quite the same."

"I know."

He was standing so close to her she caught the lingering odor of cigarette smoke on his bathrobe.

"Bill, I really don't—"

Before she could move away, he placed his hands on her shoulders and kissed her lightly, then pulled back and studied her intently. His eyes had turned the deep blue of the Mediterranean. "Do you mind?"

She shook her head.

"I care what happens to you, Alex MacFarlane."

"Thank you." She smiled, overcome by the rush of her feelings for him, her eyes swimming with unexplainable tears.

Chapter Thirty

Ed Keating sat up, threw his legs over the side of the bed, and scratched his chest thoughtfully.

The modest room on the third floor of the Congress Hall Hotel was not a palace, but it was shelter, and the price was right. Other members of the congressional freshman class boarded here. The biggest problem was missing Margaret.

But neither his savings nor the salary of a congressman covered the cost of a house in the District, so during the session his darling kept the home fires burning in Pueblo and he bached it in D.C.

All the way back to Washington, he'd thought about how to force a congressional investigation of the Colorado strike. He'd told Alex only that he'd try to see the president, but he'd seen enough of the conditions in the southern coalfields when he visited last fall to know Rockefeller and his buddies had to be restrained. As a kid, Ed had known men dying of lung disease thrown out of their jobs at the smelters in Denver. It had convinced him early that no man had the right to a profit at the expense of another man's life.

Then came Alex's telegram about the women marching, enough to convince him not only that she had the right idea but that he might have a chance for an investigation. Ultimately, public opinion was probably the only tool to get the right laws enacted. But a person didn't attack something as big as this alone.

He stood up and gave a gentle pull on the cord to the green window shade. Absently, he contemplated the patch of gray January sky that hung above the narrow courtyard dividing the two sections of the hotel.

Once an old gentleman who called himself a colonel had told Ed that if you want to speak to God, you don't stop to chat with His archangels. Today Ed was going to see the president.

141

The chief usher led Ed down the corridor of the west wing of the White House. Joe Tumulty, President Wilson's secretary, waited at the entrance to the Cabinet room. "Five minutes, Mr. Keating."

"Thank you," Ed said, masking his nervousness with a smile. Working for a man's election, even seeing him deliver his inaugural address, was a far cry from facing the president of the United States alone.

The Cabinet room struck him as a strange meeting place, but Ed wasn't particular. He entered, striving for an air of confidence, only to stop dead at the sight of Woodrow Wilson standing beyond the long table surrounded with imposing chairs, hands clasped behind him as he studied the portrait of Lincoln on the opposite wall.

Ed made no move to go farther. Wilson seemed oblivious of his presence. Finally, Ed cleared his throat and the president turned.

"Mr. Edward Keating, the congressman from Colorado, Mr. President," said Joe Tumulty, who had entered the room unnoticed by Ed.

"I appreciate your seeing me, Mr. President."

"Not at all."

This close the man had an ascetic appearance. He looked haggard, the eyes behind the pince-nez severe.

For the next five minutes, Ed concisely explained the problem. Only after he finished did the president ask questions. The door opened, and Joe Tumulty appeared, presumably to terminate Ed's appointment. Wilson waved his secretary away.

"I'm not certain what you think I can do, Mr. Keating. After all, this is a state matter."

"Mr. President, everything I know tells me it won't be a state matter for long. I've seen two strikes like this before. This is the worst. It's setting a pattern for the country."

The slender man regarded Ed. "And what do you wish me to do, Mr. Keating?"

"May I suggest, Mr. President, that you call both sides to the White House and urge them to work out a peaceful settlement?"

"I don't think I can do that," he said slowly. "I will write to the Rockefellers and endeavor to persuade them to meet with the union leaders."

It wasn't what Ed had in mind, but it held some hope. He thanked the president and left.

That night he wrote Alex as he'd promised.

Almost by return mail, Ed received a reply. The letter was brief. It told of Alex's being thrown out of the hotel, the growing tensions in town as soldiers intimidated citizens at will, the threat of a return to violence around the camps. She begged him to continue trying for an investigation.

The lame-duck session of the 63rd Congress was under way. Like other freshman congressmen, Ed had been assigned to a string of committees generally considered unimportant; happily, one of them the Labor Committee. Child labor issues were mounting, and the Committee decided to throw its support behind a bill being carried by the congressman from Pennsylvania for the National Child Labor Committee.

But the southerners to a man weren't having it. They pleaded states' rights, fooling no one. The plain truth was that the textile manufacturers wanted to keep their low-wage employees. To even get the bill before the House was going to require a good deal of tricky maneuvering.

Still, there was no way to put off Alex's pleas. The next night, he sat down and drew up a resolution calling for a congressional investigation. Finally, he sat back, satisfied but aware that the writing was the simple part. The test was getting it through the Rules Committee.

He wrote Alex about what he'd done, warning her not to get her hopes up too high.

Chapter Thirty-One

Alex tucked Ed's latest letter in her purse, put on her coat, hurried down the hall to the front door. She glanced through the door's glass panel and saw Bill, hatless as usual, his brown hair tousled, as he leaned against the Ford, waiting for her. In the week she'd been living at Mrs. Willard's, he had become part of her life.

Sometimes after dinner as they settled down for the evening musicale, Alex would sit too close to him, accidentally brushing his hand while she handed him a sheet of music. The warmth of it shot through her like fire. She had to catch her breath. At meals they'd look at each other and smile at nothing in particular. A few times she'd caught one of the boarders or Mrs. Willard watching them, but Alex really didn't care.

Bill continued to go to the courthouse, as if he still had a job to do. When he'd told her about Judge Southard's threats, she wasn't surprised. But as arrogant as the companies seemed to be lately, she worried about his safety.

Yesterday she'd gone with him to finally start the title search of the land occupied by the union camps. It might take another day to finish the project before she was satisfied and was ready to send the list to Ed.

But today her first order of business was to stop at the union headquarters. Her conversation with Leslie Baxter at the hotel had convinced her the companies were kept well-informed by their Washington sources about Ed's activities. It was important that John Lawson know just as much.

She went outside to the auto, basking in Bill's grin as he held open the passenger door for her. She got in. As he came around and climbed in beside her, she was conscious of the size of him, the muscular look of him even his overcoat couldn't hide. His presence filled the small space, and a flick of desire tingled in her belly, expanded, stirred her loins as it did every time he came near now, every time he even casually touched her. When he held her close, the smell of him, the feel of his arms around her, took her breath away.

It had been a long time.

He smiled at her, and she saw the desire in his eyes. "You're some lady. You know that, don't you?"

She laughed, enjoying his wanting her, knowing he was aware she wanted him, too. She had almost forgotten what sexual longing felt like, how it could overtake everything else in your head.

He leaned over and kissed her hungrily. "We could go for a ride in the country."

She pushed him away gently, catching her breath. "We have things to do."

"Coward."

Alex's laugh was close to a giggle. She glanced toward the windows of the front room, which faced the street. "Mrs. Willard is probably watching us."

"So?" He leaned over to kiss her earlobe.

"Bill . . ."

"Okay." He settled himself behind the wheel. "Where to?"

"I thought I should stop off at union headquarters first."

"Not by yourself you don't."

"I'm a big girl, Bill. I really am."

He grinned at her. "I know."

As Alex and Bill entered the tiny office on the second floor of the union headquarters, John Lawson rose so abruptly he nearly knocked over the neat pile of folders on the desk before him. She noted the tight set of his jaws.

He came around the desk, pulled up two folding chairs. She and Bill sat down. Almost as an afterthought, John Lawson asked what he could do for them.

"I think we have good news for you," she said.

Lawson ran his thick fingers through his brown hair, gave a deep sigh. "I could use some."

"You probably know Congressman Ed Keating is attempting to get the necessary votes to call for a congressional investigation of the strike."

He nodded.

"He's talked to the president."

John Lawson's gaze dropped to some papers on his desk, as if the news were either of no interest or no importance to him.

"It looks very hopeful," she said.

He glanced up at her. She noticed his eyes were bloodshot. "If I don't seem too enthusiastic, Mrs. MacFarlane, it's because—from where I sit—it won't be any different than the grand jury investigation they held in Pueblo last month."

"But the warrants were never issued then."

"It served its purpose. It was a setup, from start to finish."

She bridled at the implication. "You think this investigation will be—a setup? Is that what you think?"

"Won't it?" His look was filled with cynicism.

"Not with Ed Keating in charge."

"No offense, Mrs. MacFarlane, but Mr. Keating is a newcomer back there."

"I know Ed Keating. You do, too. You know his pro-labor voting record."

"So?"

"He plans to line up enough Democratic votes to get the resolution through the Rules Committee."

"Just because the Democrats have the majority in the House doesn't mean they'll back an investigation," John Lawson said. "Most of them do the bidding of the bankers and coal company owners in their own states."

"Ed can be very persuasive."

John Lawson gave a hard smile. "Judging by the way the militia is stepping up its harassment tactics, I'd say the congressman is running out of time."

The sharp sound of a telephone ringing came from the first floor. "I'm afraid you'll have to excuse me."

Alex rose. She and Bill had been dismissed. "Mr. Lawson, you must understand how important it is for the strikers to stay calm. Violence will only harm our cause."

John Lawson looked at her with tired eyes. "What do you suggest I tell the men?

"Tell them the country must get the true story about the conditions in the soft coal industry, that the only way that can happen is through evidence brought out at a congressional hearing."

"It has a nice ring to it, Mrs. MacFarlane. But it's a very thin hope to hang on to," he said, ushering them to the door.

She glanced at him. "I know, but it's the best one they have."

Standing outside in the pale winter sunshine, Alex recalled the dark circles under John Lawson's eyes. The strain of holding his men together was about to push him to the breaking point. If only there were someone else, someone he respected, whom she could convince of the investigation's importance. Louie, the man who was the second in command, impressed her as a hothead. It had to be someone else. Then it occurred to her. Maria Ferrera.

Maria was folding bandages when Alex stepped inside the hospital tent. Bill had decided to wait at the headquarters and talk to Louie Tikas, see what else he could find out about the state of the strike.

Alex stood at the entrance, conscious of the strong smell of antiseptic. She felt a little awkward, uneasy now that she was here. The tiny stove glowed red but did little to warm the cold air. Until this moment, Alex hadn't realized how much taller she was than Maria.

"I did not expect you to come," Maria said, regarding her with a level look.

Alex smiled, ignoring the abrupt manner. Today it was important to win her over. "I need your help."

Maria raised an eyebrow as she arranged the pile of bandages neatly into a box and placed it on a shelf. "For what?"

Alex glanced about for a chair, but saw only a cot. "Could we go somewhere and sit down?"

"There is work to do."

"Of course. I'm sorry. I came unexpectedly."

Maria motioned toward the cot. "Sit there if you want."

Alex sat down, hands clasping her pocketbook, not quite sure how to begin.

"Did you meet any guards on the way out?"

Alex shook her head. "Mr. Henderson has a pass."

Maria gave a hard smile.

Suspecting that this conversation was not going to be any easier than the one with John Lawson, Alex pulled in a deep breath and began. "The reason I wanted to speak to you, Miss Ferrera—"

"My name is Maria." The tone was cold.

"Mine is Alex."

Maria cocked her head, a puzzled look on her face. "Alex is a name for a boy."

"My real name is Alexandra."

"Like the wife of the czar."

Alex had to laugh. "Not quite."

But Maria was not amused. Stone-faced, Maria leaned back against a table, painted white, perhaps used for examining patients, her arms folded. "You were saying about why you wanted to talk to me."

Alex sat up a little straighter, determined not to let this woman get under her skin. She told her about the investigation, about Ed working to get the votes, why an investigation was so important.

Maria boosted herself up to sit on the tabletop, revealing mended black cotton stockings and high-topped shoes that had seen much better days. "Do you really believe what you are saying?"

Alex bristled. "Of course. And you must believe it, too."

"How long do we have to wait for this vote?"

"Not long. A week. Two, at the most," Alex said. "You've got to persuade Mr. Lawson not to give in to the pressures to start all the violence again, no matter what the militia does. Speak to the other women. I know they listen to you. Have them talk to their husbands. If the shooting starts again, it will only confirm what many people believe, what the companies want them to believe."

Maria raised her eyebrows. "And what is that?"

"That coal miners—strikers—are socialists and hoodlums."

"What do you think?"

"I think they're fools if they don't wait for the investigation."

Maria pushed herself off the table and straightened her skirts. "People here can't afford to believe in miracles."

"I appreciate that."

"No, you don't."

"Maria—"

"There are times when my heart cries aloud to see the children so thin." Maria turned her face aside for an instant before she gazed into Alex's eyes again. "It is not miracles we need."

Chapter Thirty-Two

After Mrs. MacFarlane left, Maria helped serve supper and thought of their conversation about the investigation. In her heart, she wanted desperately to believe it might come to pass. But like so many other dreams, it was a mistake to count on it.

Tonight was one of the times Frank Bellamy came to the camp to care for anyone who needed attention, and Maria hurried to the hospital tent to help him. As she ducked inside, she saw him bent over a child lying on the cot.

He straightened, glanced over his shoulder at Maria. "Cold compresses, broth if she'll take it. It's about all we can do. Just pray it doesn't turn into pneumonia."

His eyes were dark with concern, and she thought of the eyes of their child, which she carried inside her, wondering whether they would be brown like hers or cobalt blue like Frank's. It was his eyes that had drawn her to him the night they'd first met last year—sharp and anxious as they had examined Dom on the edge of death in the narrow hospital bed at St. Joseph Hospital.

Miners did not come to the hospital. The CF&I mines supplied their own doctors, such as they were. That day the doctor at Hastings, where Dom worked, was nowhere to be found. Desperate, Maria had loaded Dom in the back of a borrowed buckboard and had driven to town for help.

On the point of despair when she'd pulled open the heavy front doors of the hospital, she had stood for a moment to get her bearings, smelled the iodine, noticed the gleaming wood floor beneath her feet. A few yards away was a desk with a green shaded electric light on it. Behind it was a nun.

Carefully wiping the snow from her shoes, Maria pushed her shawl off her head and stepped forward. "I need a doctor, please," she'd said quietly.

Glancing up at her, the nun did not reply. Her features were sharp, like a buzzard's.

Her skin was sallow against the stark white wimple that framed her face. Her cold expression held none of the saintly goodness Maria had believed all nuns had. Perhaps life had not been kind to her either.

"Please, my brother's dying out there in a wagon," Maria said, pleading now.

"I'm sorry," the nun said, looking back at the papers on the desk.

"We can pay," Maria said, desperate. She would steal the money if she had to.

The nun ignored her.

"Please."

The beak-nosed woman glanced up. "You must leave," she said.

Maria looked around her. There had to be a doctor somewhere to take care of Dom. Maria ran down the dimly lit corridor.

The sister called out, demanding she stop. A nurse stepped out of a room, staring at Maria as she ran by. She was nearly at the end of the corridor, but still she'd seen no sign of a doctor. She remembered seeing a staircase beyond the reception desk, but that would mean retracing her steps and getting past the sister.

Suddenly, a door opened, and a man stepped out.

"Oh, doctor. Thank God," she said, grasping at his coat sleeves.

The furious sister hurried up behind them. "I'm sorry, Dr. Bellamy. I told the girl—"

The slender man glanced at the sister, then at Maria. "What's the problem?" he asked Maria, gently loosening her hold on his sleeve.

"My brother's outside. In the wagon. Please. He's dying."

"I told her we are not supposed to take patients from the camps." The sister tried to drag Maria away, but Maria broke free of her grasp.

"This is no night for a sick man to be out in a wagon, Sister. Have the orderly get him inside and put him in the men's ward."

"Doctor Bellamy, I really don't think—"

"That's an order, Sister."

The nun shook her head in obvious disapproval.

Frank Bellamy took Maria by the arm. "Come on, we won't wait for the good sister. Show me where he is. I think together we can manage."

Dom's fever broke four days later. Except to relieve herself, Maria never left his side. Frank came by morning and night. When he pronounced Dom well enough to go back to Hastings, Maria was forced to confess she had no money to pay.

"I can work at the hospital. Cleaning maybe," she suggested.

He regarded her with a solemn expression. "I'm not sure that's the best arrangement. At least not from the sisters' point of view."

She reached for ideas of how she could earn the money she owed. "I could clean your office."

"You could. But that wouldn't pay the hospital bill."

"I know," she sighed. "But your bill—that would be paid."

Frank had placed his hands on her shoulders and smiled. "Miss Ferrera, you don't owe me one cent."

"But—"

"I'll tell you what. You come to my office when you can. It hasn't had a good scrubbing and tidying up for as long as I can remember. In the meantime, I'll settle your bill."

She tried to look inside him, to get to the truth, eager to accept his offer but uncertain whether to trust him. He seemed like a kind man, but he was still a man. But what else could she do? If sex were hidden behind his offer, she'd deal with that later.

Maria smiled to herself. In the beginning, she had known nothing about Frank Bellamy. As she had cleaned the office and learned to sterilize instruments, as she rode with him sometimes back and forth to the coal camp, his goodness was so new to her that she refused to believe it was real.

Then, insidiously, steadily, his every look, the most casual touch, gripped her heart. There were times, standing next to him, when she couldn't breathe. To lust for Frank Bellamy was a sin. But on a warm September night, just before the strike was called, as they were on the way back to Hastings, he parked the Overland touring car in the yard of an abandoned farm, and she wrapped her arms around his neck. They crawled into the back seat. He had gently undressed her. At the height of their passion, the thought of pregnancy flashed, too late, into her head. A month went by, then another, and her worry left her. But on the night after Thanksgiving, in the midst of their lovemaking, her heart had told her with certainty she would have his child.

Now, remembering that magical night, Maria thought of the baby growing within her, a high price to pay for the love she had known. But one she would never regret.

"The child should be inside out of this cold," she heard Frank say, and she glanced over her shoulder at him. "This damn strike. How long does John Lawson expect people to live like this?"

"It must be done," she said, quietly, trying to soothe Frank, who did not share the militant views of union leaders. Decent living conditions and food, not a closed shop, were his chief concerns.

"Maybe so. But I can tell you this, Maria, much more of this weather and there won't be a child in the camps who isn't dying or dead."

"If the companies will not listen to reason, maybe there is no other choice."

He took off his stethoscope and placed it on one shelf of the battered cupboard someone had donated to the camp. In the shelves above were a collection of medicines and boxes of bandages.

"If the rumors around town are true, it might be over before we know it," he said.

"They're just company rumors. Nothing more," she said defiantly. "Mrs. MacFarlane came out this afternoon and told me about the Congress investigating the strike."

"When does she expect the vote?"

"Soon. Any day now," she said.

He glanced at her tenderly. To do more, to take her in his arms, here in the camp, was unthinkable. "If that's what you want, then I hope it's true."

Chapter Thirty-Three

Wisps of smoke from the tents' stovepipes floated into the clear blue sky. A slight breeze stirred the shirts and pants and underwear already strung out along one of the clotheslines at the south end of the camp. The sun soaked through Maria's blouse, soothing her back muscles, which ached from hours bent over the washboard.

Dom put down the wicker wash basket he had carried for her. His face held a defiant look, as if he had no intention of apologizing for being out the entire night without leaving word of his whereabouts. She hadn't slept, worrying for his safety. When he had finally returned in the gray light of dawn and she demanded an explanation, he had glanced about as if someone might be listening, and she had told him to follow her to the clotheslines, where they wouldn't be overheard.

Clothespins clamped between her teeth, Maria leaned over to pick a wet shirt out of the basket beside her. Grasping it by the shirttails, she snapped it open, hung it over the clothesline, and waited with dread for Dom to tell her where he'd been.

"We will attack Trinidad," he finally said.

Her heart stopped. She glanced at him, saw his ferocious brown eyes like shiny objects boiling in a cauldron. All the pleading to keep the peace that she'd done for the last days with the women in the camp apparently had been ignored.

She removed the clothespins from her mouth. "This was decided last night?"

He nodded.

"When is this to happen?"

"Soon."

"Was John Lawson there?"

"For awhile."

Maria shifted her gaze to the field on the other side of the wire fence and the army camp beyond. Through the months of the strike, John Lawson had appealed for calm, patience. For him to be at such a meeting could only mean that even he had given up hope.

"What did he say?"

"He talked of the investigation."

She felt the hope return. "And Louie Tikas was there, too?"

"It is his signal that will tell us when to wipe out the militia."

She snorted, stabbed a clothespin into each end of the shirt. "What with?"

"Rifles."

She eyed him, visualizing the kind of guns that might have been smuggled from friendly farmer to friendly rancher until they reached Louie Tikas. Ancient blunderbusses, probably. Rusted, little better than stout branches.

"What did Louie say about the investigation?"

"He claims the newspapers say it will never happen."

She bent over to pick up another shirt, looked at Dom as she straightened. "Doesn't he know the newspapers say what the coal companies want them to say?"

Dom's eyes stayed hard. "We have gone too far. There's nothing else to do."

The wet shirt felt cold in her hand. "The killing will solve nothing. The investigation will come. You'll see."

"Maria, this is not a matter for women."

She stared at him, instantly seized with such fury that she hurled the shirt at him. "Not a matter for women?"

"No," he said.

She slapped him. "I am not women, Dominic."

He rubbed his cheek, a shocked look on his face.

"I am your sister. I am your family."

The defiance wavered. His gaze fell to the ground.

"Do you think I am afraid to fight?"

He shook his head.

"Do you think I am stupid then?"

He said nothing.

"Do you?" she repeated, more sharply.

He raised his eyes, met her gaze. "You are the smartest person I know."

She gave a small laugh, ran her hand along the black stubble on his cheeks. "Then you do not know many people."

His eyes smiled shyly at her, and she hugged him.

If only she could make him understand the uselessness of this battle, he might convince other young men before it was too late. "Dom, it is when we fight with our minds that we win. John Lawson knows that."

"Mr. Lawson was at the meeting."

Maria tried to picture how it had been last night with men who had stolen out of the union camps in the dark, sitting on their haunches around the glow of a small fire in the hills somewhere, their hearts filled with years of anger and frustration. The talk had surely been of seeing wives and children nearly starve for too long. Someone, probably Louie, had stepped forward, his sharp features framed in the firelight, to declare that there were times when to face himself a man had to be willing to meet his maker. Now was such a time. Heads had nodded. There might even have been cheers.

Maria gazed at Dom, the brother of her heart, her hope. He had said the battle was to begin soon. But how soon? Tonight? Tomorrow? The pent-up fury of thousands of men would be hard to contain for long. She shuddered. Had she been the fool to count on something John Lawson himself might have already given up on?

Chapter Thirty-Four

It was ten days before Ed Keating was told the president wanted to see him.

"Mr. Keating, those damned operators won't yield an inch," he stormed.

Ed couldn't believe his ears. Woodrow Wilson was not a man given to profanity.

"I have decided only one thing will shake them," he said. "A congressional investigation."

Ed tried to keep his eagerness in check. "I had thought of that, too, Mr. President. In fact, I have introduced the necessary resolution, but I can't get it out of the Rules Committee. However, the Democratic members of the committee might listen to you."

"I'll see to it."

By the end of the week, Ed learned that Wilson had stuck to his word, had seen every Democrat on the Rules Committee. But no one budged. Their respect for the president wasn't strong enough to override practical political considerations. Their bread was buttered by Rockefeller. The Committee announced its decision not to report out his resolution.

That night as he sat in the hotel dining room, Ed pushed his food around the dinner plate, uninterested in eating until he figured a way around the dilemma. Then it occurred to him that it might be the perfect time to use his fellow freshmen for a good cause.

The next morning he called six of them and asked them to come up to his office. Though he hadn't told them what was up, he could tell by their amused expressions that they thought they were about to hear another of his harebrained schemes.

"Okay, Keating. Let's have it," said the man from Wisconsin.

Ed solemnly handed him a copy of the petition he'd drawn up. "I've got five more like these. It's a resolution to call a Democratic caucus. I haven't told the Speaker or the Democratic floor leader about it because I was afraid they'd think I was a blooming radical."

The man from Utah grinned.

"Anyway, I've divided the list of Democrats so each of you will have a share. Your job is to persuade them to support my resolution. I'll give you two hours to line up the signatures. Agreed?"

The red-headed congressman from Washington stood up. "You're on."

It wasn't yet time for lunch when all six returned with more than enough signatures. About to burst with pleasure over the results, Ed clapped them on the back. "Now I'll go over and file this baby."

But as he emerged from the Speaker's office, he bumped into a friend, the chairman of one of the powerful committees. Before he realized it, Ed had blurted out the news of what he'd done.

"You made a bad mistake, Keating," his friend said, frowning. "You can't run roughshod over leading members of the House like that. I'd be surprised if you're able to get a quorum when the caucus is called to order."

But Ed felt like an engine with a full head of steam rolling down the track on a steep hill. He appreciated the warning that the same men who had turned down the president would try to keep fellow Democrats away from the caucus, but he couldn't stop now.

Heading back to the office, he telephoned his six henchmen, and everyone went back to work. The caucus was the only end run around the Rules Committee. A quorum was essential.

That evening, the caucus convened in the House. Behind locked doors, the press and stenographers excluded, the floor leader called the meeting to order. The roll call revealed a quorum and then some. But among those present were several members of the powerful Rules Committee that had turned him down originally. Ed knew he was in for a fight.

"The young man from Colorado is determined to make us look like fools," one man groused. "As a member of the Rules Committee, it's my obligation to kill undesirable legislation. Now we are told we must support a federal investigation of a coal strike in his state."

A number of men nodded solemnly. "Furthermore," one added, "the strike has no interstate significance. If Congress starts investigating every strike that pops up around the country, it won't have time for any other business. No, sir. I am against it."

Ed sagged as other reasons for rejecting his resolution were aired. He was on the verge of thinking it was hopeless when David Lewis—the chairman of the Rules Committee, who represented the Cumberland, Maryland, district—stood up.

Slowly, with the skill of all great orators, he unwound the story of how he had gone to work in a coal mine at the age of nine, how he had never spent a day in school. He told of the dampness, of the air so thick a person couldn't breathe. He told of the weighmen in the pay of the companies who cheated a man of the money he was due for the coal he'd mined.

Sitting in the back row, tears in his eyes, Ed knew he had never heard a more eloquent case presented. The roll was called. The resolution went through: 156 ayes, 17 nays.

He wanted to jump for joy. Instead, as the members filed out of the hall, he thanked them solemnly for their support. Then he dashed down the corridor to head to the nearest telegraph office.

Chapter Thirty-Five

Alex pulled the bedcovers up over her shoulders, dimly aware of a knock on a door. The knock sounded again, more sharply. Insistent.

She sat up, wondering what time it was.

"It's me. Bill. Open up."

Alex groggily felt for the electric light knob, turned it. She drew on her dressing gown and opened the door.

Fully dressed, Bill held a telegram in his hand. "It came."

She was instantly awake. "Come in," she said, smoothing her disheveled hair. Bill handed her the telegram, and she tore it open with shaking hands and read.

EUREKA STOP INVESTIGATION ON STOP DETAILS TO FOLLOW
ED

Her heart beat wildly as she reread it. She glanced at Bill. "How did you get this?"

"Jed Larkin, the night telegrapher, delivered it himself. I told him to be on the lookout for it, just in case. A few years back, I cut through some legal red tape for him when his brother died. He and Lawson are friends."

"Does Mr. Lawson know?"

"I doubt it. Jed hinted at something about to blow. He wouldn't say what. Just said he hoped the telegram had come in time."

Alex stared at Bill, her head filled with visions of thousands of men killing one another. "My God! We've got to tell him."

"I'll meet you at the car."

Bill raced the coupe along the deserted streets through the early morning darkness, pulled up in front of the UMW headquarters. They got out. The quiet was absolute. Not even a dog barked. An ominous feeling hung in the cold air. Alex glanced about but saw nothing.

Bill pounded on the headquarters door. They waited for a moment. When no one appeared, he tried the handle. It was locked. Stepping back, Alex looked up at the second floor and saw a pencil-wide frame of light around one of the drawn window shades. Someone was up there.

"Mr. Lawson," she called. "Whoever is up there. It's Alex MacFarlane and Bill Henderson."

No one answered. She went to the door, pounded with all her strength. "Please. We've got an urgent message." She squinted through the large plate-glass window into the dark interior, praying for someone to be there.

She called again. This time a faint light, maybe that of a candle, appeared. The front door opened a crack, and the gnome-like man she'd seen before poked his head out.

"We have an urgent message for Mr. Lawson," she said.

The electric lights came on, a lock turned, the door was opened, and the man beckoned Bill and Alex to come inside.

"Where's Mr. Lawson?" she asked.

The small man glared at them.

Grim-faced, Bill pulled the telegram out of his pocket and thrust it at him. "You need to get word to him that the investigation is on. Understand? The investigation is on."

The man folded his stubby arms across his chest, the telegram crumpled in one hand. "I'm goin' nowhere."

"Listen here. The world is about to explode out there. An hour, if you're lucky, is all you've got."

"The hell ya say," the man growled.

"Read the telegram," he demanded.

The man didn't move.

"Okay then. Tell me where I can find him," Bill said, grabbing the telegram from him. "But for God's sake, don't wait till I get back. Spread the word."

The man regarded him sullenly. "It's too late."

Alex's heart stopped. "What do you mean it's too late?"

"Just what I said."

She turned her pendant watch over. "It's a little before four." She looked at him. "Something is happening right now?"

The man eyed her coldly. "Over a thousand of the boys are out there, surroundin' Trinidad and the militia camps, ready to kill everythin' on two legs."

Alex gasped. "How can they? They don't have any guns."

"Oh, they have 'em. Believe me."

"But the militia has machine guns and armored cars," she said. She turned to Bill, her eyes wide with thoughts of the impending terror. "We've got to do something."

The little man grimaced. "I told ya it's too late. Daylight, them soldier boys won't know what hit 'em."

"But there are informers everywhere," Alex said. "The militia will be prepared. It's going to be a bloodbath."

Bill turned to the small man. "Tell me where I can find Mr. Lawson."

"Dunno."

"Where?" Bill grabbed his shirtfront.

The man broke loose of Bill's grasp. "Simpson's Ridge maybe."

Bill glanced at Alex. "Go on back to Mrs. Willard's. I'll be back as soon as I can."

"There is not a way in the world you're going to leave me behind."

He put an arm around her shoulders, gave her a quick, fierce hug. "Please, go back where it's safe."

"Bill, I have to go."

Chapter Thirty-Six

Bill braked the Ford to a stop. "No matter what happens, stay put and keep the engine running," he said to Alex, kissing her lightly as he cursed himself for letting her come.

She nodded.

"Well, here goes." He climbed slowly out of the auto, his hands clasped on his head. "If anyone's out there, I'm Bill Henderson," he called. "I'm unarmed."

A figure pushed through the bush. In the moonlight, Bill saw the man's hand resting on the handle of the revolver stuck in his belt. "State your business, Henderson."

Bill recognized the voice, breathed easier. "John Lawson. Thank God." He started to lower his hands.

"That's far enough. Keep those hands on your head."

"The investigation's on. The telegram's in my pocket."

Lawson approached.

"Left pocket," Bill said.

Reaching his hand into Bill's coat pocket, John Lawson drew out the envelope containing the telegram.

"If you let me put my hands down, I'll light a match and you can read it."

"I'll use the headlights."

With Lawson right behind him, Bill moved in front of the car. They stood in the wavering, yellow light while John Lawson pulled the telegram from its envelope and read. He glanced up at Bill. "We've got to get the word out fast."

"Can I help?"

"You're not a familiar face, Henderson. They'd shoot you before you could open your mouth."

"Where's Louie Tikas?" Bill asked.

"He's up on the ridge above us. Or was. He's probably on his way down.

I'll need a ride back to town."

"Glad to oblige."

"Do you have a gun?"

"A revolver. It's in the car."

Twigs snapped and willow branches parted. A man stepped into view, a rifle in one hand. It was Tikas.

"Keating got the votes for the investigation." John Lawson held out the telegram to Tikas.

Louie Tikas hunched toward the light as he read.

"So all bets are off," Lawson said.

Tikas glanced at him.

"That was the deal," John Lawson said. "With the investigation called, there's no fight."

Louie Tikas tightened his grip on the rifle, looked away.

"Go out and tell the men." Lawson's voice was flint hard. "That's an order, Louie."

The two men stared at each other for a long moment, will testing will. Louie Tikas was the boss of Ludlow, the largest of the tent camps. He commanded the respect and, Bill suspected, the fear of thousands of men. But if he refused to call off the assault against the militia, if he went against John Lawson's orders, everything the congressman had managed to do would be wasted.

Shifting his rifle from one hand to the other, his jaw working, Tikas glanced at Bill, then back at Lawson. "The men won't like it."

"They'll do what I say," Lawson snapped. "Now go tell them. And make it quick."

Alex sat between John Lawson and Bill as the Ford tore over the rutted road toward town. None of them spoke of their fear that they might not reach Trinidad in time to stave off an explosion.

Finally, it was Lawson who glanced at him and said, "How come you brought the telegram?"

"Anyone would have done the same."

"Not anyone around here."

They lapsed into silence again until Bill asked, "You ever sorry you got into this business?"

"Into the union?"

"No, into organizing."

Lawson gazed out the passenger window into the graying dawn. "It was something I had to do."

Bill heard the stubbornness behind the simple words. Circumstances beyond Lawson's control had pushed him into becoming a union organizer. To live with himself, he'd had no other choice. Once Bill would have said the same when he'd first made the decision to run for district attorney. Now he suspected it had been more a case of falling for a play to his vanity.

The shadowy clusters of houses came into sight. They were at the outskirts of town. Lawson sat forward, peering through the windshield, already poised to leap from the car. "Drop me at the headquarters."

The clock outside the bank on the corner showed six-ten. Bill searched the streets for signs of strikers or militia, but saw no one. As he drew up in front of the headquarters, Lawson pushed open the door of the auto even before it had stopped, and raced toward the entrance.

Chapter Thirty-Seven

In the half-light of dawn, Bill pulled the car into the parking space behind Mrs. Willard's and braked to a stop. Neither he nor Alex moved or spoke. Finally, they got out and walked toward the back porch. Halfway there, Bill caught her in his arms and hugged her to him. "It's okay. We made it in time."

Alex laid her head against his chest, listening to the steady beat of his heart, feeling safe in the warmth of his arms. "Do you think it's true about the war?"

He let her go. "I'm pretty sure that another hour, it would have been too late."

She shivered, still unable to digest the reality of what had almost happened. "Let's go in."

He put an arm around her shoulders as they walked. A crow cawed. From down the street came the clink of milk bottles being delivered, the intermittent thud of morning newspapers against front stoops. The rhythm of the day was taking hold, and Alex felt a reassuring sense of peace settle over her.

As they walked into the kitchen, the hired girl was starting up the stove. A mixing bowl filled with biscuit dough was on the table, waiting to be rolled out. Alex was suddenly famished, dying for a cup of coffee.

February 8, 1914. A week since near disaster had been averted. Alex stretched luxuriously, eyed the faint light of morning. She couldn't sleep another wink. She flung back the covers, eager for her day to begin, and reached over to shut the window. The growing band of brilliant blue sky made her feel as giddy as the first time she'd had French champagne. Tomorrow, in Denver, the first of the hearings to be conducted by the Committee on Mines and Mining would begin.

Ed had written that the investigative committee was to be made up of five members, with Martin Foster, a physician from Illinois, the chairman.

They were to investigate conditions in seven Colorado counties where coal was mined and later look into another bitter strike in progress in the copper-producing counties of Michigan. The committee was granted full powers to subpoena witnesses and documents. The investigation would be thorough, Ed had assured her. He had every confidence in the men who would be asking the questions.

Perhaps in an effort to put his best foot forward, the governor had called all but two companies of the militia back to Denver. Unfortunately, one of those remaining was Company B, commanded by Karl Linderfelt, whom Alex remembered all too well from their encounter at Sandoval.

Alex got up, put on her robe, and took her turn using the bathroom. She dressed in a new navy blue suit and white silk blouse she'd bought at Jamieson's Department Store the previous week. As she stood in front of the mirror to pin on her lapel watch, she was pleased with how she looked. Her hair had a nice sheen. She looked amazingly rested. The relief of knowing the hearings were about to begin agreed with her.

After a breakfast of canned peaches, fried eggs, bacon, and biscuits, she and Bill lingered over coffee while they reviewed the list of potential witnesses to line up for the hearing when the committee eventually traveled to Trinidad.

"Of course, once we see who testifies in Denver, we might want to pare down the names here," Bill said as he pushed away his cup.

"I don't think I'll go."

His eyes widened. "But this is your show, so to speak."

She regarded him with tenderness. In a way, he was right. Yet she didn't want to go back to Denver just now. Her father would press her for a full accounting of her stay in Trinidad. Besides, she wanted time to get prepared for the hearings that would come to Trinidad. "I think I'll just stay put."

"The hearings may take weeks. I don't like your staying here alone."

"Why not?" She smiled. "If I need looking after, Mrs. Willard will do a fine job of it."

"If you came, you could see your father."

"I know."

Bill studied her for a moment, as if he wanted to pursue the matter, but he let it go. Perhaps he understood. She hoped so.

Alex saw Bill off and drove his car, which he had urged her to use, to the outskirts of town to a high spot with a view of the plains below. She got out and leaned against one of the front fenders. She took in a deep breath, feeling the sun soak through her, and she thought of her father again.

It wasn't that she didn't appreciate what he had done for her over the years, but it had been a mutually satisfactory arrangement. She knew his every habit, that he liked kippers for Saturday breakfast, a fresh salad for Sunday supper, that his shirt collars were to be starched but not enough to irritate his neck, that housecleaning should never take place when he was at home. Soon she'd write to tell him to search for someone to replace her in the firm, to hire a full-time housekeeper. It was time to finally cut the cord.

More difficult would be explaining how she had fallen in love with a man whose upbringing was so different from hers. It would make no sense to her father. If her mother were still alive, she would scoff at the suggestion that Bill even come to dinner.

Alex could recall how, when she was fifteen, convinced she was madly in love with the grocer's delivery boy, she had confessed her passion to her mother.

"Oh, my sweet darling, don't be absurd," her mother had said. "One doesn't fall in love out of one's class."

When Alex had called her mother a snob, she had agreed. "Snobs run the world, darling. Don't ever forget it."

Alex sifted her mother's words through her mind, thought about Bill. He was his own person. He didn't give a hang how he looked. He tended to be a trifle bossy and overprotective. Yet he had more courage than any man she'd ever known. What she felt for him was already beyond her control. Like a rusty gate, finally opened, her heart would not close easily again.

She was beginning to understand what Juanita Nevil had said about not being able to live life without Charlie. Bill had been gone less than a few hours, and already her heart ached with missing him.

The breeze had picked up, and there was a chill to the air. Wrapping her coat close around her, she climbed back in the car.

On her way back to town, her thoughts returned to the coming hearing. She'd heard about a physician in town who treated miners. As she recalled, his name was Dr. Bellamy. She decided to stop by the hospital to find how to get in contact with him. If he'd defied Trinidad's polite society, he'd probably agree to be a witness.

Alex was directed to a small building off Main Street. Inside, she was greeted by an older woman in a starched nurse's uniform and stiff white cap pinned to her gray hair. Giving her name, Alex asked to talk with Dr.

Bellamy. The nurse disappeared through a door. A few minutes later, she returned with a man behind her.

"Dr. Bellamy?"

"Mrs. MacFarlane, what can I do for you?"

The doctor appeared to be in his late thirties, trim, clean-shaven, with light brown hair and a complexion probably permanently tanned from the hours he spent traveling about the countryside visiting patients. He had the brightest blue eyes she'd ever seen. They looked kind.

"I have a favor to ask," she said. "But I don't want to interrupt your work with patients."

"You're not interrupting a thing. Come back to my office, won't you? Mrs. Elbert—" He turned to the older woman. "Do you suppose there's any hot tea left?"

"I'll check, doctor."

He smiled at her and indicated to Alex that she should follow him back to a room at the end of a short, narrow hall. The office was no more than eight by ten feet, with a desk, a chair for the doctor and two for patients, a bookcase filled with what Alex presumed were medical books. In one corner was a full-sized skeleton suspended from a chain bolted to the ceiling.

"Please, have a seat," he said. He glanced at the skeleton. "That's Sir George."

She laughed.

"The children love him. Their parents aren't so sure."

Alex already liked this man immensely. "Dr. Bellamy, I have a strange request."

"Name it."

"I'd like you to testify before the congressional committee hearing that will come to Trinidad in a few weeks about your experiences treating patients from the various company camps."

He smiled. "I think you need to know something about me before you decide whether you want me on the stand," he said, wryly.

"All right."

"I'm a graduate of Princeton and Johns Hopkins Medical School. Pretty weighty stuff for Trinidad." He laughed. "The normal course of events would have been to set up a practice in Denver. But treating wealthy matrons wasn't up my alley. So I came back home to take care of people who needed me.

"At first, the town liked the idea of a native son with eastern credentials," he went on with a grin. "Until they discovered my true intentions."

"I take it they don't approve of your treating miners and their families," Alex said.

"The CF&I camps generally have a doctor and a rudimentary infirmary. There's a company hospital in Pueblo. But it seems most miners would rather go untreated than use them."

"So they come to you instead."

He gave a crooked smile. "If it weren't for old family ties, I suspect I'd have been run out of town long ago. You see, my father came here as a young man for his health. He had an inheritance large enough to raise a family comfortably, so he chose not to follow any particular profession. But he had a keen interest in local history."

Mrs. Elbert appeared with two cups of tea and placed them on the desk. Dr. Bellamy thanked her, and she left.

"Anyway, my dad—Elmore Bellamy was his name—was a pleasant, quiet kind of man. Scholarly. Some people thought he was a bit eccentric, but he had money, which made him generally acceptable. I am quite another sort of person."

Alex laughed, took a sip of tea. "From the sounds of it, you'll make a perfect witness."

"Whoa! I haven't agreed yet."

She smiled, put her cup and saucer on the edge of Dr. Bellamy's desk. "If it would help you decide, let me assure you I am not interested in promoting either the companies or the union."

He sat back in his chair, crossed his legs. "That's not the story I hear."

"Oh?"

"What you did for that child during the march—you've earned yourself quite a reputation."

She raised an eyebrow.

"Trinidad's a small town, Mrs. MacFarlane. Word gets around."

"I guess it does." She smiled at the thought of the nurses at the hospital telling other nurses who told friends until who knows who was aware that a stranger, a woman who was obviously not from Trinidad, had brought a miner's child to the hospital.

Frank Bellamy uncrossed his legs, sat up. "But back to your proposal."

Alex smiled, pleased it had taken so little persuasion to get him to agree. "You'll do it then."

"Only if you agree to a proposal I have."

"Which is?"

"The children in the union camps have no schools. There's a young woman acting as a teacher at one of them who needs help."

Alex smiled. "Miss Maria Ferrera."

"You know her?"

Alex nodded.

"She's amazing, isn't she?"

"Indeed she is." Alex thought of the stubborn younger woman as she glanced at the absurd skeleton, then back at the doctor. "I hope you're not about to suggest I go to the camp and help her with the school."

"I certainly am."

She smiled. "I am an attorney, Dr. Bellamy. I have no children of my own. The only children I've anything to do with are the orphans at the Denver Children's Home, where I serve on the board of trustees. And at a distance. I'd say that hardly qualifies me as a teacher's assistant."

"But you have worked with orphans."

"I only read to them for a few hours at Christmas. That kind of thing. I've never taught anyone in my life."

"Well, I do have children, Mrs. MacFarlane. Three of them, who have the advantage of schooling, which many of the children in the camps have never had. I assure you, with or without experience, those children need you."

"You are most persuasive, doctor." She rose. "But I don't believe it's a good idea."

"At least think about it."

"Only if you will do the same." She opened the office door, paused. "I'll telephone tomorrow."

Chapter Thirty-Eight

Bill swung down from the train, suitcase in hand, and strode down the platform of Denver's Union Station and up Seventeenth Street toward the Albany Hotel. It was a good commercial hotel, its rooms came at a reasonable price, and its bar was the watering hole of reporters and local politicians. The hearings would be rehashed in minute detail. All in all, it was an excellent spot for his purpose.

Once in his room, it occurred to him he should send Alex a telegram, just to tell her he'd arrived safely. He missed her, knew she would be missing him. He understood about her father. The old man had ruled her life for a long time, and would not take kindly to anyone threatening to take his daughter from him.

Jonathan Russell wouldn't have said anything, but the message would have been clear that Bill Henderson, district attorney of Las Animas County, was not what he had in mind as a proper suitor for his daughter.

Bill decided to hold off on the telegram for a while and went out to roam the streets instead. Back at the hotel, he had a sandwich and a beer in the hotel bar, and went to bed.

The next morning Bill took a front-row seat in the already crowded gallery overlooking the floor of the Senate where the hearings were to take place. Voices filled the high-ceilinged room, rising and ebbing like a swelling tide. An unfamiliar feeling of euphoria stirred in him at the prospect that the days ahead held real hope.

On the floor below, committee members were seated at a long table placed in front of the chamber. A lectern had been set up for those called to testify. The attorneys occupied padded benches along each wall. Representing the companies were a half dozen men, among them Leslie Baxter and a man Bill knew to be a former Huerfano County judge. All of them appeared relaxed, almost jovial. Across from them, on the union side, sat three men. To his astonishment, he saw that one of them was Ellis Chapin.

On the surface, it seemed to Bill that Chapin's Harvard law degree and his austere manner made him an unlikely advocate for the union. But the man had made a name for himself when he came out as a Progressive and worked for Teddy Roosevelt's election. Ten years ago, he had astonished his fellow Republicans when he fought for the breakup of the trust that controlled Denver's public utilities. But fighting trusts was a far different situation from defending unions. Bill was anxious to hear the approach Chapin would take.

The chairman, Representative Foster, was tall and spare with a white mustache, the ends drooping down along his cheeks. He wore the stiff collar and morning coat of earlier days, but his step was firm and quick as he moved about the room giving last-minute instructions. At the dot of nine o'clock, he rapped the gavel, called the hearing to order, and read the congressional resolution.

At its conclusion, he glanced up. "If either side of this controversy wishes to be represented by counsel, the committee asks that the name of counsel be indicated at this time."

Leslie Baxter rose. In pious tones, he informed the committee that because the coal companies had no organization, each of the three majors would use its own counsel for the purposes of the hearings. The chairman nodded, turning toward the union team. As the apparent spokesman, Ellis Chapin made the introductions.

The preliminaries over, the audience had barely settled back when General Chase, in full uniform, tromped down the center aisle. Bill leaned forward for a better view.

"Mr. Chairman," he bellowed importantly.

Representative Foster regarded the general calmly.

"I insist that the military organization of the state be represented."

The committee members exchanged glances and the chairman solemnly agreed to the demand. Looking a bit deflated at his easy victory, the general took his seat.

The hearings began.

The first hours were taken up setting the stage. State geologists provided information about the state's coal resources and their development. The state coal mine inspector testified there were so many accidents and such a heavy loss of life, his office simply did not have the personnel to carry out its statutory duties. There was a general stirring within the group of attorneys representing the coal companies, but none of them rose to protest. It was when the state labor commissioner claimed that politics pressured men to violate state laws that Leslie Baxter jumped to his feet.

"Mr. Chairman, I rise not for this case but for the fair name of Colorado. If this witness has any facts to substantiate his charges, the committee is entitled to know them."

Foster's reply was sharp. "Let me assure you, Mr. Baxter, the committee is ready to protect the State of Colorado in whatever rights it may have."

Bill almost cheered. The attitude of the committee was still unknown. But he had the feeling that at least the chairman would apply an even hand.

The parade of witnesses continued. The chairman called a noon recess for lunch until two o'clock. Bill went downstairs and searched through the crowd of men milling around the entrance to the Senate hearing room, hoping to find John Lawson. No one had seen him yet. The thought that there might have been foul play along the way between Trinidad and Denver crossed Bill's mind. He went back up to the gallery and took his seat.

It wasn't until the sunlight faded and lights were turned on that John Lawson finally appeared through a side door. Several men seated along a back bench, whom Bill presumed were union officials, greeted him. They talked in low tones. Finally, the chairman called him to the stand.

As he walked down the center aisle with shoulders squared and head high, coal company types strained for a better view of the man they'd learned to hate but whom Bill suspected they'd never seen until that moment.

Ellis Chapin came forward. He orchestrated his questions to allow Lawson to tell what had led up to the strike and about the strike itself. John spoke easily, projecting his voice so everyone in the gallery could hear. Bill watched the committee members as they listened. Occasionally, one would nod, another would make a note of something John said. They were paying attention. Alex would be pleased.

After an hour, the chairman interrupted. Due to the late hour, the hearing would continue in the morning. He invited Mr. Lawson to continue his testimony then. With a rap of the gavel, the first day of the hearing was over.

Immediately, Bill made his way through the crowd and down the stairs, anxious to catch John before he left. He wanted to tell him how well he'd done, but there was no sign of him. Undoubtedly, he'd gone off with the other union officials for supper. Or maybe he was conferring with Ellis Chapin about tomorrow's testimony.

Bill moved with the men and women streaming out of the capitol building and down the steps to the street below. It was dark. His stomach grumbled, and he decide to stop somewhere to eat on his way back to the hotel. A beer might taste good, too.

The night air was mild. A good night for walking. Passing the shop windows, he caught his reflection. A man alone, apart from those around him, hurrying home from work to a family and a warm dinner. He thought of Alex again.

Over the years, he'd sometimes thought of getting married. There'd been Judge Broadhurst's daughter. Hair the color of straw, fair skin, full breasts. She'd been nice enough, had seemed to like him, but that indefinable attraction, almost like a chemical reaction, was missing. Marriage was a risk. Look what had happened to his dad.

But since Alex . . . He'd never known a woman like her. Lord but she was beautiful. He realized now he'd lusted for her since the moment he saw her ten years ago. He admired her spunk, her bravery that sometimes went to the point of foolishness. She was smart. Truth was he'd never taken to stupid women. Most amazing was her openness to looking at the other side of a situation. And she was a person who gave a damn.

A display in a department store window of women's fashionable clothes caught his eye, and he stopped to gaze at it, imagining Alex's reaction. In some ways, they were as different as two people could be. But it couldn't be helped. The truth was he loved her, always had.

The following day Bill arrived early to make sure he had a good seat. The chairman of the committee called John Lawson back to the stand.

Chapin resumed his questions on behalf of the United Mine Workers, drawing from John one story after another of assaults, beatings, and general intimidation.

After the lunch recess, Leslie Baxter stepped forward to cross examine. He asked John about the union's budget. Lawson calmly insisted he was only a union organizer, not the treasurer. Bill glanced about and caught sympathetic nods from among the spectators.

The hearing proceeded. Dozens of witnesses for both the union and the companies were examined.

Days became a week, then two. The national press was giving the hearings front-page space. When A. C. Felts, a supervisor for the Baldwin-Felts Detective Agency, took the stand, he readily admitted hiring guards on orders from the companies, also arranging for the purchase of four machine guns paid for by the Rocky Mountain Fuel Company. Finally, after skillful questioning by Chapin, he conceded he had been charged and tried for numerous felonies, including robbing a bank. There was a collective gasp from men and women sitting in the gallery.

That night Bill wrote to Alex, detailing the testimony of the day. He was tempted to sign it "with love, Bill" but decided to only use the customary "Yours, Bill." A matter as serious as love needed to be said face to face.

The next day the visitors' seats were still at a premium. The crowd of spectators gave no hint of losing interest.

When Jesse Welborn, president of CF&I, took the stand, Bill hoped the companies' attitude toward the union and the miners who belonged would be laid out in the full light of day.

"Mr. Welborn, do you have personal knowledge of the purchase of machine guns?" Chapin asked him.

"Most certainly. I ordered eight guns myself and had them set up in the CF&I mines. With the number of guards we've lost, they're quite necessary."

The chairman's eyes widened.

Chapin proceeded with several questions about company ownership until, almost as if it were an afterthought, he asked Welborn, "By the way, did you have a talk with Governor Ammons before the last election or during the campaign about your influence in the southern coalfields?"

"Indeed," Welborn admitted. "In fact, the governor came to my office. We talked about the company's connection with politics. I said we would not oppose him down there."

"You vote down there, do you?" Chapin asked in a casual way.

"No, I do not."

"So when you say 'we,' you refer to the company?"

"Yes, sir."

No one in the chamber moved, as if struck simultaneously with the significance of what Welborn had said. A minute passed, and another.

"Tell me your opinion, Mr. Welborn, about the Guard's action against the wives and children. I refer to their march in protest against the importation of non-union miners."

"The march was illegal, of course."

"In what sense?" Chapin asked.

"General Chase did not grant permission for the march."

"I see." Chapin clasped his hands behind him. "Would you comment, sir, specifically about the Guard's actions."

Welborn settled back in the chair, his legs crossed, apparently as unconcerned as if he were sitting in a living room discussing the time of day. "If you mean was the decisive action of the cavalry appropriate, my answer is most definitely."

"The cavalry involved were armed, were they not?" Chapin asked.

"Only sabers, General Chase informed me."

"They used the sabers, did they? Against women and children."

"When necessary, yes."

Chapin turned slowly to face the committee. "No further questions." Bill tried to read the members' expressions. Had they truly understood the full horror of that day?

At the lunch recess, Bill found a hole-in-the-wall cafe on Sixteenth Street, ordered a ham sandwich, and stared out the window at the passersby, missing Alex but glad he'd decided to come.

The hearings in Denver were scheduled to end in two days. From Denver the Committee on Mines and Mining would go to Trinidad to hold more hearings. Bill approved of the chairman's fair and business-like conduct of the proceedings. Chapin's emphasis on legal rights also pleased him. Yet he couldn't help wondering if it had gone almost too well.

Chapter Thirty-Nine

Three weeks after Bill had left for Denver, Alex sat on her narrow bed, a breadboard borrowed from the kitchen on her lap for a desk, and wrote her father a short letter to tell him she was well and little else. She made no mention of the tradesmen and local residents she'd talked to about testifying at the hearings when they came to Trinidad. As she addressed the envelope, stuffed in the letter, slid her tongue along the flap, and sealed it, her thoughts returned to Dr. Bellamy.

She had put off her decision about going to Ludlow for too long. Yet what possible good could she be to the children at Ludlow? She'd be a veritable duck out of water. But the stay wouldn't have to be more than a day or so, and while she was there, she could also talk Maria into testifying. She'd be back in town in plenty of time before the hearings moved to Trinidad.

The next morning, she telephoned the doctor. He told her how pleased he was at her decision, confessed he'd already talked about his plan to Maria, who insisted Alex could stay with her. As she hung the receiver back on its hook, Alex was stunned at what she'd actually agreed to do. It was one thing to drive out for a visit, quite another to actually sleep and eat there.

She went back to her room, not certain she'd made the right decision. Yet it was too late to change her mind. She packed a change of clothes, a nightgown, and left word with Mrs. Willard where she'd be. Dr. Bellamy arrived a few moments later in an old touring car, took her small valise, and stowed it in the back seat. They climbed in and drove off.

As the car rolled north out of town, Alex gazed out the window, every detail of the passing scene unimaginably clear and bright. The afternoon sunlight held an unearthly brilliance, turning the leafless cottonwoods into columns of burnished pewter, etching them knife-sharp against the sapphire sky.

The anxiety she'd felt about going to the Ludlow camp slowly took on a different perspective. The sharpness of the passing images, the clarity of the landscape seemed to make everything come into focus. Whatever ambivalence she had felt about plunging herself into the real life of the camp had vanished.

She wanted to ask Dr. Bellamy about what he knew of the camp and the people who lived there, but he seemed wrapped in his own thoughts; she sat back, comfortable in their silence, and tried to prepare for whatever she might encounter.

Frank Bellamy parked in front of the tent with the flag on its roof where Alex had first met John Lawson. A little girl emerged from a nearby tent and, seeing him, waved timidly. He smiled and motioned to her. When the child ran up to him, he caught her up in his arms and walked on. Every man they passed doffed his cap. A few women bobbed little curtsies. To the children, he tossed hard candy, which he pulled out of his pockets in seemingly limitless supply. Clearly, Dr. Bellamy was the camp's patron saint.

At the cook tent, they went inside. Remembering her previous visit with the watchful men playing cards and the aging women by the stove, Alex was surprised to see children of all sizes and ages sitting on benches set up in rows. A dozen men and women stood at the rear.

Maria sat on a high stool in front of the group. Her feet barely touching the bottom rung of the stool, she looked almost young enough to be one of her students. As usual, her thick blue-black hair was braided and pinned on top of her head. Tiny gold rings hung at her ears. From the adoring looks fixed on her pupils' faces, she was another saint, like Dr. Bellamy. Yet there was a dramatic, decidedly earthly quality about her beauty that couldn't be dismissed.

As Alex and Dr. Bellamy moved closer, Maria looked up.

The doctor's face broke into a broad smile. "Please don't let us interrupt you, Miss Ferrera."

She put the book aside. "No, it's all right. We just finished the lesson about whales."

Alex caught the warmth of the glance exchanged between the two and wondered if there was more to their relationship than they would have it seem.

Maria eyed her. "You came," she said dryly.

Alex smiled, pleasantly. "So it would seem."

Maria took Alex to the small tent she ordinarily shared with her brother. After the drive, Alex needed to urinate, and Maria directed her to the row of privies at the edge of the camp. As Alex walked toward them, she could feel Maria watching her. Without hesitating, she selected one, knocked, and entered. The stench was overpowering. She nearly gagged as she lowered herself onto the wooden seat.

As she stepped outside, gulping in the fresh air, she saw Maria on the path directly in front of her, waiting, still watching, as if judging whether Alex had passed some kind of test.

Dr. Bellamy stayed in the camp to attend a Serbian woman who was within hours of delivering her fourth child. After supper, Maria announced she was going to the hospital tent. Not knowing what else to do, Alex went with her.

"You must be tired."

"I want to help."

Maria looked dubious.

"I really do," Alex repeated, but Maria had already disappeared into the tent.

Feeling awkward and unneeded, Alex looked around her for a time, hearing a woman's soft moans inside the tent, watching the people who passed and trying to imagine their stories, then gazing overhead at the black dome studded with stars, listening to the sounds in the tents, people readying for sleep. Gradually, she began to get cold, and she thought she might go back to the cook tent.

The woman's moans grew louder, and Alex could see the shadows of Dr. Bellamy and Maria moving about inside. Someone, probably Maria, crooned softly in Italian. The moans continued, became more urgent, finally turned into screams.

Alex shut her eyes. She had expected to work with children, not this. She was seized with the desperate wish to be someplace—any place—else. The screams diminished, stopped. Quiet settled over the tent, but no one came out to tell her what was going on.

After awhile, she heard Dr. Bellamy's firm, low voice. Then Maria lifted the tent flap and appeared, holding a small bundle wrapped in a blanket. Alex pulled in a breath, afraid to look.

"It's dead, isn't it?" Alex asked, already knowing the answer.

Maria nodded.

"Is the mother all right?"

"For now."

"There must be something I can do," Alex said, automatically.

"Mr. Cazak is waiting with the other children in the cook tent. If you would get him—I need to stay here to help Dr. Bellamy."

Alex wound through the maze of paths, taking several wrong turns, until she finally reached the big tent. Inside was a rough giant of a man, sitting on a bench, leaning over as if in despair, his head in his hands. Three small children were sleeping atop the next table.

Alex called his name, and he looked up, eyes wide with apprehension. She wasn't sure he spoke English, so she merely gestured for him to follow her. Gently, he roused his children. He carried the youngest in his arms, the other two followed behind, out into the dark toward the hospital tent.

Alex held open the flap, and the Cazak family went inside. Letting the flap fall back into place, she stood for several moments, staring at the figures silhouetted inside; then she decided to go back to Maria's tent.

Once inside the small space, Alex fumbled for the kerosene lamp, realized she didn't know where the matches were kept. She groped for her valise, finally pulling out her nightgown. She undressed, slipped on her nightgown, its silk inadequate against the cold. As she arranged her clothes so they wouldn't be in the way, she wished she'd brought something more substantial to wear.

She lay down on the cot, hard and unyielding, pulled the rough blankets over her, listened to the unfamiliar noises—people walking by, low conversations in foreign tongues, the scurrying of a mouse or maybe a rat across the tent floor. She couldn't get comfortable. Her feet stuck out over the end. After awhile, she heard someone stop outside the tent, and she sat up.

"Maria?" she called out softly, anxious.

A figure stepped inside.

"Did I wake you?" Maria whispered.

"I wasn't asleep."

Her eyes were accustomed to the dark now. She could see Maria undressing.

"How is the Serbian woman?" Alex asked.

"She died. She had been in labor for too long before her husband called us. Some of the women are not accustomed to doctors," Maria said, her tone remote, matter-of-fact, as she lay down on the other cot and covered herself.

"Oh." Out of habit Alex added, "I'm sorry."

"It is the way we live," Maria said, turning slowly on her side, her back to Alex. *I said you wouldn't understand*, the back seemed to say. *You with your high-flown words, you are no different than the others who come to tiptoe through the vermin, among people who can't speak English, shabby and ill-kempt people in threadbare clothes. They scare the hell out of you.*

Alex glared at the back. *You're right, Maria Ferrera. They do scare the hell out of me. They smell. There isn't a one of them who probably ever took a hot bath. Their strangeness terrifies me. Maybe I don't like them. I'm not sure. But I came to find out. I'm here, and I'm going to stay. If that isn't enough, it isn't. But it's what I'm about.*

Chapter Forty

In the dim light of dawn, Maria stared at the sleeping form on the other cot. Before the strike, well-dressed women had come to Hastings each year on the day before Christmas with baskets of food held in smooth white hands, tipped by clean, carefully shaped nails. She'd often been tempted to spit in their pasty faces. But word of the incident eventually would have been relayed to Dom's foreman, which would have meant trouble.

So instead, she had merely watched them, enjoying and loathing their uncertain smiles, their eyes darting nervously at the ragged children gathered about, as if they were so many mangy curs begging for scraps.

Last night, when she'd asked Alex MacFarlane to go to Jan Cazak and tell him about his wife, Maria had seen the fright in her eyes. To her, the Cazaks were foreigners, people she'd see only if she lost her way and landed in the Denver slums.

Alex stirred, turned over, opened her eyes and blinked as if to figure out where she was. When she saw Maria looking at her, she smiled and said good morning.

Maria rose, began to dress. "I must go prepare breakfast," she said in a near whisper so as not to wake those in the surrounding tents.

"I'll go with you."

Maria shrugged, as if it made no difference. Secretly, she was pleased.

Later, after the breakfast was over, as she and Alex were setting up the schoolroom, Alex asked her how she'd decided to teach.

Maria eyed her. "Education is our children's future. It's the children who keep alive the hopes of every man and woman in the camps."

"But there are schools in Trinidad."

"That's seventeen miles away. A three-hour walk."

"What about the coal companies? Surely, they provide schools."

"Some do. The men teachers are mostly drunks. They only stay a year. No one lives in a coal camp unless he has to."

Alex frowned. "I suppose not."

The tent flap opened and children began to stream in. Maria introduced them to Alex. Clothes patched but clean, faces scrubbed, they smiled up at her with a mixture of uncertainty and curiosity in their eyes, as if wondering what this straight-backed, beautiful stranger with her fine clothes was doing there.

Maria asked Alex to read to the smallest children while she worked with the older ones. At first, Alex sat primly on one of the benches, book in hand, the children grouped in neat rows at her feet. By afternoon, she was down on the floor, cross-legged, one little girl in her lap, the others listening with rapt attention.

Maria almost protested. Proper schoolroom decorum was part of what she wanted the children to learn, but she decided to keep silent.

The school day was almost over when Maria returned to the blackboard to demonstrate a long division problem. Behind her, where Alex was reading from Rudyard Kipling's *Jungle Book*, came peals of children's laughter, heart-warming sounds in the midst of the grim surroundings. They had been roused by a stranger.

The following day passed quickly. Alex seemed to know what to do and when to do it, giving Maria time to work alone with two of the older boys who had been struggling to make out the words in even the simplest readers.

It was nearly dark when a man brought word the doctor had returned. He had asked that Maria come to the hospital tent when she could. Only a few children remained. Alex said she thought she could manage until the women came to prepare supper.

Walking toward the hospital tent, Maria's sadness nearly overwhelmed her. The child inside her had been moving for several weeks. She would memorize Frank's face, the sound of his voice, the way he moved, to keep it in her memory forever after she left.

She turned at the street sign with the careful drawing of a caduceus and an arrow pointing the way to the hospital tent. A woman with a child in her arms, another clutching her skirts, was coming out. There was no time now for personal feelings. There was work to do.

Maria entered, and Frank's smile nearly broke her heart.

"Miss Ferrera, I'm just finishing with Rosa here. It's head lice all right. It looks like we'll have to have another camp-wide inspection very soon."

Rosa, a dark-haired child, feet dangling over the edge of the cot, beamed at Maria, wiggled her fingers at her in a kind of wave.

"I gave her a good check and—except for the lice—she's fit as a fiddle." Frank grinned at the child. "You're fine, little one."

Maria helped the child into her jacket and held open the tent flap. "Rosa, tell your mamma I'll come by to talk to her later."

The little girl nodded and ducked outside.

"Have you had supper?" Maria asked Frank.

"I'll get some later."

"That's what you always say, and look at you. Thin as a rail." She shook her head. "Come with me to the cook tent."

"It's okay. Really."

His kind gaze touched her as softly as a kiss, and she felt the blood rush to her head. "It's not okay."

She took the stethoscope from his neck and laid it on the table where he kept a crude sterilizer and some instruments. Lifting his coat from the rack that stood behind one of the cots meant for patients, she held it as he put it on.

"Nurses are never supposed to question the doctor," he said with a soft chuckle.

"Hah!" she said, scornfully. The scene they played was always the same. It kept their passion at bay, most of the time. He held back the tent flap, she stepped through, and they walked side by side, never touching. At the cook tent, Frank ate, drank some coffee, told her of his patients that day.

After the meal, they walked toward his automobile. He asked about Alex MacFarlane.

She shrugged. "She's not what I thought."

He eyed her, smiling, seeing inside her. "You like her, don't you?"

She regarded him solemnly. "It doesn't matter if I like her or don't like her. It is the children I care about."

Frank smiled at her sadly but with great tenderness. "It shouldn't be."

"What?"

"No one so beautiful should always be so serious," he said quietly.

Boldly, she took his hand in hers.

They had reached the end of a row of tents. Twenty yards ahead, unseen, she knew, was one of the men who stood guard around the camp at night. Standing together in the dark, Frank wrapped his arms around her, and for several minutes they stood silently, her head against his chest.

"Lord, how I love you, Maria," he murmured into her hair.

"*Cara mia.*" She raised her face, and they kissed deeply.

She trembled and closed her eyes, letting herself surrender to the touch of his hands as they moved over her arms, her back. Finally, breathless, they let each other go, knowing it was time for Frank to go. They continued walking toward his car. "I have a baby to deliver at the Caruthers, east of town. Chances are I won't get out for awhile," he said in a voice loud enough now for anyone who might be nearby.

"We can take care of the lice inspection."

"Good."

Frank got the crank out of the car and fit it in place. With a couple of sharp pulls, the engine started up. Her arms held her shawl closely around her as she watched him walk to the door on the driver's side.

He opened the door, one foot on the running board. "Keep me informed about what you find, will you?" he asked, stretching out the remaining seconds, saying words that had nothing to do with what lay in their hearts.

Now these moments were more precious than gold. "Just bring us more books when you come."

"You've got yourself a deal, Miss Ferrera." He got in and closed the door.

A moment later, he swung the car around, and disappeared into the darkness.

Chapter Forty-One

Bill stood by the door of the cook tent, Alex's valise at his feet, watching her with love in his heart as the children clustered around her, tugging at her skirt, one of them waving a book at her. Her gray eyes were held wide as if to hold back tears. Her lips trembled as she tried to smile, and she kept patting a little girl's dark curly head.

"Children," Maria Ferrera finally said. "Mrs. MacFarlane will be back to see you soon."

Alex looked over the children's heads at Bill. He nodded.

When he'd returned from Denver that morning and Mrs. Willard told him about Alex going to the Ludlow camp, he hadn't liked the idea at first. If General Chase and his gang got it into their heads to cause trouble at a union camp, Ludlow was a likely target. But the congressional committee was due to arrive tomorrow, and Ellis Chapin had already told him they planned to visit this camp. Alex was in good hands. As to why she'd come, he could only guess. Except for her impassioned approach to life, there was nothing predictable about her.

"You see, I told you Mrs. MacFarlane would return," Maria said, dropping to her haunches and gathering several children into her arms. "She gave me her solemn promise to come back for Greek Easter. Remember? We talked about that?"

Some of the children smiled eagerly, but from the confused looks of the others Bill knew they didn't understand what Maria had said.

"Now, Mrs. MacFarlane has to go." She stood up and took the dark-haired girl's hand, pulling her gently away from Alex.

"Let's sing a song. How about 'The Flowers That Bloom in the Spring'?"

"Please," Alex said, her glance caressing each child. "I'd love a song."

Maria began. After a few bars, one child after another joined in, uncertainly at first until—spying her encouraging smile—they strained harder to remember the words. By the second verse they were in full voice.

At the end, Alex and Bill clapped, and Maria gave an exaggerated curtsy.

"All right, children, it's time for school. Mrs. MacFarlane and Mr. Henderson must go. Come, come." She shooed them toward the older boys and girls who were patiently waiting.

Alex went over to Maria and took her hands. For a few moments, they stood very close, talking earnestly, their faces etched with the intensity of their feelings. Whatever had happened in the few days Alex had been in this camp obviously had drawn them together in a way Bill had no way of knowing or understanding, unless Alex told him. Whether she would do so was anyone's guess.

The next day there was a tour of the Forbes camp, the union camp closest to Trinidad. Bill and Alex strolled out of the cook tent where they and the visiting dignitaries, including several state legislators and the union's attorney Ellis Chapin, had gathered for lunch and an impromptu concert given by some of the strikers.

Miners and their families lined the paths, smiling and gawking, a few waving, as John Lawson led the group through the camp. The members of the investigating team smiled and nodded amiably. The mood of the unseasonably warm early March afternoon was festive.

The entire county was like a kid, scrubbed and combed, fingers crossed, standing at the top of the stairs on Christmas morning. The governor had ordered all but two hundred of the six hundred troops home. Tomorrow the hearings were scheduled to resume.

As he and Alex followed the other visitors back to the touring cars that had brought the group out from Trinidad, they passed John Lawson talking to Ellis Chapin.

Alex touched his arm. "We need to talk to Ellis about the testimony for tomorrow's hearing."

He glanced at her. "Who else did you line up?

"Dr. Bellamy. Maybe Maria, though I doubt if she'll agree to leave the children. It's almost as if she doesn't dare waste a minute that could be spent with them." She sighed. "And I spoke to the woman who does my hair about her father's experiences working at Cokedale. Apparently, he died last year of black lung disease."

He nodded, his eyes on Ellis Chapin, now standing in a group of men. Six feet tall, slender-framed with a long horse face, Chapin glanced past the men he was talking to. Alex waved, and hurried over to him.

As Bill came up behind her, Alex turned back, introduced Chapin.

"Alex tells me you're the district attorney," Chapin said, his piercing dark eyes behind the pince-nez he wore surveying him carefully.

"That's what they tell me."

Chapin smiled wryly. "She also says you were at the hearings in Denver."

"I thought they went well."

Chapin cocked his head, nodded. "A good bit of valuable information came out. Now we're going to get down to brass tacks."

Alex glanced at Bill and gave him a didn't-I-tell-you-so look. He grinned at her. The sight of her satisfaction over the scenario thus far made him think that sometimes dreams did come true after all.

As he and Alex walked along with Chapin, Bill decided he had to ask him a question that had been nagging at him ever since the Denver hearings.

"Say, if you don't mind my asking, Ellis, why are you down here defending the union? If my information is correct, you're a Republican. Your work for Roosevelt's election and against Denver's public utility trust makes sense. But defending the union doesn't seem to fit."

Chapin looked at him with unexpected sternness. "It's about a principle—I underline the word principle—that guarantees men's rights in general."

Bill grinned. No wonder Alex liked Ellis Chapin. "Sounds good to me."

"Excellent." Chapin's eyes softened. He almost smiled as he pulled a notebook and pencil from his vest pocket. "Now tell me what witnesses you would suggest."

Alex told him about Dr. Bellamy and the woman who dressed her hair, the tradesmen she'd spoken to.

"Perfect." He scribbled down the names.

"And there's also a local rancher—his name is Charlie Nevil," Alex said. She told him about how the company guards had killed Charlie's nephew.

Chapin said, "I take it this Mr. Nevil lives by a coal camp."

"A place called Sandoval," Alex said. "It's owned by CF&I."

"Excellent." Chapin again scribbled in the notebook.

"If you're wondering about his connection with the mines, his wife's cousin worked in one over near Walsenburg some years back," Bill said.

"That's a connection, but not enough to explain the boy's killing. Can you get in touch with him?"

"Alex and I'll drive out there tomorrow."

"You think he'll agree to testify?" Chapin asked.

Bill shrugged. "We won't know till I ask."

Charlie Nevil's eyes were full of doubt as he listened to Bill explain the purpose of the hearings.

"So what do you think?" Bill finally asked.

The only sound in the kitchen was the steady thud of the iron as Juanita thrust it down across the shirt spread over the ironing board.

Bill looked over at Juanita, but she refused to raise her gaze from her work. Alex cleared her throat, and he glanced across the table at her. On the way out to the ranch, they had talked about the possible danger of Charlie testifying, knowing they couldn't guarantee his safety after the hearing was over.

Alex rose and put an arm around Juanita's sturdy shoulders. "I know it's a great deal to ask."

Juanita turned to look at her, dark eyes swimming in tears. "This evil is a well with no bottom."

Alex hugged her close. "I know," she said softly.

Charlie got up and lifted the coffeepot off the stove. Holding it in mid-air, he said, "It might not do any good, me speakin' up."

"There's always that chance." Bill tipped back, balancing the chair on its back legs, biding his time. He had laid out the reasons why Charlie's testimony was important. Charlie Nevil was a man who couldn't be pushed. There was nothing more to do but wait.

The next morning, Alex and Bill entered the West Theater on Main. The building was grand by any standard: a graceful balustrade over the main entrance with twin Corinthian columns on either side, three stories ornately carved with a double-tiered balcony in the back and private balconies running along each side of the main floor. It was an appropriate setting for the hearing.

They chose seats off the center aisle, close to the stage. The maroon velveteen curtain had been drawn back for the day's event. In the center of the stage was a long table for the five committee members. At either side, sitting at smaller tables, were the counsels for each side of the dispute, as the newspapers liked to call the strike. A chair, apparently for the witnesses, had been placed next to the committee table. The theater hummed with an undercurrent of excitement and anticipation.

Bill glanced at Alex affectionately. Sitting there, she seemed every bit the duchess he'd seen that first day in law school. She smiled at people who looked her way, as if completely confident in the outcome of the day. But beneath her calm exterior, he knew, were all the uncertainties about how the day would unfold.

She'd put her heart and soul into this. That the hearing was taking place at all was due in large measure to her. The case for justice and men's rights would be skillfully represented by Ellis Chapin. Yet even he would not be able to control the testimony. Hopes and dreams rode on the next few hours.

"Looks good," he said.

She glanced at him, smiling for those who might be watching them, though her eyes were filled with anxiety. "Lord, I hope you're right."

Chapter Forty-Two

Alex looked around, curious to see who was in the audience. The balconies were filled with men in work clothes and women dressed in their shabby Sunday best, miners and their wives, talking among themselves, their faces eager with anticipation. The mayor and his wife, the publisher of the *Chronicle* sat in one of the private boxes. What appeared to be townspeople nearly filled the main floor.

Seated in the first two rows reserved for witnesses were men who looked like miners and mine superintendents, even a few shopkeepers. In the row behind them were men with bored expressions, draped casually in their seats, whom she guessed were reporters. Missing was Charlie Nevil, but it was only nine o'clock.

The five committee members emerged from offstage and took their seats. Behind them came Leslie Baxter and Judge Southard, Ellis Chapin, and a young man unknown to Alex. He looked too young to be an attorney.

"Horace Hawkins." Bill whispered in her ear. "From Virginia, I think. He's a new law partner of Senator Patterson, your old boss at the *News*."

Alex nodded as she studied the attorney. "If it weren't for the thinning hair, I'd say he was a college boy."

"Don't let the baby face fool you," Bill replied. "He's as sharp and tough as they come."

Congressman Foster conferred with his fellow committee members for a moment, straightened a pile of papers on the table in front of him, and gaveled the hearing to order. Alex held her breath.

"General Elmer Chase," the chairman called.

The audience stirred, heads craned. General Chase did not appear.

"Was the general informed that he was to testify?" the chairman asked Leslie Baxter.

Mr. Baxter rose. "He was, Mr. Chairman."

Committee members exchanged glances.

"As general of the National Guard ordered to Las Animas and Huerfano Counties by the governor, the committee believes his testimony to be vital to these hearings," the chairman said.

He turned to address a sheriff's deputy who was standing at the back of the stage. "Deputy, I want General Chase found and escorted to the theater."

Clapping erupted from the balconies.

The chairman glared at the audience. "Ladies and gentlemen, I warn you the chair will not tolerate interruptions of these proceedings."

Out of the corner of her eye, Alex caught the complacent smiles of those sitting in the box, like so many old cats who knew more than they chose to reveal.

"While we are waiting for General Chase, I will ask Mr. Baxter to call his first witness."

Smoothing his white hair, Leslie Baxter rose and gave a brisk little tug at the cuffs of his shirt so that each hung at exactly the same length beneath the edge of his coat sleeves. "We call Mr. Malcolm Thurmond, superintendent of the Hastings mines."

Mounting the stairs with a relaxed, confident air, Mr. Thurmond crossed the stage to the chair next to the committee table. A county court clerk pressed into service for the day took his oath, and Thurmond sat down.

Led by Baxter's friendly questioning, Thurmond painted a picture of a coal camp efficiently but benignly managed in the best interests of both owner and worker. Cross-examination, however, revealed a company that still paid its miners in scrip and had no provision for caring for sick or injured workers.

Two other witnesses followed. The same stark contrast emerged between what the coal companies stoutly maintained occurred and what Ellis skillfully pressed them to admit. Nearly two hours after the hearings began, at least in Alex's opinion, the score was even.

Suddenly, there was a commotion outside of the theater, and with members of the high-booted cavalry preceding him, General Chase, in full-dress uniform, appeared. He strode down the aisle, shoulders back and chest out as if to show off the brass buttons and ribbons to best advantage, then stopped halfway to say, "Mr. Chairman, I gave my testimony in Denver. I refuse to be cross-examined any further."

Gasps issued from the audience.

"I beg your pardon," said Representative Foster.

"I believe I made myself quite clear, sir."

The gaunt, hawk-nosed chairman regarded the general coldly. "You did, sir. But be advised we are pledged to seek the facts, and we shall have them."

The general's nostrils flared in indignation as he looked to Leslie Baxter sitting on the stage, perhaps expecting some sort of direction or at the very least a sign of support. But the puffy face of the counsel for CF&I was blandly noncommittal, and like a recruit cut off from reinforcements, General Chase wheeled and stomped back up the aisle.

Catcalls and boos tumbled from the balcony. Someone threw down a rotting apple core, barely missing the general's bald head. If the chairman didn't take control, the hearing would turn into a Roman circus. Alex looked toward the stage. Representative Foster grabbed the gavel, banged for order, called for a ten-minute recess.

Some people stood to stretch. Conversation hummed through the auditorium. Alex let out a sigh of relief. She leaned toward Bill. "I wonder if Charlie's going to come."

"Let's go take a look."

Bill and Alex nearly collided with Charlie as they went out the front entrance. His face was sober.

Bill shook his hand and smiled. "Thanks for coming."

"Let's go find Ellis Chapin," Alex said.

They worked through the crowd of spectators milling about the lobby and down the aisle toward the stage where Ellis and Horace Hawkins were talking. Leslie Baxter and Judge Southard sat at the small table, watching her.

Ellis came forward, and Alex introduced him to Charlie and went back down the stairs to her seat. The two men talked for a few moments, and Ellis pointed to several empty seats in the front row reserved for witnesses. The chairman came back on stage and gaveled the hearing back to order.

Charlie was the next witness. The chairman indicated where he should sit. The clerk administered the oath. Ellis Chapin approached, adjusted his pince-nez, gave Charlie a business-like smile.

For the first few minutes, his questions centered on personal information: Charlie's business, where he lived, how long he had lived there, what he knew about the strike.

"If you mean do I know what the union's after, I don't. Heard it's about wages and havin' their own weighmen. That's about it."

"Have you ever worked for a coal company, Mr. Nevil?"

"Nope."

"Then you have had no personal association with the coal industry?"

"Not exactly." Charlie studied his Stetson held stiffly on his lap.

"Please explain," Ellis asked.

Charlie looked up, suddenly alert. "A day last November. The twenty-ninth. It's not likely I'd forget." He raised his chin ever so slightly. "Anyway, two company guards came ridin' into our yard and shot Rogerio point blank."

"Rogerio?"

"Rogerio Valdez. My wife's nephew. We raised him since he was knee-high, since his Ma died."

"Rogerio Valdez was how old at the time of his death?" Ellis asked.

"Seventeen."

The theater was quiet, waiting.

"You saw the shooting?"

"Yep. Rogerio and I were in the barn when we heard an automobile drive in. Rogerio went out to see who it was. I could hear talkin' and I didn't like the sound of it. Mean. Like there might be trouble, so I went to have a look-see. There were these two standin' by the car. One of 'em with a shotgun, pointin' at Rogerio." He paused.

"Continue, please," Ellis urged in a kind way.

"Well, the men—"

"Could you identify them?" asked Ellis.

"Dark-haired. Big. Burly. One of 'em with a mustache. The other's nose was flat—like he might have been a prizefighter once."

"You said initially, Mr. Nevil, that they were company guards. How did you know that?"

"They said so. Said they was from Sandoval—about four miles from my place."

"And these men, company guards, what were they saying to your nephew?"

"They said Rogerio helped some scabs get away from Sandoval."

"By scabs you mean strikebreakers?" Ellis asked.

"Yes, sir."

"Mr. Nevil, please explain to the members of the committee what you mean by helping some scabs to get away."

"Well, I guess there's some who hire on that don't care about whether there's a strike goin' on. But others have no idea. One way or the other, though, most of the scabs come without so much as a light for their caps. They have to buy their equipment from the companies, who take it out of their wages—wages usually half of what was promised. So what with char-gin' for rent and food at the company store and paying for the equipment, the companies have 'em hog-tied. If they try to quit, they get the devil beat out of 'em."

"Isn't it true that the same conditions exist even without a strike?" Ellis suggested.

"Sure. But here's the difference," Charlie said. "The scabs don't come with families. So there's no women and children for 'em to look after."

"Are you suggesting the strikebreakers are freer to take risks?" Ellis asked.

"Can't say about risk. But if a man finds out he's been lied to and cheated, and he's bachin' it, he's more apt to climb the fence and hightail it out of there than if he's got little ones to think of."

Ellis nodded. "Tell me, Mr. Nevil, are the coal towns enclosed by fences?"

"Yep. They got guards, too."

"And it was two of these guards who came to your ranch and accused Rogerio Valdez, your nephew, of assisting the escape of several strike-breakers?"

"Yes, sir."

"How did Rogerio Valdez respond?"

"Said he'd never laid eyes on any scabs—strikebreakers. Which was the God's honest truth."

"You knew that to be a fact?" Ellis glanced at the committee.

"Yes, sir." Charlie took in a deep breath. "Because it was me who seen the scabs."

Ellis swung his gaze back to Charlie. "Would you explain, please."

"The night before, I went out to the barn to check on a mare that was about to foal. It was after midnight. There they were. Poor devils couldn't speak a word of English. It's too far from the tracks for 'em to be hobos, so I knew who they were. They babbled at me, got down on their knees. Like they were beggin' me to help. I told 'em to stay put, that I'd be back with some food."

"Through sign language?"

"Yes, sir. Rogerio was asleep. But my wife, Nita, she was up, anxious about the mare. She didn't ask any questions and I didn't tell her, but she packed some meat and bread and tied it up in a piece of oilcloth. I went back out, gave it to 'em, and they took off."

"You told the guards what you did?" Ellis asked.

"Never had a chance. The next thing I knew Rogerio was on the ground with a hole blown through him as big as your fist."

"Thank you, Mr. Nevil." Ellis turned to the chairman. "Mr. Chairman, that concludes my questions of Mr. Nevil."

Leslie Baxter rose, his thumbs hooked into his vest pockets, and walked slowly over to Charlie Nevil. "Mr. Nevil, am I correct in understanding you have never worked for a coal company?"

"That's so."

Baxter studied the stage floor as if pondering his next question. "Then, tell me, sir, how it is you know so much about Sandoval and about its practices?"

"Talk."

"You've heard about the guards and the company's policies regarding the issuance of equipment, for example, from friends, have you?"

Charlie Nevil gave Baxter a long look. "Say what's on your mind, mister."

Alex was seized with a ridiculous urge to giggle. Charlie Nevil might look like hayseed, but he was as intelligent as anyone she knew. He wasn't about to put up with Baxter's devious tactics.

"Mr. Chairman—" Leslie Baxter began.

"The witness is quite right, counselor. Restate your question."

"You associate with strikers?" Baxter asked.

"I've met some miners over the years. Passed the time of day with 'em. They're people, like the rest of us."

Alex smiled.

"Indeed." Leslie Baxter gave him a stony look. "Then you knew the men who came to your barn that evening had broken a legal contract. By helping them, you were abetting their crime."

"I dunno know about any contract. If you mean by abetting that I helped them, you're right. You people hold men against their will, like prisoners in jail. They don't know English or their rights, and you know it. So if helpin' a man who's down and out is against the law, I'm guilty."

Cheers came from the balcony.

The chairman banged the gavel. "Order." He turned to Leslie Baxter. "Any further questions, counselor?"

"No, sir," Baxter said, assuming a look of indifference.

"Then I shall call a recess for lunch," the chairman said. "The hearings will resume at two o'clock."

Alex and Bill invited Charlie to have lunch with them. As they walked toward the Newhart Cafe, she heard people around them discussing the morning and what it meant. In spite of her private resolution not to expect too much, Alex was buoyed with confidence. The hearing was going well.

They ordered fried chicken and Charlie had a piece of lemon meringue pie. He said he had to get back to the ranch, and Alex promised they'd come out to tell him and Juanita what happened in the afternoon. They parted outside the cafe.

During the afternoon, Horace Hawkins took Ellis's place as attorney for the union. A man who had been a foreman in the Hastings mines testified he'd been forced to discharge miners because they were union men.

Leslie Baxter called a hardware merchant from Pueblo. He told the committee that the owner of a general store in Walsenburg, over in Huerfano County, had purchased guns from him, .30–.30 caliber carbines for the most part, and that the guns were picked out by a union organizer, though he couldn't remember his name.

As each witness spoke, Alex tried to judge the reaction of the committee members. If their intense interest and nods were any indication, the testimony elicited by Horace Hawkins and earlier by Ellis was making the kind of impression that would have a strong impact on the final outcome.

Finally, John Osgood, owner of the Victor-American, settled in the witness chair. His dark eyes glittered, cold and hard like bits of coal, she decided, noting the irony. He was of medium height, gray-haired with a mustache that covered his upper lip. His aloof, disdainful manner was just as Alex remembered. It was no secret Osgood detested unions, and Alex suspected Horace Hawkins was about to prove it to the investigative committee.

Though her contacts with John Osgood had been mercifully few, she'd never liked him or his loud, garish wife, who had once been his paramour.

Horace Hawkins approached the witness. "Tell us, sir, what is your opinion of the United Mine Workers of America?"

"I refuse to do business with them," Osgood said, curtly. "Now or ever."

"I see." Horace Hawkins looked appropriately somber. "Would you also tell us, sir, your opinion of the union's demands?"

He regarded the attorney with distaste. "All of them?"

"If you wish."

Osgood glanced at the committee and back at Horace Hawkins.

"First, there's increase in wages. Absurd. No justification whatsoever."

Hawkins folded his arms and nodded, waiting.

John Osgood shifted his position. "As to the eight-hour day, I've always thought it was nonsense. Always opposed it. In the first place, no coal miner has ever worked eight hours. I mean really worked. They refuse to timber or clear away debris because we won't pay for it. But let's say, just for the sake of argument, they wanted to work not just eight hours but more than eight hours. The union says no. I say, that's an infringement on a man's rights."

So far so good, Alex thought. The questioning was going in the right direction. As Horace Hawkins continued down the list of union demands, John Osgood's face reddened in anger. It wasn't until Leslie Baxter began his cross-examination that he sat back in his chair and smiled.

The choice of John Osgood as the final witness had been a stroke of genius. If Ellis and Horace Hawkins had searched far and wide, they couldn't have found someone whose testimony so graphically expressed the companies' attitude that individual rights were of no importance.

A hush fell over the hall as the committee members conferred. Representative Foster announced that the hearings of the Committee on Mines and Mining were in recess. They would resume in Washington on April 1. A rap of the gavel closed the Trinidad hearing.

If Alex had any regret it was that Stefan Vaska should have been present to testify. Otherwise, she was satisfied. A dramatic picture had been painted of thousands of people denied the very rights guaranteed to every American. She could hardly wait for Ed Keating to read the record. After the Washington hearing, Congress couldn't help but take some kind of action.

Alex and Bill filed up the aisle and retrieved their coats from the cloakroom. A small knot of people standing across the foyer talked for a moment and pushed out the front doors. A quiet settled over the theater. Buttoning her coat, Alex found it difficult to believe that ten hours ago, in that very entryway, she'd had to elbow her way through a noisy crowd.

Outside, the streetlights were on, and the windows of the buildings along Main Street shone yellow in the settling dark. From the saloon across the street, men's raucous voices drifted out into the crisp night air. It was the end of a day like any other day in Trinidad. Yet, of course, it wasn't.

She took a deep breath as she took Bill's arm. "How did you think it went?"

"Hard to say."

"Ellis and Horace Hawkins did an excellent job. And Charlie coming. What a brave and noble thing to do."

Bill smiled at her.

"I prayed it all would happen, and it did."

"Well, give the congressman a little credit."

She laughed.

"You should be damn proud of yourself," Bill said, his eyes warm with feeling.

"I guess I am," she admitted. She had concentrated for three months on working to make this day a reality. Her only fear had been that it would never happen. She smiled at Bill. "Thank you."

They joined Ellis Chapin for dinner at a corner table in the hotel dining room. Ellis spoke enthusiastically though quietly about the day. Alex switched the conversation to what lay ahead after the final hearing in Washington. The conversation was serious, practical.

In the morning, Ellis and the committee members would return to Denver, the committee members to change trains and go on to Washington. When the evening ended, Alex felt as if they were bound together by a magical thread. Impulsively, she gave Ellis a hug. They said good night and parted.

In a week, the last of the hearings would be over. Her purpose in staying in Trinidad would be gone. She still had not come to grips with what her next move should be.

Chapter Forty-Three

The next morning, as Alex lingered over breakfast, the sharp ring of the telephone in the hall broke the quiet that had settled over the house.

"Someone wants you on the telephone, Miz MacFarlane," came the voice of Mrs. Willard's hired girl.

Alex got up. "I'll be right there."

She went out into the hallway, picked up the telephone receiver, and held it to her ear.

"Alex? Phil Van Howe here."

"Yes?"

"I'm afraid I have bad news of you."

She waited.

"Stefan Vaska's body was found earlier this morning on the tracks just outside the strikers' camp at Forbes."

She stared at the empty umbrella stand by the front door, stunned. "You've made a positive identification?"

"I'm afraid so."

She caught in a breath to steady herself. "I'll be over as soon as I can."

Alex hung up, went back to her room, put on her hat, grabbed her coat, and went over to the Columbian Hotel.

Facing Phil Van Howe in his office, she was struck again by how officious he was in his uniform and gleaming cavalry boots. Three months in Trinidad must have been comfortable for him, she decided, for he had developed a paunch.

"I want to know what happened," she said, firmly.

"According to the report, a routine patrol found him about dawn."

Their eyes met, and in that instant Alex knew he was lying.

"I want an autopsy performed."

"Alex, the body is mangled."

"That may be. Nevertheless, I want Dr. Bellamy to do an autopsy."

"Dr. Ingram is the county coroner."

"I want Dr. Bellamy to assist."

Phil Van Howe leaned across the desk, his expression set. "Surely, I don't need to remind you this county exists in a state of martial law. General Chase still makes the rules around here."

"Which means what?"

"Which means there will be no autopsy. With or without your Dr. Bellamy."

"You know I'll report this to Congressman Keating."

Phil's eyes were cold with contempt. "I expect you will."

The man infuriated her. But if she lost her temper, she'd also lose her chance to learn what had happened to Vaska. Aside from the possibility he'd been so drunk he'd passed out as he crossed the tracks, the circumstances of his death were suspicious.

"Look, Phil, I didn't mean to be rude. But as you can imagine, Vaska's death comes as a shock."

His mouth pulled into a hard smile.

She continued. "To be run over by a train . . ."

"On the contrary. The man was murdered by your union friends."

"What union friends?" she snapped.

He glared.

She had to control herself. "I'm sorry, Phil. You were saying?"

"He was murdered and left on the tracks to give the appearance that death came at the hands of the Guard," he said, glaring at her. "I need not remind you we were sent here at great expense by the State of Colorado to restore order and to keep the peace. When the governor decided to withdraw some of the troops a few weeks ago, General Chase gave his word the Guard would not be responsible for any incident that might trigger a return to violence."

Her impatience welled. "Exactly what are you getting at?"

"The union intends to blame Vaska's death on the Guard. It wants the world to believe the Guard broke the peace. But let me assure you, Alex, if they think we will simply stand by and let this happen, they are wrong. At this very moment, we're taking measures to clear out the troublemakers who are responsible for this Vaska affair."

"You mean you have suspects?"

"Exactly." He stood up. "Now, I have a great deal of business to attend to."

Alex entered what apparently served as the morgue and froze with cold horror at the sight of the figure on the narrow table that nearly filled the small room. She could feel the thud of her heart, a macabre reminder of life in the presence of death.

She took a few steps closer to the remains of Stefan Vaska, conscious of the bile rising in her throat, filling her mouth. She glanced about frantically, ran to the tin-lined sink in the corner, and vomited. She straightened, only to be seized with the need to vomit again. Finally, her eyes still closed, leaning against the edge of the sink to steady herself, she straightened. She drew her handkerchief out of her suit skirt pocket, wiped her mouth.

Drawing up all her courage, she went back to the table where Vaska lay. The smell of formaldehyde filled her nostrils. The light from the bare bulb hanging on a cord from the ceiling cast eerie shadows over the mangled body parts spread out on the enamel-covered table.

It was evident Vaska had been literally sliced in half by the train wheels that had rolled over him. He was covered with blood; dark curly hair matted against his head; his nose was smashed in; lips were slit and grossly distended. He had the appearance of a man who'd been in a brutal fight—or the victim of a terrible beating—before he died.

She was almost certain the union wasn't responsible. An outbreak of violence would destroy the positive image John Lawson had fought so hard to maintain and to reinforce during the hearings. A killing would only justify a continuation of martial law. She had to find out what was going on.

Alex recalled the first day she'd gone out to the Ludlow camp to talk to John Lawson, how he had refused to tell her anything about her client. At the time, she'd wondered about it. Now she had more than a few suspicions that he had known all along Vaska was more than he appeared to be. She'd barely known the man, but she'd taken on an obligation for his well-being. With his death, John Lawson owed her the truth. She'd find Bill. It was time for another visit to Ludlow.

The sun warmed the automobile enough to make it almost hot. Alex lowered the window as Bill steered the Ford north along the main highway toward the Ludlow camp.

The fields on either side of the road were greening, but the snow-capped mountains to the west were silent reminders a blizzard could sweep down across the plains tomorrow. Ahead, off to the right, was the Forbes camp where, only three days ago, she and Bill had been part of the grand tour for the congressional committee members and visiting dignitaries.

As she looked more closely now, she saw men, women, and children grouped around its gate. A dozen soldiers were shoving them at rifle point away from the camp. Shouts and curses mixed with cries rose in the clear morning air. On the pretext of hunting down Vaska's killers, a full-fledged confrontation was in the making. Alex wondered if the militia had deliberately chosen this camp to flaunt its power.

Then, about twenty yards farther down the road, she saw an odd-looking vehicle with the appearance of a touring car, yet covered with armor plate. She glanced at Bill. "Look, there. Isn't that Linderfelt's war machine with the machine gun?"

He followed her gaze, frowned. "It must mean Company B is involved. The scum of the world."

"Do you think they're the ones who killed Vaska?"

"Probably." He shifted gears. "If we're smart, we better back up and take a side road to get to Ludlow."

As Bill and Alex walked toward the headquarters tent at the Ludlow camp, they discovered the news was already out about the militia's harassment at Forbes. Speculation raged about what it meant, what might happen next.

The guard at the headquarters asked their business, ducked inside the tent, and came out a moment later with Horace Hawkins behind him.

"Mr. Hawkins, I thought you were back in Denver," Alex said, surprised to see him.

"Mr. Lawson thought I should stay for awhile."

The news made Alex uneasy. "I need to see Mr. Lawson."

"I'm afraid he's tied up with the Vaska incident."

"I understand," Alex said. "Stefan Vaska was my client."

"My sympathies," Horace Hawkins said, gravely. "Can you wait?"

"Of course."

As they waited to see John Lawson, Alex and Bill walked through the camp until they reached the edge facing the militia camp. From there, they could see men running across the parade ground. Trucks were driving in and out of the gate. All the activity could only mean General Chase was either about to or had already decided to tighten his control even more. Vaska's death was his excuse. No wonder Horace Hawkins had stayed.

She glanced at Bill. "Is that where Company B is quartered?"

"I'm not sure."

She sensed someone behind them and turned to see Dom Ferrera. Cap in hand, he asked to talk to her alone.

Bill excused himself, telling her he'd be back at the headquarters tent, and disappeared around a row of tents.

Dom glanced about to see if they were alone before he said, "Maria says you were Stefan Vaska's lawyer."

Her pulse quickened. It had never occurred to her to ask Dom about Stefan. Now perhaps she'd learn what happened. "Yes, I was."

"I thought you should know how it was."

"I'd appreciate that a great deal," she said. "I saw him only once, you know. I asked him about his arrest. But he really didn't tell me much."

"When the word came he was dead, Maria told me to go find you." Dom cocked his head. "She says you're one of us and will keep your mouth shut."

"Your sister is a good person. I'll hold whatever you tell me in the strictest confidence." She smiled. "But you should know, Dom, that I'm not a union sympathizer."

He cocked an eyebrow, his eyes hard and angry. She wouldn't be surprised if he decided he'd made a bad mistake to come to her. Thrusting his hands in his pants pockets, he turned to face the prairie, his back to her. She sensed that whatever he was about to tell her was something few people knew.

A minute later, he wheeled and began. "Before the strike, there were organizers."

"The men who persuade miners to join the union?"

He nodded. "We had twenty, maybe. Or more. Nobody but Mr. Lawson was s'posed to know exactly how many or who. They got special training in Denver to find out the new way. See, up to then, no matter how careful we are, company spies find out who joins. And they get fired."

"So Mr. Lawson and the others get this better idea," he continued. "Two men work together. One is what's called the active organizer. He works out in the open. The company and everybody thinks they know what he's up to.

"The other organizer pretends he's a miner who's lookin' for work. He cusses the unions and Mr. Lawson. So the company hires him. He makes friends with the company big shots. Gets in good with them."

Alex nodded, trying to follow what he was telling her.

"So this inside man—the one who the company thinks hates unions—gets himself hired as a spotter."

"You'll have to explain."

"Spotters. They get paid extra—twenty bucks a month—to squeal on men who join the union or who even think about joinin'."

Alex was puzzled. "But the two men—the organizers. How are they connected?"

"Simple. The outside man everybody knows is the organizer starts to get new members in the same mine where the phony spotter is. But instead of the names bein' handed over to the company, they're handed to the phony, who keeps mum. So none of the new members are fired. You understand?"

"I think so."

"Now, let's say a man says no, he don't want to join the union. Well, the phony spotter goes to the pit boss and makes up the story the man is really goin' to join. So quick as anything, they send the slob down the canyon. In other words, we get rid of the troublemakers."

"Because the company fires them."

"Right. The companies fire the wrong men and hire union men, and they don't even know it. Nifty, huh?" He smiled at the thought. "One, maybe two, thousand union members were hired that way. It was important to get as many members as we could before the strike."

"I can see that." Alex couldn't help marveling at the cleverness and effectiveness of the system. "And Stefan Vaska was one of the organizers?"

Dom concentrated on stabbing the toe of his shoe into the dry ground for a minute before he looked up at her. "He was one of the inside men. The best."

"Do you think the companies found out how the system worked? Do you think they found out they'd been tricked and killed him?"

"I dunno."

Alex remembered the angry man at the Sandoval camp who had spit at the mention of Stefan Vaska's name. "Did miners kill him? Men who thought he truly was a spotter for the companies? Is that who you're saying might have killed him?"

"Could be," Dom said. "Mr. Lawson's the only one who knows who's who."

"Then how . . ." Alex studied the careful eyes, blank of anything that might betray what else he knew. "Dom, if Mr. Lawson was the one person who knew the organizers, how do you know about Stefan Vaska?"

His face remained a mask.

"Were you an organizer, too? Did you work with Vaska?"

His expression gave no indication of his answer.

"I'm sorry. I shouldn't have asked."

"I wanted you to know, missus. Vaska was a good man. He gave his life to the UMW."

Alex watched the boy's face, aged beyond its fifteen years by a world that forced men and their sons to do things they should never have to do. Once this strike was over, she would do what she could to find him a decent job that wasn't in the mines.

"The companies say it's us—the union—that murdered Vaska. They say we're after trouble now that those men went back to Washington."

"Are they right?" Alex held her breath.

He looked wounded. "Mr. Lawson gives the orders. He tells us stay calm, we stay calm."

"Thank God." She gave a long sigh and placed a hand on one of his arms. "Dom, would it be all right if I told Mr. Vaska's sister?"

She caught the alarm in his eyes.

"I will simply say he died standing up for what he believed in. I won't even hint to her he might have been an organizer," she said. "Besides, I don't really know it's true, do I?"

He gave her a crooked smile.

"But if something ever came out that he worked for the companies on the sly—that he was a traitor, of sorts—I don't think she could bear it. He was her whole life, you see."

He nodded, gravely.

"I'll write her about his death, of course. When I go back to Denver to visit my father, I'll call on her."

They began to walk toward the headquarters tent, and she thought of Linderfelt and the machine gun again.

"Dom, what Mr. Lawson said about staying calm . . . It's so important," she said, anxiously. "The last hearing begins in Washington next week. If there's any violence from the union . . ."

The prospect of what the militia might do was too grim to even contemplate.

Chapter Forty-Four

Ed Keating took his seat in the House Chamber, smiling and nodding to the dozen or so congressmen around him. Judging from the vacant seats on the floor, smart politics apparently said to boycott the hearing. But the gallery was packed. Not an empty seat was to be had from the looks of it. All the press as well as the great unwashed of Washington were there to listen and to gawk as young John Rockefeller explained his father's operation in the southern coalfields of Colorado.

Outside, buds on the cherry trees were on the verge of bursting into bloom. The lawn around the Capitol was emerald green. The air was fresh. The promise of new life and new hope was everywhere. It was Ed's favorite time of year.

The babble of voices suddenly quieted as the committee members took their seats at the table placed below the Speaker's chair. The union's counsel, Chapin, and a young man new to Ed sat down across the room from Leslie Baxter and Judge Southard. But today only the committee would do the questioning.

Martin Foster, who would continue as chairman of the proceedings, was a good man. He didn't put up with malarkey from a soul. Not even a Rockefeller.

A moment later, a man of medium height, dark haired, and well dressed, who looked to be in his mid-thirties, entered the chamber. A half dozen men, a retinue of assistants from their subservient manner, followed. They took their seats on either side of their employer at a table placed in front of the committee.

The chairman sounded the gavel, calling the hearing to order, then explained that Mr. John D. Rockefeller Jr. would be the only witness called. From where Ed sat he had a good view of the man whom until this morning he'd never laid eyes on. Square-jawed, clean-shaven, Rockefeller had the look of a man used to giving orders. Unruffled, cool as could be, he leaned toward one of his minions and said something. Being the sole witness apparently didn't faze him.

"Mr. Rockefeller."

The witness nodded. "Good morning, Mr. Chairman."

"The committee appreciates your appearance today. So that we may have a full picture of your interests involved, would you tell us, sir, exactly the degree of your investment in the affected companies located in Colorado where the coal strike is going on?"

Rockefeller nodded. His family owned forty percent of the preferred and forty percent of the common stock of Colorado Fuel and Iron.

"You are a member of the board of directors?" Foster asked.

"I am. However, I have not attended a meeting for over ten years." He had "not the slightest idea" who was present when the directors of the corporation were elected.

"I see," the chairman said in an even tone. "Tell us, sir, do you recall the date the Colorado strike was called?"

"No, I don't."

"An approximate date, perhaps?"

"I'm afraid not," the young Rockefeller replied, blandly, and reached for a stack of papers on the table before him. "However, if that's important, I'm sure I can find the date you're after here in our records."

A murmur riffled through the chamber.

A congressman seated at one end of the committee table motioned to the chairman.

"Mr. Schmidt, your question."

"Thank you, Mr. Chairman." The white-haired committee member turned his attention to Rockefeller. "Sir, do you realize that since last September this strike has been reported in the press of the country, that the governor of Colorado has called out the militia to police the disturbed district, that the conditions prevailing in the district were shocking, according to such reports, and that the House of Representatives deemed it a duty to undertake this investigation?"

"I've been fully aware of all those facts," Rockefeller replied, coolly.

Frank Schmidt eyed the chairman.

"You may proceed with your questions, Mr. Schmidt."

"Thank you, Mr. Chairman." He shifted in his chair. "You say you are fully aware of all those facts, and yet neither you, personally, nor the board of directors has looked into the matter?"

"I cannot say as to whether the board of directors has looked into the matter or not," the witness said. "Its meetings are held in the West."

"What have you done to find out about the trouble in Colorado?"

Rockefeller held up a sheaf of papers. "This correspondence will give the whole thing."

"But what have you done, personally, as one of the directors, aside from correspondence?"

"I have done nothing outside of this. That is the way in which we conduct business."

The committee members exchanged glances.

Frank Schmidt sat back. "Mr. Chairman, I will hold further questions."

Foster nodded and regarded the witness again. "Can you tell us what remedies you have suggested to end this industrial disturbance?"

"The management of the company is in the hands of the officers, and so long as they have our entire confidence we shall stand by them. We could not conduct the business in any other way," Rockefeller replied.

The chairman glanced at a yellow legal pad on the table before him for a moment before he asked, "Mr. Rockefeller, will you tell us what you believe to be the central issue in this strike?"

"The issue, Mr. Chairman, is not unique to Colorado. It is a national issue. Namely, it concerns whether workers shall be allowed to work under such conditions as they may choose."

Ed crossed his legs and leaned back. He should have known the union's demand for a closed shop contract would be the linchpin of Rockefeller's argument.

"Our company is only part owner of the properties in the southern coalfields. But our interest in the laboring men in this country is so immense, so deep, so profound that we stand ready to lose every cent we put in that company rather than see the men who have been employed thrown out of work to suffer conditions not of their seeking and that neither they nor we can see are in our interest."

"What percentage of the men working for you would you say prefer an open shop?"

"Ninety percent."

The chairman raised his eyebrows. "And you have personal knowledge of this? You have been out there in Colorado and talked to the men?"

A gray-haired man in a morning coat whispered something to Rockefeller, who nodded. "No personal knowledge. But I have been assured by Mr. Bowers and Mr. Welborn, officers of the CF&I, that that is the case."

Martin Foster asked, "No personal knowledge, Mr. Rockefeller? You are willing to let men lose their lives on either side, endure the expenditure of large sums of money and all this disturbance of labor rather than go out there and see if you might do something to remedy those conditions?"

"So far as I understand it, Mr. Chairman, there is just one thing that can be done to settle the strike, and that is to unionize the camps. But our interest in labor is so profound and we believe so sincerely that the camps should be open camps, that we expect to stand by the officers at any cost."

"And you will do that if it costs all your property and kills all your employees?" Foster asked.

John Rockefeller sat back in his chair. "It is a great principle."

Ed glanced up at the astonished faces looking down over the gallery railing.

"And no matter what the costs, you would do that rather than recognize the right of men to collective bargaining? Is that what I understand you to say, sir?" the chairman asked.

"No, sir. I believe that outside people should never be allowed to come in and interfere with employees who are thoroughly satisfied with their labor conditions," Rockefeller said firmly. "It was upon a similar principle that the War of the Revolution was carried out. This, sir, is a great national issue of the most vital kind."

Ed stared at the scion of one of the world's great fortunes. To compare the medieval ruthlessness of the CF&I with the War of the Revolution was absurd. The man was a wonder.

When the chairman asked Rockefeller to explain his views in more detail, the entire chamber sat a little straighter and listened. What unfolded was the usual picture of an organization with international ties, headed by agitators and thugs who used intimidation and force to persuade otherwise contented employees into conflict with their employers.

"And the object of this conflict?" asked Foster.

"Why, to increase its dues-paying membership, of course, directly enriching the leadership," replied Rockefeller. "Absolute selfishness is at the root of it. Without concern for employees or employer."

George Taylor from Utah caught the chairman's eye.

"Congressman Taylor."

"Thank you, Mr. Chairman." He leaned across the long table to peer at John Rockefeller over the top of his wire-rimmed glasses, which had settled at the end of his nose. "Sir, beyond your stated concern for the freedom of your employees to choose whether they wish to join a union, what would you say is the major focus of your attention?"

"The general well-being of the company. Of course."

"Sales, finances, profits. That sort of thing. Is that right?"

"Of course."

"Do your companies provide housing for your workers?"

"I—"

"Schools?"

The congressman pressed Rockefeller further, building a picture of a man who knew nothing of the company he controlled. Yet Rockefeller was completely unruffled, as if he saw nothing amiss. The human side of matters was of absolutely no interest to the man, Ed decided.

The questioning went on. Ed looked around him, studying the reactions of his fellow congressmen. The expressions varied from curiosity to boredom. The gallery was another matter. But the gallery didn't vote. The gallery didn't depend on men like Rockefeller for reelection. Congressmen did.

The same men who had helped him push through the resolution might go along with labor reform legislation. They might not. An investigation was one thing. Finding the votes for a piece of legislation when you had nothing to trade was another situation entirely. Young Turks like he was had no favors to offer. And when you put yourself on the line for a losing cause, you could kiss any support from the party leadership good-bye.

After the noon recess, John Rockefeller returned, cool and collected as ever. Every space in the gallery was filled. The questions resumed. Ed felt a pain in his stomach, tried to tell himself it was due to the pork chop he'd eaten. Slumping in his chair, he folded his arms over his chest and continued to listen to the man no older than himself explain away the deliberate neglect of men whose lives he controlled.

It was after six and dark when the hearings were concluded. Ed headed back to the hotel. He knew in his gut, the fight—if you could call it that—was over. Not for good. There'd be a flurry of indignation in some of the newspapers. But not enough to change anyone's mind. It was over. He was certain of that. Some day the issues at stake would rise again and be addressed, because they were too fundamental to be ignored. For now, there wasn't a prayer.

Rockefeller and men like him ran the country. Because leadership took some guts and a modicum of intelligence, the Congress, which by and large had neither, went meekly along. Though democracy was the greatest system of government in the world, it had its flaws.

Ed didn't consider himself a quitter. Just the opposite. A feisty Irishman, some called him. His years in politics told him to back off. Well, not back off. Just not push. The right to collective bargaining, a closed shop, safety regulations with clout—all the rest of it—were states' rights issues. Lord knows, he'd heard that song often enough. But one man or a handful of men didn't change the world by themselves. He knew he couldn't come up with the votes to give the big boys even a decent run for their money.

He turned in at the hotel entrance and collected his mail from the desk clerk, hoping to find a letter from Margaret. When God made Margaret Lennon Keating, He created a saint with a head on her shoulders and a sense of humor to boot. But there was no envelope addressed in the familiar, strong hand, and he took the elevator up to his room.

Automatically, he took off his suit coat and draped it over the back of the chair by the desk. The room was stuffy. He went over to the window and pushed it open, enjoying the cold air. Through a lighted window across the courtyard, he could see a woman preening in front of a mirror. A rush of longing for Margaret swept through him, and he turned away.

His thoughts returned to Alex and to his own disappointment. He had been wrong to give her hope. He knew how the game was played, yet he'd persisted in believing that if the cause was just, right would win the day.

Lord, have mercy on my soul. Give me the wisdom to explain to Alex what happened today. Give us both the courage to try again.

Chapter Forty-Five

Alex slowly put the pages of Ed's letter in order, refolded them, and placed them on the dresser. Sick at heart, she sat on the edge of the bed and stared out the narrow window as she went back over Ed's account of the hearing and what it meant.

There was no doubt about his conclusions. There was no hope of making substantive changes in the conditions that had triggered this and every other strike. At least for now.

Ed was sorry. He'd let his idealism take over when his political sense knew better. He'd done her a disservice. A terrible disservice. He hoped she would forgive him. More than that, he hoped she wouldn't give up. He wouldn't. Now, yes. But there'd be another day. Bank on it, he said.

There was a huge, swollen lump in her throat. She was on the edge of tears. She'd counted on him. The men and women in the camps had put their faith in him. Now he was telling her the matter was dead before it ever had the chance to become a debatable issue.

She thought about incidents that had occurred in two different camps during the last week. In both cases, Linderfelt and his men had busted in, arresting men on some trumped-up charge or another. So far John Lawson had kept a tight rein on the strikers. But now that the hope for congressional action was gone, God only knew what would happen.

She stood up, then forgot what she had intended to do. She felt lost. There wouldn't be a big announcement about the failed hearings. It didn't work that way. So maybe—hope against hope—the small amount of peace that existed would continue.

Damn. She didn't care about the companies. Or the union. She did care about the people. Why should you have to be rich and educated before it was acceptable to demand your rights? Why should men have to join a union in order to have a safe place to work? Why should women be forced to risk their lives and that of their children to fight for their rightful piece of the American dream? Justice under the law was a reality only if you knew the powerful people, spoke the king's English, lived in the right part of town.

Someone knocked and, reluctantly, not wanting to see anyone, she went to the door. It was Bill.

"I'm sorry about the hearings."

"Come in." She went over to the dresser and handed him Ed's letter.

"I should have known." Her voice was a monotone, masking her anguish.

Bill stood by the window and read the pages.

Finally, he raised his eyes and looked at her; at that instant, she began to cry. Still holding the letter, Bill came over and pulled her gently into his arms.

"It isn't right," she said, sobbing now.

"I know."

She drew back, wiping at her eyes. "Oh, Bill, martial law will go on forever. Then everything in the coal towns will be go back to the way it's always been. Nothing will have changed."

He dug into his pocket and gave her his handkerchief.

"I really thought there was a chance."

"These people are good at surviving. They've been through this before. They'll be all right. You'll see."

She blew her nose, unconvinced. No one's strength lasted forever. "What do we do now?"

Bill kissed the top of her head. "Take a deep breath."

She looked up at him, tried to smile.

"I brought an invitation you might like."

She blew her nose again.

"It's from Maria." He pulled a piece of paper out of his coat pocket and handed it to her.

Dear Alex,

I hope you remember your promise to help celebrate the Greeks' Easter the Sunday after next. Please come. Bill is invited, too.

There will be special food. Louis Tikas says it is called the Feast of Feasts. Though there will be no priest, it will be a happy time. Please come.

Your friend, Maria

Alex reread the note written in lovely, flowing Spenserian handwriting. From its appearance, it could have been written by a college-educated woman brought up with every advantage. She glanced at Bill. "I can't face her. Not now."

"You don't think she'll understand?"

The note dangling between her fingers, Alex gazed out the window. Nothing daunted Maria. She would try anything, do anything if she believed it might help the people in the camps. Maria was the most remarkable woman she knew. She felt her own courage return.

"Well?" Bill asked. "How about it?"

The sky on April 19 was a brilliant blue and nearly cloudless when Bill pulled the car up at the edge of the Ludlow camp. In the distance, fields of alfalfa glowed like great patches of emerald velvet amidst the dun-colored miles of prairie. As she climbed out of the car, Alex took off her coat and rolled up the sleeves of her blouse. Maria would have heard the disappointing news, but today was not the time to discuss it.

The pathways between the tents were filled with people milling about, laughing and singing as if it were a Greek Easter Sunday no different than any other. Some children dashed in and out of the crowd as they played hide and seek. A man playing a concertina strolled by. The entire camp seemed to be in a holiday mood, as if hope were still possible.

As she looked about for Maria, she saw a man dressed in a flaring white skirt. Beneath it he wore white tights. Over his full-sleeved shirt was a bright red vest, rich with embroidery. A red scarf was tied pirate fashion around his dark hair. She realized it was Louie Tikas.

"Christ is risen!" he called to them as they approached. His smile was broad. Did she detect a certain smugness beneath it, or was that her imagination? She recalled her first impressions of him as he'd stood behind the old men playing cards in the cook tent, how he'd seemed dark and sinister, somehow. Leslie Baxter once told her the Greeks in the camps were ruthless troublemakers, and she thought of the night, less than two months ago, near Simpson's Ridge when Louie had almost refused to obey John Lawson's orders. She almost smiled. For Louie, the investigation's failure must be a kind of self-fulfilling prophecy.

Bill stopped when he reached Louie. "You look like you're going to a costume party."

Louie laughed and struck a pose. "It is our native costume. I wear it in celebration of Easter."

"Is Mr. Lawson here today?" Alex asked.

Louie's smile disappeared. "He's in town."

Alex felt a stab of apprehension. "Not trouble, I hope . . ."

"Just rumors." Louie shrugged, then spread his arms in a welcoming gesture. "But tonight we forget that. There will be good food. Dancing, singing. Soon a baseball game. Stay awhile, enjoy."

Alex glanced at Bill, saw his frown. He had an instinct for danger. Still, Maria had counted on their coming. "We can go back to town right after the feast." She smiled into Bill's troubled eyes. "Besides, you need to prove just how good a baseball player you really are. And I can hear the songs the children promised me."

An hour later, the sweet clear voices of the children still ringing in her ears, Alex left the cook tent with Maria, walking slowly, talking of this and that, toward the outskirts of the camp where Bill and Louie had gone to join the baseball game already in progress.

She could hear the crack of a bat and cheering. The rumors of trouble must be just that: rumors. She sighed with relief. But as they approached the baseball field, she became aware of movement in the distance: horses. There were three of them, coming out of the canyon toward the camp at a full gallop. She tensed. Fear raced through her. As they neared, she saw the riders were in army uniform. They didn't slow until they reached the far edge of the baseball field. It was then Alex saw that each man had a rifle, held at the ready.

Chapter Forty-Six

Maria's heart stopped at the sight of the riders. She had prayed the promised trouble wouldn't come. But now, prancing up and down the edge of the baseball field, there it was.

She and Alex exchanged glances, and she saw the apprehension in her friend's eyes. "Pay no attention," Maria said. "If we pretend they are not there, they'll go away."

The men on the field glanced around, taking the measure of the rifles, trying to judge the mood of the riders.

As if unaware of them, Louie cupped his hands over his mouth and shouted, "Hey, we playing ball or not?"

Heads turned back toward the pitcher and Bill, who was at bat. The game went on.

Maria looked around her and smiled to reassure the fearful women and children who stood nearby. "It's all right," she said to them. "Nothing will happen."

But the women gathered the children close around them and kept their eyes on the riders.

The men on horseback put the rifles to their shoulders and aimed. Alex caught in her breath. The men grinned and guffawed, as if they were playing some kind of ghastly game.

Then from the distance came the sound of an automobile moving very fast, and she glanced toward the road. Her heart stopped as she recognized Linderfelt's war machine.

Calling something out to Bill, who nodded, Louie started to walk in the direction of the headquarters tent. At first, his pace was steady, deliberate, but it soon quickened to a trot. Bill and the other men on the field stayed where they were, watched.

What seemed like hours went by. Maria held her breath, her eyes on the rifles, until, as if on cue, the riders lowered their rifles and spurred their horses to gallop, also toward the headquarters tent. Instantly, everyone followed.

Maria elbowed through the strikers clustered outside the tent, heard a man shouting, "I said get the sonofabitch to me now. We're bringin' him in for the murder of Stefan Vaska."

She stood on tiptoes and saw it was the dreaded Lieutenant Linderfelt who had spoken.

Louie stood behind the makeshift desk. "He isn't here. I told you that."

"Don't give me that shit, Tikas."

"I'm telling you. Dom Ferrera isn't here."

Maria gasped. Dom was no murderer.

"Well, guess what, Tikas? We're goin' to search the place, and make you out a lyin' bastard."

"Please do," Louie said with elaborate courtesy.

Lieutenant Linderfelt waved to the three soldiers. "Go to it, boys."

Instantly, the flap on one tent after another was thrown open, soldiers stomped in and threw out precious belongings. Finally, Linderfelt called the men back.

Though no taller than Louie, Linderfelt was fifty pounds heavier. He grabbed Louie's shirt and lifted him off the ground. "Listen up, fucker. I'm comin' back here tomorrow a.m."

He glared at the men and women grouped around him. "Till then, nobody is leavin' here. Get me?"

Maria glanced at Alex, over at Bill, wondering if it was safe for them to try to get back to Trinidad.

Linderfelt shoved Louie away. "And when I get back, Tikas, you better deliver Ferrera."

With deliberate calm, Louie straightened his shirt. Linderfelt's eyes went narrow and black. "Just remember, tomorrow a.m. Or else."

Maria could almost reach out and touch the fear. No one moved or spoke for several minutes after Linderfelt and his men had left. Finally, Louie turned to them. Be calm, he said. He'd telephone John Lawson. Linderfelt wanted to push them into a fight, he said. Stay calm. He forced a smile. In the meantime, go to the cook tent and have some of the best food God ever invented.

Alex and Maria stood aside as the men left the tent.

"It's a witch hunt," Alex said, glancing at her.

"It's nothing." Maria fought to control the dread in her heart, and placed a hand on her friend's arm.

"What do you mean, nothing? You heard him. Linderfelt is after Dom."

"Dom is probably in town with Mr. Lawson."

"You don't know that for sure, do you?"

Maria smiled. "Who is sure of anything now?"

Alex stopped, glared at her. "Oh, my God. How can you stand there and pretend it's all going to work out? Linderfelt says he'll be out here tomorrow morning. You heard him."

Again Maria smiled.

"If Dom does get back, the militia will take him off to jail. If he doesn't, they'll probably shoot him on sight."

Maria fixed her attention on a hawk, circling over its prey in the field to the west. "They've threatened us before."

Alex frowned, her eyes dark in her exasperation. "Maria, it isn't like before. Don't you see? It's different. Everything has changed. The militia wants to flex its muscles. It wants a fight. A real fight. A battle. And they want the union to start it."

"I know." Maria felt tired to her bones.

"There's nothing else for Dom to do but to turn himself in."

Maria shot her a glance. "No."

"But he didn't kill Vaska," Alex said. "We can prove that, I'm sure."

"No one cares about proof. They will kill him as they killed Stefan Vaska." The child inside her stirred.

Alex opened her mouth to say something, then closed it. Perhaps she sensed Maria was right, for there was a kind of lifeline of trust that stretched between them.

Finally, Alex took her arm. "I've thought of you so often over the last days. I've been worried about you."

"Me? No. I'm always fine." Maria laughed. They walked on for a moment. She had few friends among the girls and women she knew. The love she felt for Alex should have surprised her, but didn't. How different they were and yet the same. Each a fighter in her own way, Alex with her law books, she with her schoolbooks.

They stepped inside the cook tent. She breathed in the delicious aroma of roasting lamb.

Louie approached, grinning now, as if Linderfelt had never come. "Moussaka. Souvlakia. Roasted lamb. Soupa avgolemono. Baklava for desert. Red wine." He kissed his fingertips. "Ah, ladies, it will be a feast."

Maria felt her spirits rise. She'd been hungry too often. But as she moved through the crowd of men and women and children, nodding to this one, patting the arm of another, her thoughts returned to Linderfelt's threats. She told herself whatever happened she would deal with it. She had to.

She glanced at Alex, who had gone over to help some of the women who were cooking. They laughed easily together. Some embraced her. Watching her friend, Maria was struck by what an amazing woman Alex was to have entered a world so foreign to her and taken its people to her heart with such grace—and courage.

The feast was served in the evening chill on long tables outside the tent. Louie led the singing. One man played a mandolin, another strummed a guitar. People ate and talked among themselves. If a stranger were standing on the sidelines, he would see an ordinary celebration of Greek Easter going on. But the fear was everywhere—in the eyes of women cradling their babies, in men's faces as they stood with arms around their wives' waists.

It had been a part of their lives, as pervasive as the air they breathed, for nearly nine months, but tonight there was a different, sharper edge to it. Once she thought she felt a hand on her shoulder and started, looked around. But there was no one there.

After the dishes were washed and the tables returned to the tent, Louie collared the concertina players. They struck up a lively polka. A husband and wife came forward. A cheer went up as they began to dance. Bachelors danced together. The tent filled with men and women and children clapping, keeping time to the music with their feet.

Bill Henderson approached Alex, took her hand and led her toward the dancers. As Maria watched them together, her heart ached. Frank was out there in the dark somewhere, probably delivering a baby. He had told her to expect him tonight, but she'd learned not to count on it. Now she almost hoped he didn't come, for she wasn't sure she wanted him caught up in whatever might happen. Yet if trouble came tomorrow, he might be desperately needed.

She sat down on one of the benches, letting the merry music wash over her. She tried not to worry about Dom. Was he with Mr. Lawson? Was he safe? She stood up and went outside, fighting back her despair. She looked up at the starry sky. So vast. So unknown. Like the life ahead of her.

Hugging herself against the chill, she turned back to the tent. Tomorrow was another day. God grant that Dom was safe and that Linderfelt burn in hell.

Chapter Forty-Seven

Alex put the last of the breakfast dishes away in the makeshift cupboard, took off a borrowed apron, and folded it over a chair by one of the stoves. For safety's sake, she and Bill had decided to spend the night at the camp. As soon as he came back with the latest news, they would return to Trinidad.

Alex stepped outside and breathed in the clear, cold air. By noon, it would probably be as warm as it had been yesterday. Across the way, several women were setting washtubs outside their tents, as if it were any normal Monday.

Impatient, she decided to find Bill, but as she approached the headquarters tent, she realized no one was there. She looked around for a moment before she spotted several dozen men lined up at the edge of the union land. She felt a dart of foreboding as she scanned the group. Thankfully, Bill was not among them.

In the field beyond, a lone figure carrying a white handkerchief in each hand was walking toward the railroad tracks and the water tower. From the broad shoulders and close-cropped, dark hair Alex knew it was Louie Tikas.

The water tank was on a slight rise above the prairie. On one side were the tracks and the Ludlow depot, no bigger than a tool shed. A variety of vehicles belonging to the militia were parked around it. Militia were everywhere, it seemed. She could see, even from where she stood, that all of them carried rifles and belts of ammunition.

An officer, judging from his uniform, whom she didn't recognize, stepped out of the depot and walked toward Louie. It worried Alex that Linderfelt and his war machine were nowhere in sight. Louie and the officer talked. The officer gestured angrily. A glint of something in the vicinity of the water tank caught her eye. She squinted, trying to make out what it was. A field glass perhaps. Maybe the barrel of a gun. Linderfelt's machine gun.

The strikers stirred uneasily, maybe thinking the militia had taken the safeties off their rifles. Someone came up behind her. She glanced around to see Maria. Neither of them spoke.

Louie and the officer continued talking for a moment. The officer wheeled in the direction of the depot, and Louie headed back toward the camp. He was walking fast, almost running, waving the white handkerchiefs over his head. Just as he reached the line of strikers, a bomb exploded. Then a second. And a third.

Pistol shots sounded, interrupted by the sharp rat-tat-tat of machine-gun fire.

Louie ducked low, dashed past strikers who were scattering toward the nearby arroyo and breastworks they had built, past Alex, toward the headquarters tent beyond. She looked over her shoulder to say something to Maria, but she was gone.

Not knowing what else to do, Alex ran toward the tent. Inside Louie Tikas was on the telephone, shouting into the mouthpiece that it was an attack. He paused, listening, probably to John Lawson as he relayed instructions.

A minute later Louie hung up and pushed past her down the central pathway of the camp, shouting, "Stay down. Stay inside the tents."

Alex glanced around for Maria, knowing wherever she was, she was gathering children separated from their mothers. Alex ran down the main path, calling her. Bullets whined overhead, tore through the canvas of one of the tents she passed. Alex saw the cook tent and Maria, a child in one arm, holding the hand of a toddler. Behind her were a half dozen other children.

Alex caught up with them, scooping the littlest of the stragglers into her arms. Flinging open the cook tent door, Maria shooed the children inside. Alex grabbed Maria's arm.

"Come on," shouted Maria. "Close the door."

As Alex pushed the children down onto the floor, Maria went to the center of the room and strained at a large ring-handle until, slowly, a piece of flooring lifted. Alex hurried over to help. Together they folded it back, revealing a hole large enough to hold several people.

Maria told Alex to get in. One by one, she handed down the eight children until, finally, she grabbed the rope dangling from the underside of the trap door and pulled it down over their heads.

They sat, crammed together on the dirt floor of the small, dark space. Even in the few minutes they'd been there, the air was close.

Alex wondered how long they could stay before they would suffocate. Above her came the sound of bullets ripping through canvas, women screaming, children crying out in terror. She thought of Bill, prayed he was safe.

"You never told me about a cellar," she said.

"Many people dug them for such a day as this one."

The youngest of the children began to whimper.

Alex glanced up at the trap door. "Maybe we should try to get them to their mothers."

"It is too dangerous."

"Do you know where they live?"

"Mostly."

"Their mothers must be frantic."

Maria didn't reply. They continued to sit, cramped, barely able to breathe, for what seemed like hours. Alex could stand it no longer. "Maria?"

"All right," she answered, her deep sigh telling of her own frustration, her worry for the children's safety. "We will take them home."

The high-pitched screams of terrified women pierced the air as Alex and Maria ran, bent over, from one tent to the next. At each stop, they thrust a child, sometimes two, into the hands of a hysterical mother.

At the last tent, Maria turned to Alex. "I must go to the hospital tent. Someone might be waiting for me."

But when they got there, it was empty. Grabbing a box of bandages, Maria ran outside again, shouting over her shoulder that she'd be at the headquarters.

"Wait," Alex called after her, but Maria was already well down the path.

Alone, Alex glanced about at the rudimentary equipment. If anyone was seriously injured, without a doctor, there would be little she could do. A head poked in. It was Louie Tikas.

He thrust his red neckerchief at her. "Not that it will keep you safe, but make some kind of an armband out of this so it looks like a red cross. Put it on. Bring some bandages. Whatever is in here."

Alex stared at the square of red cloth, not certain for an instant how to proceed, then ripped it in half. She found a roll of adhesive tape. Tearing off several strips, she fastened the two lengths of cloth together, attached the rude cross onto a length of bandage she wrapped around one coat sleeve. She pulled iodine and rolls of bandage off the shelves and wrapped them in a sheet as a makeshift carryall. She started out of the tent.

"This wasn't how it was supposed to happen," Louie said when she caught up with him.

"What do you mean?"

"The men in the arroyo were supposed to draw the fire from the women and children." One side of his mouth pulled into an ironic smile. "Jesus, we should've known better."

Time and sanity ceased to exist. Later all Alex could remember was running, Louie beside her, bending over women with bullet wounds, trying to stop the bleeding, sweat streaming down her face, blood caking her coat and slick like grease on her hands, the screams of the children wide-eyed with terror. A bullet grazed the heel of one of her shoes. For an instant she stopped to look down, thinking it had struck her foot. But it had only hit the heel, slicing it off. She kept running in and out of the tents, canvas so bullet-riddled it had the appearance of lace.

Suddenly, she saw Maria, racing across the clearing toward a lone toddler. Machine-gun bullets sprayed around her. Spits of hard-packed earth flew up. Just as she lifted the child, a bullet found its mark. She stopped, staggered. Then slowly, like a rag doll, she crumpled to the ground, the child still in her arms.

Alex crouched and ran to her, pulled her body into the protection of her arms. Maria's head fell back, her dark eyes sightless. Alex clasped the slight body more tightly. "Please, not you. Maria, not you," she moaned as she smoothed a loose strand of black hair from Maria's dirt-streaked face.

Hands reached down, took Maria from her. Prisms of tears blinding her, Alex looked up at Louie. "We were hiding in the cellar, but I wanted to get out."

"Come," Louie said. "Bring the child."

Louie found an empty tent nearby and placed Maria's body gently on the rough plank floor. Alex laid the dead child beside her. She took off her coat and put it over them. Then she knelt beside Maria, kissed her forehead, aware that it was still warm. "Forgive me, dear brave heart. Sleep well," she whispered.

Tears coursing down her cheeks, she rose and, as if she were a sleep-walker, she followed Louie to another tent to tend another woman and another child.

The shooting in the arroyos stopped at 4:30. Alex remembered the time because for some unknown reason she looked at her watch, still pinned to her blouse. The silence held. She straightened up from what she was doing and looked at Louie.

"We're out of ammunition," he said, matter-of-factly.

She stared at him dumbly.

"I need to go around and tell everyone to stay calm. With no way to keep them out now, the militia will be here soon."

It was dusk when the trucks rolled over the single strand of wire that served as a fence into the camp. With rifles in hand, militia strode through the camp, bursting into the tents, looting the meager possessions of men and women who had nothing—a guitar here, a concertina there. One soldier had three quilts draped over his shoulders.

Numb with horror and exhaustion, Alex was helpless to do anything but stand outside the cook tent and watch. The chaos continued. Dark settled on the camp. Alex had not moved from where she stood.

A shadowy figure appeared for an instant, then ducked behind a tent. "Pssst." She knew it was Louie, and she moved to where he waited, unseen.

"Any of them see me, I'm a dead man," he said in a low voice.

She knew he was right.

"I need your help to get as many of these women and children out of here tonight as we can," he said. "When John gets here with the reinforcements, the shooting will start up again. This time it's liable to be a full-scale war."

Within a half hour, they had managed to elude soldiers and gather nearly fifty women and children. Louie took the lead, the women and children followed, Alex in the rear. They headed silently across a field through the moonless night toward the relative safety of the arroyo.

One of the women dropped back, waited for Alex. "Missus, one of Mary Petrocco's kids is still back there," she whispered.

"At the camp?" She caught up with Louie and told him.

"I'll go check," he said.

"Let me. These women need you, Louie."

"Do like I say." He gave her a gentle push. "Go on now."

"Please be careful," she said, but she wasn't sure he heard, for he had already started back to the camp.

Alex and the others went on. They were nearly at the arroyo when a roar like a speeding train as it enters a tunnel suddenly filled the night. All of them froze, turned to see the tents, one after another, burst into flame, until the black sky turned into an orange holocaust.

They stood, transfixed, hands to mouths to stifle their cries. Finally, realizing that in the brilliant light of the blaze they were easy targets, Alex led the women on.

As they approached the arroyo, dozens of men scrambled out to scoop up children and guide the weeping women into the deep trench nature had provided. As hands reached out to help Alex, she asked if anyone had seen Bill. No one had.

"Dom gave himself up," someone said.

"Dom?" she asked, certain the person was wrong.

"Missus, it's true," an old man said. "He made it back here after the shooting started. He said it was his fault. He was out of his head."

Other men around them nodded.

"We told him it didn't do no good to surrender to Linderfelt. He'd as soon kill ya as look at ya, we told him. But he don't listen."

"Where'd he go?" asked Alex.

"Over there," the old man said. He pointed into the darkness.

"I don't see where you mean."

"The militia camp, missus."

"Oh, my God." She stared at him. "How long ago?"

The old man shrugged.

"An hour? Two hours?"

"Before dark. Before we ran out of bullets."

Alex felt her heart plummet. God only knew what Linderfelt might have done to him by now.

She surveyed the steep sides of the arroyo for only an instant before she reached above her and grasped some clumps of weeds to pull herself up.

"Missus, where you goin'?" a man called to her.

She reached the top and straightened. "To the camp. To find Dom."

Chapter Forty-Eight

Alex held up her skirt as she ran across the field toward the militia camp. The gate was open. There was no guard to stop her. She glanced around, saw no one, no movement, no trucks. She suddenly realized no lights shone. She felt a stab of fear. Immediately in front of her was a large tent with a flagpole next to it, perhaps the headquarters.

Glancing about, she ran toward it. As she reached the entrance, she pulled in a long breath, paused for an instant to collect her courage.

Inside, the dark was absolute, and, instantly, the vision of the cellar with Maria and the children returned. Her heart pounded wildly as she stood, listening. Apparently, Linderfelt and his men had gone to the union camp. She remained in the open doorway for another moment, trying to decide what to do, when she heard something. She froze. Something moved. She heard a low moan.

Could it possibly be Dom? She called his name very softly. "Are you in here?" She waited. Silence.

"Dom, it's me. Alex MacFarlane."

Still nothing.

"I'm alone. They said you'd come over here to surrender, so I came looking for you. No one's here though. Linderfelt must have gone over to the camp." She paused, breathless, hoping against hope it was Dom across the darkness.

A chair, something, at the other side of the tent suddenly crashed against the plank floor of the tent. She started at the sound, fear racing through her.

"I'm over here." The voice was Dom's. "Don't light the lamp."

"I won't," she whispered. "Are you hurt?"

"Beat up a little. A bullet grazed my head. I can't seem to stop the bleedin.'"

She remembered the bandages she'd had were in the pockets of her coat, still lying over Maria and the child, back at the camp. Her slip was silk, not very satisfactory for a bandage. It would have to do. Raising her skirt, she yanked at it until she heard it rip and the fabric fell loose around her ankles.

"I can't see a thing. Where are you? I've got something that might work as a bandage."

Then, without warning, he was beside her, weaving slightly. As she caught his arm, she felt the sudden weight of him leaning heavily on her for support.

"We need to get where there's a little light so I can look at your head," she said, still whispering. "Hold on to me. We'll have to go outside."

They sat on a bench next to the tent. The night had an eerie quality to it, and she realized the light came from the tents still burning, a mile away. She could see Dom's profile. She folded the remains of her slip into a long strip and tied it tightly over the wound. "It's better than nothing."

He gazed in the direction of the union camp. "It's on fire."

She adjusted the makeshift bandage. "Louie and I managed to get most of the women and children to the arroyo."

"So Maria's okay."

Alex pretended she hadn't heard. She would tell him about Maria later. "What happened to you?"

"I came over to surrender, and they shot me before I could say a word. I think I passed out for awhile," he said. "Linderfelt musta gave me up for dead."

"Thank God."

He moved to get to his feet. "We gotta get outta here."

Alex took his elbow. "Are you sure you can walk?"

He shrugged away her hold. "They'll be back."

"Somehow we'll have to get to Trinidad," she said. "The militia has taken over the camp."

The night was alive with the staccato bursts of machine guns, near-constant rifle fire, as they set off toward Trinidad. Here and there patches of fire glowed red against the black sky. She tried to tell herself Bill was all right.

Now and then Dom had to stop to rest. Twice she explained she had to urinate, and Dom turned his back while she relieved herself with the darkness as her only privacy. He insisted they avoid the main highway, stick to the back roads. Occasionally, bands of men loomed out of the darkness, frightening men, armed, eyes bright with terror, demanding money, eyeing Alex. Dom spoke to them in rapid Italian until they withdrew into the night again.

The heel of one foot was blistered raw. Alex tried to estimate how far they had come. The distance between Ludlow and Trinidad was seventeen miles, but they'd backtracked, gone the long way. She was without a coat and said a little prayer of thanks that the night air was mild for April. Finally, as dawn spread across the eastern sky, Alex felt she could not put it off any longer.

"Dom, Maria is dead."

He stopped, crossed himself as he stared at her. His breath started coming in short, quick spurts. Tears streaked down his blood-caked cheeks.

He suddenly hid his face with his hands and sobbed. "May God forgive me. It was my fault."

Instinctively, she patted his arm. "You're wrong, Dom."

"If I had—"

"The militia used you as an excuse to make trouble. They were trying to goad the union into doing something violent."

His hands fell to his side. "You don't know the whole story."

"If you're talking about what you did for the union . . ."

Their eyes held.

"That's something I know nothing about. What I do know is that I came looking for you because I loved your sister, because I know how important you were to her. All those children she taught to read, she thought of them as little Doms. Did you know that?"

He glanced at her almost timidly, tears swimming in his eyes.

"It's true."

"I dunno."

"Well, I do." She patted his arm again. "Maybe we should go on. We still have a way to go."

They had avoided the farmhouses they passed. But now, as they approached what appeared to be a deserted barn, they decided to risk a short stop. Tufts of weeds clung to the base of the posts along the fencing. A rusted wagon wheel lay in the yard. The barn's huge doors stood ajar, half off their hinges. Dom and Alex approached cautiously.

They paused for a moment as they peered inside to let their eyes adjust to the dark. No one seemed to be about, and they went in. The air was dry and cold.

Suddenly, a half dozen ragged men stepped into sight, their rifles cocked. Red bandannas were tied around their necks, bulging gunnysacks slung on their backs.

Dom hailed them in Italian. He glanced at her as he spoke, and the men eyed her suspiciously. One of them, a tall, wide-shouldered man who must have been the leader, replied in a tense, hard-edged voice. The men's dark looks frightened her. But, as before, Dom seemed to have matters under control. After a few minutes, gesturing with their rifles, the men told them to leave.

A huge feeling of relief swept through her as she and Dom set off down the road again. She could feel the men's eyes. They might decide they'd made a mistake to let them go. She was tempted to run, but knew her legs wouldn't let her.

Finally, clusters of small houses surrounded by a few trees, signs of a town, began to appear. They had reached the outskirts of Trinidad.

John Lawson frowned at Dom's pale face and the bandage, now filthy and bloodstained, as he handed them each a cup of steaming coffee. "Looks like you got nicked."

"It ain't nothin' serious," Dom said, clutching his cup with shaking hands.

Lawson ordered them to sit down. "We're holding Trinidad and all the territory around it for about seventeen miles."

"Bill? Have you seen Bill?" Alex asked. Her voice echoed in the cavernous room of the union headquarters.

"He made it here, but I told him to go stay put in his office."

She gave a deep sigh of relief. "And Ludlow? How bad is it?"

The cords of his neck tightened. "Twenty women and children shot or burned alive in the cellars is the count so far."

She started to shake so violently she nearly dropped the cup. "You know Dom's sister, Maria, is dead."

"That's what I heard." Lawson glanced at Dom. "I'm sorry. Maria was a fine woman."

"Where's Louie Tikas?" she asked.

"The militia's got him. It doesn't look good," Lawson said. "Right now we're trying to get a truck out to pick up the dead in Ludlow so they can be buried. But the machine guns are blocking the highway."

She told him about the men they had seen on their way to Trinidad. "Were they union men?"

"Most likely." Lawson shook his head wearily. "Whoever they are, we've got to get them under control. The fires you saw were coal camps being torched. Some of the men are like packs of dogs on the loose."

"Does the governor know what's happened?" she asked.

He gave a hard smile. "He was in Washington. But the president was too busy to see him. Seems he was all caught up in the arrest of American marines in Tampico." He shrugged. "Anyway, Ammons is on the way back to Colorado. He's ordered three companies down here. But the word is that half have mutinied and a good many of the others are suddenly out of town and unable to report for duty." John Lawson grinned.

"And Chase?" she asked. Everything was happening so fast.

"He's in Denver. I talked to him this morning by telephone. He says he's coming down with three hundred troops in the interest of peace."

Alex had to smile at the irony. "And what did you say?"

"I told him there's no peace when there's no justice. They started this war of extermination. We don't fire on women and children. Our war is strictly against the militia and the gunmen."

"So a trainload of soldiers is on its way right now?" she asked.

"They're bringing three-inch guns and about a thousand rounds of shrapnel. I'm told machine guns are mounted on a flat car in front of the engine."

"Oh, Lord," she murmured.

"Orders went out for the train to stop just north of Aguilar. We've sent men with derailers and dynamite." Lawson paced the large room, lined now with cans of food and boxes of ammunition and rifles.

"Mr. Lawson," Dom said, "I want to go out to Aguilar."

Lawson glanced at him.

"For Maria's sake. I got to."

"A truck's already left," Lawson said. "Besides, you're in no shape for something like that."

"They'll need all the men they can get," Dom protested.

The union leader studied him.

For an instant, John Lawson's blue eyes softened with affection, as if he were looking at his son. Yet when he spoke, his tone was cold. "Handling dynamite calls for cool heads."

"I've loaded charges, Mr. Lawson."

"You'd be a drag on us."

"I'm a crack shot with a rifle. Ask anybody."

Lawson turned from Dom, shutting off his pleas. "Mrs. MacFarlane, you need to get out of town. Is there somewhere you can stay? Out aways?"

"The Nevils. They're out beyond Sandoval."

"I'm afraid I can't spare a truck," he said.

"Bill has a car."

"You'll have to have someone with you to get through our lines," Lawson said, glanced at Dom. "You go with Mrs. MacFarlane. See that she gets to where she wants to go."

"Boss, please."

"That's an order."

Three men came into the room, diverting Lawson's attention for an instant. "The dynamite's over in Waite's garage, boys."

They nodded and left.

"Boss . . ."

Lawson glanced over at Dom again. "You've got a job to do. Now do it."

Dom gazed at him dumbly.

"And Dom . . ."

"Yessir."

"Don't come back. You're through working in the mines and for the union."

Dom stared for a second, uncomprehending.

"Hear me?"

"Yessir." His chin quivered ever so slightly.

"Don't forget it."

Alex squeezed between Dom and Bill. The ride to the Nevils' was slow going. Occasionally, they met union patrols, and Dom explained who they were either in Italian or through a kind of sign language, showed them a note John Lawson had given them that served as a pass.

Alex watched him. Dom was where he'd lived most of his life. But he couldn't go back to the mines, that much she knew. John Lawson had also made that plain. She thought of the Nevils. Maybe . . .

When they finally pulled into the yard, Bill got out and went into the house. Dom's face was a mask as he climbed out and looked around.

"It's nice, isn't it?" Alex asked, hopefully.

He gave no sign he'd heard her.

"The Nevils had a nephew who lived with them. He was their right-hand man, I guess you could say. About your age. Seventeen, I think. Two guards from the Sandoval camp came and accused him of helping some scabs get away. They shot him in the back."

Dom crossed himself.

"It's been very hard on them. Mr. Nevil's getting on in years. Their nephew's help was really all that made it possible for them to keep the place."

Dom mumbled something she couldn't hear.

"Sorry?"

"It ain't good to get old," he said.

Alex nodded, earnestly. "And Mrs. Nevil, she misses her nephew very much."

Dom shoved his hands into his pockets.

"Come see the barn," she said, beckoning him to follow her.

He poked his head inside. "Mules is the only animal I ever worked with."

She smiled, reaching to think of what might persuade him to see the opportunities on the Nevils' ranch. "I remember your mentioning that once."

He walked over to the corral fence, staring, expressionless, at the fields beyond, giving the top pole a shake, as if to test its sturdiness.

"Mr. Lawson wants you to have a chance he never had, Dom. That's why he told you not to come back."

He ignored her.

"After this strike is over, you know the companies will be hard on any union member."

"It's all I know," he said simply.

"It won't be easy. But you're smart. And you're brave. You've proved that."

He looked past her, his eyes heavy with misery and anger. Then he said, low and trembling with feeling, "I hate 'em. All of 'em."

"I know," she said gently.

"She's dead, missus. Dead." His eyes spilled over with tears. "They killed her."

"Dom . . ."

He turned away so his back was to her, held his head in his hands. Sobs racked his body.

"She loved you very much," Alex said, patting Dom's heaving back. "You stay out here as long you want. I'll be back in a few minutes."

Juanita peered out the window. "Why does he stay out there by himself? Bring the boy in here. He's hurt. He needs something to eat. I can see that from here."

"Nita, we have to talk about this first," Charlie said, arms folded across his chest as he leaned against the sink.

"What is there to talk about?" she demanded. "The boy needs our help."

Alex said, "I should have talked to you first about the possibility of Dom staying here with you for awhile before I mentioned it to him. I apologize."

"Why do you apologize?" Juanita asked. "You and Billie can't go back to town until the strikers leave. You will stay here with the boy until he gets used to things. It will be fine."

Charlie looked over at Bill, standing by the entrance to the back porch. "What's the story anyway?"

Bill shrugged. "Damned if I know. As far as we could find out, the union controls about a ten-by-three-mile stretch either side of Trinidad."

"Dom and I saw the frames up at Hastings burning," Alex said.

Bill said, "Even with Dom and Lawson's pass, we had a helluva time getting out here."

No one spoke. It was as if they were trying to digest the magnitude of it all.

Charlie glanced out the window at Dom, who stood gazing out across the pasture.

"You need the help, Charlie," Juanita said, as she went over to stand beside him.

"I s'pose that's right."

Neither of them spoke, each apparently lost in thought. After a few moments, Alex went over to Juanita and hugged her from behind, feeling the strength of the solid body, almost literally able to touch the love always given so freely to anyone who needed it. If Dom did stay with them, he would be with people who would help him mend his broken heart.

Finally, Charlie turned away, went past Bill, and lifted his hat from its peg on the back porch. He glanced at Juanita. "Mother, I think I'll go talk to the boy for a spell. Looks like he could do with a bit of company."

Alex watched Bill as he saddled the big roan standing patiently in the corral.

It had been a week since the battle at the Ludlow camp. She was impatient to reach the outside world, but first she had to come to grips with her feelings for Bill.

"Where's Dom?" she asked.

"Out fixing fence with Charlie. I thought I'd check to see how they're doing."

"It's got to work out. It's just got to."

"Dom's a good boy," he said. "A hard worker. He'll catch on fast."

Alex gazed across the field. "He misses Maria terribly."

She could feel Bill looking at her as he tightened the cinch.

"That kind of thing takes time to heal," he said, quietly.

She sighed. "Do you think we could get through to Pueblo tomorrow?"

"Drive, you mean?"

She nodded. "Or at least reach a telephone."

"I don't know. My revolver's in the desk drawer back at Mrs. Willard's, and there's no way to get at it."

"Maybe we wouldn't need it."

"You don't know who's out there."

"True."

He stroked the roan's neck and glanced at her. "Alex, what's on your mind?"

"I—we—need to know what's going on. For all we know, the president might have sent in federal troops. Certainly, he's not going to allow this mayhem to go on."

"What else?" He reached for her and folded his arms around her, holding her close.

"I'm going back to Denver," she said into his chest.

He released her, looking down at her with puzzled eyes.

"I must see my father for a day or two. I know he's worried about me. After that—I don't know. I may go to Washington to talk to Ed. I've thought about opening my own office."

He held her chin, kissed her gently.

"For all that's happened, what's really changed?" Her heart ached as she heard herself say the words out loud.

He waited.

"Stefan and Maria are dead. Once the violence quiets, the strike will fail, and the companies will continue to operate as they always have. So the union will try another strike somewhere else. And it will start all over again." She sighed. "The killing, the violence, none of it accomplished anything."

"You're forgetting about Dom," he said. "He's got a new start. Big problems are solved in little pieces."

"I hope so. Lord, how I hope so."

She watched a tiny bird dart under the eaves of the barn, perhaps to a nest, and she thought of Maria again. Dear, beautiful, intelligent, brave Maria. She, too, had been building a nest, filled with books and ideas for a generation of children she was determined must never go down into the mines. Maybe now some of them wouldn't.

"Alex . . ."

She glanced at him. "One thing can be said. I've learned more about the anatomy of a strike than any textbook would have taught me."

"That's sure true."

"So what would be the sense of my giving up now?"

"Never thought you would."

She looked into the intelligent blue eyes smiling at her, the lock of hair that always fell across his forehead. He had opened her heart, fired her passions, some she hadn't known existed. "What about you?"

"I think I'll stay—at least till things calm down."

She put her arms around his waist and hugged him.

"Don't you give up either."

He gave a low laugh. "Not a chance. In fact, I've been thinking about a visit to Mr. Sims and Mr. Charlton in Pueblo. See how they're coming with that workmen's compensation legislation."

"That's a wonderful idea."

"I'd probably have to bring in some other kind of work to pay the bills."

Alex nodded, her mind on his plan. Like Bill, the two men he'd told her so much about had put everything aside to pursue what they believed in. Instantly, she knew what she would do. "Bill, do you think Mr. Sims and Mr. Charlton will be bothered by a woman attorney working with their firm?"

"Alex, you're not . . ."

"It's certainly a possibility."

He started to laugh.

"What's so funny?"

"Not a thing." Bill pulled her into his arms again. "I was just thinking I never knew a woman so full of schemes."

Three weeks later, federal troops were in Trinidad. Alex and Bill stood on the platform of the depot, waiting for the 2:10 for Denver.

"If you need to get in touch with me, I'll be at my father's for awhile." She paused. "But I guess I told you that."

He nodded.

"You'll send me your Pueblo address?"

He smiled. "The minute I get there."

Belching steam, the train approached from the south, slowing as it neared. The whistle blew. The other passengers on the platform stirred expectantly.

Alex stared out at nothing and everything—the adobe houses across the tracks, Fisher's Peak looming over the town. Behind her were the canyons, riddled with coal camps. In between, the ranches—the Nevils'—the farms, the union camps full of hopes lost.

The wheels squealed to a halt. The conductor swung down and placed a step stool at the foot of the stairs. Bill and Alex looked at each other and smiled.

"Well, I guess you better get on," he said, a little gruffly.

"I guess so."

The conductor raised his arm, shouted, "All aboard!"

"Bill . . ." Her heart was too full to continue.

"I love you, Alex."

"I know."

He took her elbow and helped her to mount the stairs into the car. The train began to move. As she was about to turn away to find a seat, she saw Bill running alongside, squinting up at each window to catch sight of her. She flung open the door and, grabbing the metal rail between the cars for balance, she leaned out and called to him.

"Alex, you're going to kill yourself," he shouted.

"I love you, too," she shouted back.

His hair blowing in the wind, a broad grin on his face, he waved with both arms. "See you in Pueblo," she heard him shout as the train rounded a curve and headed north.

Afterword

The strike that had gripped the southern coalfields of Colorado since September 1913 culminated in a fiery tragedy on April 20, 1914. It was later known as the Ludlow Massacre.

The result was a massive explosion of violence, which ended only with the arrival of federal troops sent by President Wilson. The strike ended on December 10, 1914, but others would follow: in 1919, 1921, and 1927.

In October of 1914, President Wilson tried for a settlement between the union and the company owners. When he was unsuccessful, he invoked the Industrial Relations Commission, authorized by legislation passed during the Taft administration. The four-member commission was chaired by Frank Walsh, a Kansas City attorney and reformer.

Reaction to the commission's final report ranged from elation to rage. "The evidence is in," Walsh remarked at the end of the hearings. "The case has gone to the great jury of the American people."

But John Rockefeller Jr. refused to be thwarted, and he devised what he called the Representation Plan. At the heart of the plan was a grievance committee made up of representatives from workers and management. Discussion between the two sides was intended to lessen the friction between workers and management. If a miner's grievance could not be solved, he had three levels of appeal. The first was the president; the second was the committee of workers and management; and the last was the newly formed Colorado Industrial Commission. But no appeal could be sent to the commission without first obtaining permission of the grievance committee, which could not muster a majority vote without company support. The power remained safely in the hands of the company.

At the end of the 1914 strike, some miners clung to their tents for a time. Others drifted out of the state, blacklisted by the companies, with no hope of employment.

John Lawson was convicted of the murder of a company guard in the district court located in Trinidad, Colorado. The conviction was appealed and subsequently overturned by the Colorado Supreme Court. In 1919, Lawson was hired by Miss Josephine Roche, who had just taken over the management of her father's firm, the Rocky Mountain Fuel Company, upon his death. Miss Roche, a nationally known advocate of social and industrial reforms, needed an able and practical man to help her. She believed John Lawson met both qualifications. The relationship of trust he had built through the years with the United Mine Workers was the basis for his success as the firm's vice president for eleven years.

Edward Keating was the major force behind the first federal child labor law and a model minimum wage law for women and children. He vigorously supported women's suffrage. He was one of six congressmen who voted against the United States entering World War I. Though he was defeated for reelection in 1918, he continued throughout his life to work on behalf of labor.

During World War I and throughout the twenties, Rockefeller's Industrial Representation Plan became an influential form of company unions across the United States. It remained in effect until 1934 with the passage of the National Recovery Act.

Colorado was among nine states that passed a workmen's compensation law in 1917. But it was not until 1933, under the Bituminous Coal Code, that coal miners got the eight-hour day, a minimum daily wage, the right to live where they chose and to buy where they chose, payment in legal money, the services of a check-weighman, and representation by the United Mine Workers of America.

In 1937 the Supreme Court upheld the Wagner Act, which prevented unfair practices in labor relations affecting interstate commerce, and stipulated that Rockefeller's Industrial Representation Plan and other company unions were unconstitutional.